A Delhi Obsession

A DELHI OBSESSION

M.G. VASSANJI

DOUBLEDAY CANADA

Doubleday Canada and colophon are registered trademarks of
Penguin Random House Canada Limited

LIBRARY AND ARCHIVES CANADA CATALOGUING IN PUBLICATION

Title: A Delhi obsession / M.G. Vassanji.
Names: Vassanji, M. G., author.
Identifiers: Canadiana (print) 20190053089 | Canadiana (ebook) 20190053127 |
ISBN 9780385692854
(hardcover) | ISBN 9780385692861 (EPUB)
Classification: LCC PS8593.A87 D44 2019 | DDC C813/.54—dc23

This book is a work of fiction. Names, characters, places and incidents are
products of the author's imagination or are used fictitiously. Any resemblance
to actual events or locales or persons, living or dead, is entirely coincidental.

Cover and book design: Lisa Jager
Jacket images: (building) Sunny Hopper / EyeEm / Getty Images;
(texture) donatas1205; (stars) C2Lens, both Shutterstock
Printed and bound in Canada

Published in Canada by Doubleday Canada,
a division of Penguin Random House Canada Limited

www.penguinrandomhouse.ca

10 9 8 7 6 5 4 3 2 1

Penguin
Random House
DOUBLEDAY CANADA

in memoriam
Neerja Chand

The Hindus and Muslims belong to two different religious philosophies, social customs, and literature[s]. They neither intermarry nor interdine together, and indeed they belong to two different civilisations which are based mainly on conflicting ideas and conceptions.

—MUHAMMAD ALI JINNAH TO THE MUSLIM LEAGUE, LAHORE (1940)

not Hindu, not Muslim
a child is born but human

—SAHIR LUDHIANVI, LYRICS FROM THE FILM *DHOOL KA PHOOL* (1959)

Having said this, the illustrious daughter of the king of Madra, wife by law to that bull among men [Pandu], climbed onto the fire of that funeral pyre.

—MAHABHARATA, SAMBHAVA PARVA (TRANSLATED BY BIBEK DEBROY)

I will slap anyone who looks at Hindu women the wrong way!

—INDIAN MEMBER OF PARLIAMENT, 2017

Munir Aslam Khan

IT CAME AS A WHIM, a thought that flew in from nowhere and spread wings in his mind, that he should visit India. More precisely, Delhi, the city from which his grandfather had departed a hundred years ago, when it was the new showpiece of the British Raj. He had heard about that city as a child in his home in Kenya, shown no interest; and about the reason for that departure, he had caught the barest innuendo of an intrigue that had no conceivable relevance.

Munir Aslam Khan was recently widowed, his wife of many years having died suddenly in a car accident, skidding on an ice patch a block away from their home in North Toronto. It had been Halloween night and bitterly cold, the first snow had come early and unannounced, and having given its warning it had disappeared. A year later now he had not recovered; he did not expect to. His sense of loss—grief was too strong a word—he knew he would always carry as a memorial to their years spent together. The awkward sympathies from the neighbours had ceased; there remained only the friendly banter and the

occasional joke from Andy or Jim or Joanna, called out from
their porches as he passed on the sidewalk. He found some solace
in his reading, which now consisted of histories mainly. His own
writing had run into dry ground. He had no ambition left in that
direction, he had written whatever he had inside him, a few
books of fiction, with modest success; anything more now was
mere addendum or exercise, scratching at futility. And so he was
often at loose ends. There were no longer any pressing chores,
which he had disliked when she was around but had helped to
fill the days of their later years, as they'd liked to call them. They
had discussed the eventuality of death; he was assured that she,
always the better earner, would remain in comfort for the long
remainder of her life that she could anticipate. But death ignores
statistics—knows not night or day, as his elders would piously
proclaim in their fatalistic moments—and here he was, alone.
There was the numbing comfort of Scotch or a red at night.

It was the end of November and he was returning from a
long walk in the neighbourhood; approaching home he
watched a moving truck arrive a few houses down and proceed
to unload. A wiry young man, barely in his thirties, already bald
and very obviously of Indian origin, stood behind the truck,
watching stuff come down from the back; on the porch his
wife, smart in tight denims, holding a girl of about three by the
hand, also stood watching. Techies, Munir mused, with ready-
made money. We came with pennies in our pockets, he recalled
of his generation of new Canadians. Munir stared at the scene:
a sofa came wobbling down, as if riding a wave from the van,
and he felt an irrepressible surge of compassion. To be that
young . . . And with no apparent logic the further thought
occurred: I should go to India.

It had been always at the back of the mind, a journey that he should make one day, eventually. Those were her words: one day, eventually. Aileen, a Scot by descent, had no association with India; she had agreed in principle that they should go, it was necessary for him, but the thought of catching a bug, something noxious and Indian, had always held her back. For Munir, the prospect was daunting precisely because of its significance: a return to the ancestral homeland after something like a century. Munir could now vaguely recall as a child imagining India alternately as Delhi, a strange city somewhere that might appear in the *Arabian Nights*, which Sinbad might have visited. But while a lot of other travel was undertaken by Munir and Aileen during their marriage, India remained "undone," a hole in their world map of journeys. Now, watching the young family moving into his neighbourhood, the woman directing the movers through the narrow door, the child tugging at the mother, the father holding the storm door open, the revelation came without equivocation, he should visit India, especially Delhi, and fill that hole.

He realized that with a surname like Khan there might be a hitch obtaining a visa. Such were the times, it could not be helped. The world travelled nervously these days. And indeed, when he submitted his visa application at the Indian Consulate, the clerk raised her eyebrows with a pert smile, as if to say, *Fat chance.* "Will it take long?" Munir felt compelled to ask. "Depends," she said, "on when we hear from India." "Do all applications get sent to India?" "Only certain ones." He nodded. He had time. And if he was rejected as a possible threat to that nation, so be it.

But only a week later he was called for an interview; it was scheduled with the consul himself. Munir announced himself at the window on the other wing of the floor, the door was opened for him, and after a short wait alone in a quiet ante-room he was ushered into a large office with an oversized desk. Aditya Sharma, the consul, stood up and came over to shake hands. He had a warm smile. He was a small, unassuming man, wearing a dark Indian vest buttoned at the neck. He tried speaking in Urdu, and failing to get a response from Munir, continued in a plain though fluent English.

"Mr. Khan, I am delighted to meet you. Normally I would not interfere in the visa process, but your application gave me an opportunity to see you in person. I am honoured, sir."

Munir was at a loss for words. Such humility from a diplomat. People occasionally recognized his name in Toronto, and on rare occasions even his face. It was flattering but also disconcerting. Having gone through periods of literary fame such as accompany the publication of a book, followed by the relative oblivion afterwards, he had reached a phase in his life when, no longer quite a writer, he preferred solitude and anonymity; and yet there was always just that frisson, when vanity got aroused. It annoyed him to succumb to it, for with every instance of recognition came doubts. What did it mean, this flattery; how true was it, and how deserved. Did it matter. It was better to remain unrecognized, unperturbed. To get on with living.

"I am flattered, Mr. Sharma, thank you. Is this to do with my visa? I was told the application would have to be sent to India—"

"Oh, no, no. With your name—"

"I would understand it, of course, these are not easy times we live in."

"Yes. I am pleased you understand, Mr. Khan. Many people don't, and complain. But you don't have to worry. Here is your passport, with the visa. We've given you ten years, and for your inconvenience, I've waived your fee."

"Thank you, Mr. Sharma. I am obliged."

Munir took his passport and the uncashed money order. They sat down on the sofa, which was set towards the back wall, and the receptionist brought tea and biscuits. They chatted. Aditya Sharma had only recently taken up his post. He had been previously in Addis Ababa, and before that in Kazakhstan. He had been to Nairobi, stayed at the Masai Mara National Reserve. They talked about literature. Mr. Sharma asked him to recommend Canadian writers he might read. Finally he told Munir, "You should go to the Jaipur Literature Festival. In Jaipur. Rajasthan. Why haven't you done so? I'll get you invited. The organizers are known to me."

"Thank you," Munir said, though he was done with festivals too, but there was no point in sounding rude or arrogant.

He parted on the warmest terms with the consul. They agreed to meet again, and the consul invited him to the annual Indian Independence Day reception the following August.

There were the medical preparations, beginning with a visit to his doctor, who prescribed a bevy of prophylactics. There was advice from people—to drink only bottled water, to refuse ice, not to eat salads and fruit however enticing they looked. Absolutely no street food. There were all the means devised for travellers to carry money safely on their person. A SIM card was essential. He should carry passport-sized photos of himself. He flew via London, where there was a long stopover, which he spent walking along the city streets familiar to him from the past.

He dipped into a few bookstores and paid a quick visit to the
National Gallery. It was late evening when he boarded his onward
flight. The terminal was quiet at this time, but there was a long
trail of fellow passengers—grandmothers in wheelchairs, couples
with noisy children, businessmen, backpackers, and quiet men
and women who had the look, Munir felt, of going home. He recognized spoken Punjabi, the language his elders had spoken in
Nairobi. Two elderly men trotted along with their carry-ons on
their shoulders like farmers.

He found himself observing the returning Indians closely,
with fascination. Am I like them? One of them? Ever since watching the young couple who had moved into his street (he had seen
them twice since then and once had greeted the man), followed
by his meeting with the Indian consul, he had begun to sense a
greater awareness in him of other Indians. Had his marriage
deprived him of this connection? Perhaps; but he had thought of
himself as a Kenyan, and he was now also a Canadian. In Nairobi,
emulating the English had been the norm among his Asian age
group. There was an awareness of ancestry and family connection, but that was it. Perhaps now, as he passed his middle age, the
ancestors had come knocking, demanding homage. He smiled.
In high school, his friend Peter had invited him to his father's
second marriage, to a young woman of his own tribe, which was
Bukusu. Peter's mother was a Kikuyu, but now his father needed
pure-breed sons who would say the proper rites for him when
he died. This had sounded funny then. Was he, Munir Khan, now
going through a similar phase? He had his daughter to think of;
he had hardly given her anything of his own heritage.

———

In Delhi, he put up at the Delhi Recreational Club, or DRC, booked for him courtesy of the Indian consul in Toronto. It was a quiet complex set off from a moderately busy road, with a fountain and lovely front garden in which all the flora were neatly labelled; it provided everything he would need for his two weeks. The residential rooms were in the main building; across a stone patio were a formal dining room and an informal cafeteria called "the lounge." The food was decent, there was internet and room service. Adjoining the Club behind it was a park called Sikandar Gardens, where people went for walks, or did their yoga at dawn; at various places among the vast variety of trees and flowers stood the pink-and-white stone remains of past centuries, silent memorials to sultans and nobles. At the back of the main building was a small and discreet bar with glass walls, accessible from the back garden; it threw its doors open promptly at six in the evenings to its eagerly awaiting patrons. The library was excellent and there he would look up arbitrary historical subjects, toying with ideas for stories. Perhaps he was not done with writing yet. A ten-minute walk away from the Club was the fortuitously named Khan Market, where he could buy fruit and browse in the two small bookstores packed to their ceilings. He contemplated reserving a seat on a tour bus to go to Agra to see the Taj Mahal. That surely was a must. Meanwhile he visited by taxi the Qutub Minar, a lean and elegant tower of red sandstone in the south of the city, from where the first Turkish sultans had ruled, having defeated the local Rajput kings in the tenth century; and the Purana Qila, which was the site of the earliest city of Delhi, called Indraprastha, from the time of the epic *Mahabharata*. From here the five Pandava brothers had ruled in that hoary past. Delhi offered endless history. He was excited, up to the moderation that his nature demanded; his own history began here in this great, tumultuous city.

He was regularly one of the first ones in the bar and easily found a table, leaving early after a vodka and tonic (or two) and a snack for his supper. The tables around him were always lively and he caught intriguing snatches of conversations about the nation's politics or the lives of children abroad, their placements at Juilliard or Wharton, their upcoming marriages, their jobs at Microsoft or Google. His eavesdropping was a habit Aileen had found annoying, because he tended then to drift away from her presence.

On his first Saturday in Delhi, three days after he arrived, at about eight o'clock a rush of people flocked into the bar and it suddenly filled up. The room became raucous, the air turned misty. He gathered from the excited chatter that a good number of the guests had returned from an afternoon at the Jaipur Literature Festival. He couldn't hold on to his table by himself for long, it was clear, and soon enough a woman came and sat down with an audible sigh of relief, then politely turned to him and asked for permission.

"Please," he replied in consent. "I'm alone, and you are most welcome. I'm leaving soon anyway."

"Oh no, not on my account, I hope!" She smiled.

"No, I was about to get up," Munir returned the smile.

"Oh. But don't hurry. Some table will vacate soon. I'm waiting for my husband to join me." She turned and looked anxiously around, then asked, "Were you at Jaipur? I think I saw you there. That was some session, wasn't it—English versus Hindi? Fireworks! Are you an author yourself?"

He hesitated before replying, "Yes, but I wasn't there. This is a personal visit."

"I must have seen your picture somewhere. I am Mohini, by the way. And my husband is Ravi. I wonder where he is. We've just returned from Jaipur. It was quite wonderful. We heard Ronnie Kohinore, do you know him?"

"Of him. I'm Munir Aslam Khan, from Toronto."

She quickly looked around again, the waiter stopped by and Munir, with her permission, ordered her a red wine. She accepted a cutlet from his plate. She looked edgy, perhaps didn't want to be seen sitting with a male stranger who couldn't help staring at her. The fair, oval face with a high brow, a sparkle on the forehead; the hair pulled into a long braid at the back, the soft brown liquid eyes. The husky voice laced with a slight edge, and the delicious accent. The sari was brilliant beige, silk. She shone.

She stretched forward, alarming him, before he realized she was searching behind him. "He should be coming. Though he always finds his former army buddies wherever he goes! So frustrating."

Munir didn't want her Ravi to come yet. She was hardly simple, but that traditional look—shouldn't there be a red dot instead of the blue sparkle? But what did he know of being Indian?

"You are silent. What are you thinking?"

"If you could be real. I thought women like you existed only in the old Indian films."

What gave him the courage? Normally he wasn't so brash, so mischievous.

"I look old-fashioned, you mean?"

"In a nice way."

"A sari may be old-fashioned to you, but many Indian women wear it. You can look around the room and see."

"I am aware of that. But I didn't mean to offend you. And I admit I am ignorant about India."

That brought on a look of surprise. She leaned forward, searching his face.

"You are Indian and you are ignorant about India? That's a shame. Why is it that people who leave India want to forget about it as soon as possible? We should know about where we come from!"

"It's too late for me."

"It's never too late!"

"I was born in Kenya, actually."

"But you are Indian—aren't you?"

In Nairobi he would have vehemently denied this, but out in the world you had to supply all the nuances as to who you were. He said, "I suppose I am . . . in a sort of way."

Neither of them spoke, then. She took a quick, anxious look around the room. Her husband was not to be found. The crowd had depleted measurably, most people having decided perhaps it was not worth the wait for a table. She returned her gaze to him and gave a wan smile.

"Why Delhi? Ours is not the friendliest of cities."

"Well, I had to start somewhere. And Delhi has such a rich history."

"You'll need a guide. I suggest you hire a day taxi."

"I have already done that, the last two days."

She looked curiously at him. "You're seeing the tourist India."

"Why not?"

"No reason."

But then he asked, daring even further, "Would you like to show me around the non-tourist Delhi?"

What had got into him? First a flattering comment. And then asking her out. A married woman. A married *Indian* woman. As he waited for her to reply, her phone rang and she spoke briefly into it in Hindi. Then she looked up and said, "Yes! I'll show you around. I think I can trust you. But I have to go now, that was my husband, he's picking me up. Now the table is all yours and you don't have an old-fashioned Indian woman disturbing your peace!"

Rather archly.

He returned a sheepish look and signed his bill. They left together and parted at the driveway, where she waited for Ravi, and Munir went inside the building and back to his room upstairs.

The next morning she called and arrived shortly after to pick him up.

"You have a driver," he observed, as he got into the back beside her, somewhat disappointed. She was in salwar-kameez, he noticed, but the blue dot—which he had thought should be red—was as prominent as it had been the night before.

"Yes, it's impossible for normal people to drive in Delhi anymore, and it's getting more impossible every day. Tell me what you would like to see."

"I didn't think you would come. I seemed to have offended you last night."

She looked pleased. "Not offended, actually. Unless by an old-fashioned actress you meant Tun Tun."

"Who was she?"

"The round, fat one. And very silly."

They laughed. "Well? What would you like to see?"

"What do you suggest?"

"I suggest we first go to Old Delhi. The Red Fort, from where the Mughals ruled India. And the great mosque. That should interest you. You people ruled us for seven centuries, you know."

"Oh? All right, to Old Delhi then."

He wondered about *you* and *us. You people?* It amused him. He could never have come up with these designations.

His knowledge of the Mughal Empire was perfunctory—vague memories of history lessons in school and a popular Hindi film seen in childhood, which he had found exotic and barely understood, and lately a few book reviews. There seemed a certain romance attached to the period, a nostalgia, though there was hardly a hint of that in the modern city they were driving through. She told him that historically there had been several cities of Delhi. They were driving through the most recent one, New Delhi, which was the contribution of the Britishers (as she called them) when they made it the capital of the Raj. It was designed by Sir Edwin Lutyens. People were now calling it "Lutyens's Delhi," talk of colonial hangovers! She beamed as she pointed out the India Gate inside a lush green park which they circled, the presidential residence on its exclusive hill, called Raisina, the row of crafts shops from all the states of the country, and Connaught Circus, and as he watched with reflective wonder, he could feel her eyes upon him.

"You see, India is not all poor and dirty."

"I never said that."

"But all this is British-built. No architecture of significance has been built since Independence, as Ravi often says."

The streets became progressively busier and chaotic, until the driver came to a stop near an ancient-looking archway. "Here we get off," she said, opening the door on her side. They were at the Ajmeri Gate of the old city, and as he stepped onto the broken pavement and looked around him he thought to himself that this was the India he had heard and read about—and feared: crowded, jostling, cluttered, and infinitely noisy. The sun came down like a bludgeon and he was already soaked in sweat. There was the constant bustle and scream of activity, rapid changes of scene in all the three hundred and sixty degrees around him. She held on to his arm to steady him. A bicycle rickshaw stopped and offered its services, and with some difficulty, she going up first and pulling him in, the two of them clambered up the shaky contraption. "Jama Masjid," Mohini briskly instructed the driver and off he went, struggling initially to get their two weights rolling with his thin legs. The ride was wobbly and bone-shaking. They hardly spoke, pretending they were not actually touching in the confined space of their seat. The narrow street was jammed with rickshaws and pushcarts, pedestrians squeezing through any space they could find. One odd motorbike threaded its way past them, claiming rights by virtue of power and noise. This is India, he thought; would I have experienced it on my own, so close, in this rawness? The city of my forebears, even if a hundred years removed. He smiled his gratitude to her.

"I rarely come here," she raised her voice to explain, "but I thought you would enjoy experiencing the real India." She casually pulled out the end of her sari from under him.

"Thank you. And the other India, of the Recreational Club—isn't that real?"

"The DRC? A bit removed. But it's necessary, don't you think? Who can stand this *bheed* all the time?" She indicated the street scene outside with a wave of a hand.

"Most of these people live here, I presume," he said, watching her.

"Most of them, yes. Could you?"

There hid a certain aggression behind that friendly manner, he had noticed this the previous night too, it sparked out in those quick, sudden retorts. What unconscious animus could it possibly rise from? But the friendliness must be genuine, or why take time off to show a stranger a more authentic India? Perhaps she regretted it already, this adventure in the dust and heat? He watched her as she exhorted the driver to please not go over the potholes.

Suddenly a wave of brilliant warm sunlight fell upon them, and they had reached the open end of the street. Before them, behind a wall, lurked the great mosque, its immense white dome rising up into a shimmering sky. The area outside was grungy, with motor spares spread out on sidewalks, vendors selling fruit from carts, hoardings on the building-fronts advertising rooms for rent and trips to Mecca and elsewhere. The rickshaw turned shakily round the corner and proceeded to the front side of the mosque, where they scrambled out. A crowded street led off from there, lined with eating places. They turned towards the mosque and passed through the security gate where three bored-looking men in deep khaki sat with automatics on their laps. They climbed up the wide steps of the mosque, removed their shoes, and entered an arched doorway into a large square terrace. The pavement was burning hot, though a running red carpet gave respite. Tall, thin minarets rose up at the four corners. Narrow arcades ran along three sides of the square, shady shelters where weary travellers had put down their loads and stretched out their legs. On the fourth side, under the dome, was the shallow, covered recess of the prayer hall, facing, presumably, Mecca to the west.

The red runner took them straight to the centre of the square, next to a fountain, the midday sun merciless on their uncovered heads. The milling crowds were local visitors and foreign tourists taking pictures with phones and cameras; a few men did their practiced ablutions at the fountain. It was an awe-inspiring place, the tall minarets, the immense white dome over the open prayer hall, its walls—what we could see of them—intricately, emphatically carved with the message of God that spoke to some but not to others.

"Would you like to go and pray?" she asked, looking up at him.

"What? No, thank you."

She gave a look of surprise. They walked over to a side to look at the Red Fort in the near distance.

"That is where the emperors lived. The last one was exiled to Burma after the Mutiny of 1857—we call it the First War of Independence. He died there—in Burma. Myanmar nowadays. He was a great poet. Bahadur Shah Zafar."

The name meant nothing to him.

Immediately below them was a market with makeshift stalls. A man who could have been a snake charmer sat forlorn under a tree before a basket. Snatches of a vigorous vocal music rose up to them. He recognized it as qawwali. All that is imposing, mysterious, and architecturally impressive—he mused to himself—lies dead amidst all that's makeshift, crowded, dirty, and rotting—the tumultuous, organic, and living. How different from all the Western cities he'd been to. He thought of Aileen. What would she have made of this?

They came out of the mosque, both a little subdued, and walked awhile through a maze of streets, and finally entered one that looked vaguely different from the others. It was special, she told him pertly, leading the way. It was wider and neater, quieter than the others, with no eating places and no goats around. Midway along they came to a wide-open gate which they entered to find themselves in a yard surrounded by low residences. Three boys were playing cricket but stopped when they entered; two young women looked down at them from a small balcony. Mohini turned to Munir.

"Well, what do you think?"

"I don't know. What should I think?"

She smiled.

"This is a haveli. In former times an entire extended family would live here together, in the rooms at the four sides. But now it has been divided up and there's been some construction, as you can see. But this particular haveli is where Kamala, the wife of Jawaharlal Nehru, our first prime minister, was raised. Imagine, the aristocratic Nehru family coming here, Nehru himself on the bridegroom's horse, to escort the bride away!"

She was charming when she was excited—her eyes opened wider, and the smile was mischievous. She was enjoying her control over him.

Outside, further up along the street, they came to what seemed like a hole in the wall, a crooked doorway into a dark space, through which a few women were trickling in and out. By their demeanour he realized that this was a temple. "Wait here," she said, throwing off her heeled sandals outside. "I won't be a minute."

"Can't I come with you?"

"Really? Yes, certainly you can. It's a temple."

He followed her into a dark room, long and narrow with a grimy cement floor; on their right, towards the back of the room, a few women had taken shelter to rest; to their left, against the wall, was a dimly lit shrine. And right above them was the strangest sight: a large and heavy metal ring descending from the ceiling, with numerous little brass bells suspended all around its rim and centre. The shrine was modestly decorated with marigolds and an idol of a god, behind which quietly sat the priest. Mohini covered her head with her sari end, joined her hands and knelt before the idol. Munir looked around nervously, then shakily half-knelt beside her, joining his hands too. The priest gave them some water, which, following Mohini, Munir sipped from his hand, dabbing his head with what remained. The watching priest then gave them each some coarse sugar pellets.

When they were outside, back in the brightness, she turned to him and said, "But you are a Muslim."

He took a breath, then replied, "If you say so. But I don't describe myself by a faith."

He felt stupid saying that, but it was the naked truth.

"But you bowed to our gods."

"Your gods . . . Well, I paid my respects to the gods."

"What are you, then?"

"Do I have to be something?"

"How do people know you, then?"

"As just another person. A friend. A neighbour. An author."

"All right, then. Just a person. Just an author. But I'm not convinced, I can tell you that."

He laughed. "Yes, just a person. Could we go to that glittering street that we passed? The one with all the lights?"

"Dariba Kalan—the jewellery market? You *are* full of surprises! Let's go. I can help you with the bargaining, if you want to buy something for your wife."

He opened his mouth to explain, but said nothing. A bicycle rickshaw took them to the jewellery market. It was less busy than suggested by all its glitter, but she explained that many shoppers came later in the day and on the weekends.

"You cannot have a wedding in Delhi without half a dozen visits here, believe me. Invitation cards, decorations, jewellery— gold, silver, diamond and whatnot—everything you need for a wedding you can find here. Except alcohol." She smiled.

They walked a short distance down this street, and back up again. Is *this* it? he said to himself. Is this where Dada came from? When he was young, to his ears "Dariba" had been synonymous with Delhi. How fateful to find himself here. A vague sense of possessiveness had come over him. He peered into shops, stared at the owners who stared back over their glass counters. On an impulse he walked into an alley to examine the residences there. All the while she watched him with amusement. Finally they went inside a shop, and he bought a pair of gold earrings.

"A successful visit to Old Delhi, then. And you purchased something."

"Yes. Thank you. But I'm exhausted now."

"Let's eat first, then we'll return to that haven where you've put up. Do you have a strong stomach?"

"I think so. How strong?"

"Let's take a chance. Nothing ventured, nothing gained, as we say. There's a place nearby called Karim's. It's world-famous and it's been here since the time of Bahadur Shah. Karim himself was one of the emperor's chefs. Your visit would not be complete without eating here."

"To Karim's, then."

"Tally-ho."

Karim's was one of a cluster of eating places nearby that all offered the same cuisine, kebabs and biryani occupying pride of place, releasing enticing aromas into the street. Of them, Karim's had the distinction of having its entrance leading inside through a passageway to a counter. Behind it were scattered a number of modest dining rooms on two floors. They were taken to an upper room, which was less full and where a few young tourists were being served.

"You eat non-veg, of course?"

"Meat . . . ? Yes, in moderation. And you . . . ?"

"Sometimes. But I don't eat beef. Well, not usually, anyway." She smiled. "I'll join you if you do."

They had lamb kebabs and a vegetable curry with naan.

She asked, and he told her about himself. He was recently widowed. He had been an analyst at the private wealth sector of the Bank of Montreal, but left some years ago to pursue writing. Not a wise decision, it turned out. He had arrived in Toronto from Kenya as a graduate student. His wife, Aileen, had worked at the bank too; that's where he met her. They had a daughter, Razia, who was in New York.

"You did well in Canada."

"Yes, I've done well. Too well, perhaps."

That was too quick and a mistake.

"How can you do too well?"

He shrugged, and she said, "I see."

But did she? The good life, the enviable success—and he was still looking for that edge through the softness that was Canada, searching for that rawness that he seemed to have lost. Even this despair of the artist seemed somehow a luxury and false. Was anything real at all anymore? But perhaps there had been a tingle of relief, a rush of sinful release in his recent loss of his wife? He looked at her.

"And you?"

She wrote a weekly column for the daily paper the *Express Times* and taught a course in English at a college twice a week. Her family were refugees from Sargodha, which became a part of Pakistan after the Partition. Did he know about the Partition? Yes, he did. Her family migrated to Delhi, and later moved to Shimla when her father was offered a teaching job at the university. She had married early—Ravi's family happened to be holidaying in the hills from Delhi, and spotted her. She was a good catch, she informed him, with a twinkle in her eye, educated but traditional. And pretty. Again that twinkle. They had two daughters. Asha was sixteen and still at school, Priya was nineteen, at university in Hyderabad. Ravi was in the security services and travelled constantly. Very hush-hush, and let's not talk about it.

"So we could be being watched."

"Possibly," she laughed. "You'd better behave!"

"What kind of columns do you write?"

"Human interest—from different angles—social, political. The last one was on teenage dating. A lot of that goes on nowadays."

"And do you approve? What did you say in the column?"

"We have to accept that India is changing, I said. Obvious, isn't that. How we respond to the changes depends on each family. But we should trust our kids."

"That's very wise, I think."

They took a rickshaw back to Ajmeri Gate, where the young Nepalese driver stood patiently leaning against the car. Before she got in, she bought some vegetables from a street vendor, which the driver picked up and placed next to him in the front seat. They didn't speak much on the way back and before long Munir had nodded off. He thought he heard her speaking on the phone.

When they reached the Club, she got off with him and sent the driver off.

"Ravi was on the phone, he will pick me up later. I'll wait in the library. You must want to go up to your room and rest—don't let me keep you."

That was abrupt and took him by surprise.

"Well, thank you for showing me around. I would never have made it on my own—I'm truly grateful."

And they parted.

In his room he fell instantly asleep; he was still jet-lagged. At half past five, after a shower and armed with a book to read, he came outside and walked across the patio to the lounge for tea. Resisting the temptation to order one of the pastries so abundantly displayed in the anteroom, he stepped inside the cafeteria. As expected it was crowded, filled with the clamour of voices and the clatter of migrating tea trays. There was only one table he could possibly sit at, at the far end, occupied by one person;

it was Mohini. She was facing towards him and waved energetically at him to come over.

"You look fresh," she observed.

"I feel fresh—like a new person. Listen—don't let me impose—isn't your husband joining you?"

"He'll take his time. Sit. Don't be so formal."

He sat down and ordered a Darjeeling tea, feeling rather uneasy. She had dismissed him summarily after their sojourn, perhaps with second thoughts about having done the improper thing, being out with a man on a pleasure trip. Then why this change of . . . attitude?

"There are men with automatics outside on the grounds," he said. "Your husband's?"

"He's not so obvious. Or he would not be good at his job. But there are others. A lot of powerful men come here; you couldn't tell by just looking at them."

He didn't inquire, and she fell silent. Then she went on, "You see that sardarji, the Sikh with the blue turban? With the pudgy pocked face? Don't look now. He was head of security in Punjab during the Khalistan emergency. It's said the emergency was defeated using 'encounter killings.' Shoot on sight. He was responsible. Those men outside must be his protection. And the slimy-looking one in the corner at the front—in the pure-white outfit, surrounded by that crowd of adulating women and young men . . . Don't look. He's Jetha Lal from Ahmedabad. A Hindu purifier. In the business of protecting cows and Hindu women. And calling for the censorship of books. According to him, our ancient gurus invented the internet and knew about relativity. A couple of years ago he was into breaking up impure liaisons."

"Impure liaisons? Such as?"

"Love jihad." She smiled. "Hindu-Muslim relationships; also Hindu-Christian. Not to forget low caste–high caste."

"How did he go about that?"

"Not him, his goons. They would kidnap the girl and beat up the boy."

"And he got away with it?"

"Got away? He boasted of it to a newspaper! You can watch him on YouTube."

He looked around the room, aware of her eyes on him. In the corner to his right a young man was giving an interview, straining to be heard through the din. There was a book on his table. A photographer was readying her equipment next to him. As Munir looked away, an elderly couple came by and warmly greeted Mohini. She introduced Munir to them as a famous author from Canada. They hadn't heard of him. Finally a server came and told "Madam" that "Sir" was seated at another table, and she got up. Munir thanked her again for the morning and watched her leave. Ravi was at a table against the side wall, facing two other men. He too was watching his wife approach, and for a moment met Munir's eye. Lean and straight, Munir observed, just like an army man, and with his hair dyed brown. An indulgent smile on his long, creased face.

The next morning Munir spent a few hours in the library reading up on Delhi's crowded and confusing history, knowing he could only catch partial glimpses of it. The library was a long hall with a bank of computers at one end and rows of bookshelves at the other. In between were carrels where men and women sat absorbed in study. The atmosphere was hushed and, according to a stern-sounding notice, mobile phones were strictly forbidden; the staff were helpful. Later he took a taxi to ruins of the thirteenth-century city of Siri, well within the present Delhi, from where the stern Sultan Alauddin had warded off a Mongol attack. If the Mongols had persisted, Delhi would certainly have been sacked and its story different. There were now a sports complex and an auditorium at the site. Nearby was Hauz Khas, site of a water reservoir built by the sultan for his city, and now an exclusive residential and shopping enclave next to a deer park. The following morning he visited Tughlaqabad, the city that came next after Siri; collapsed upon itself, it stood high on a hill, overlooking the bustling car traffic on the plain below, as stonily ascetic and grim as the ruler who built it, Muhammad bin Tughlaq.

At DRC during those two days there was no sign of Mohini in the lounge or the bar. He would peer at arriving members as they were dropped off in their cars, glance frequently at his phone as though willing it to ring, inquire at the desk for messages. He missed her, he admitted to himself, providing perfectly innocent reasons why he did so, and quickly chiding himself not to act immaturely. But that oval face with those deep brown eyes, and the rich voice and lively combative manner, were hard to dismiss from his mind. Perhaps the attraction was nothing more than nostalgia, her Indian-ness reminding him of his Punjabi home in Nairobi's Eastleigh; and certainly he was lonely, pathetically so, and desperate. But he would be out of here in a little more than a week and this silly phase forgotten.

Meanwhile there was the library and Delhi's fantastically crowded history—in which he had found a tiny corner for himself.

——

On December 23, 1912, on the once-stately thoroughfare of Chandni Chowk that emerges from the Red Fort in Old Delhi, a bomb was thrown at British Viceroy Lord Hardinge's procession in what came to be known as the Bomb Outrage, or the Delhi Conspiracy Case. "It exploded with terrific force," a report said, "blowing to pieces the attendant standing immediately behind Lord Hardinge . . ." The Viceroy was thrown down from his elephant, unconscious and bleeding. Subsequently the police went on a rampage in the area, and four men were eventually charged with the conspiracy. One was captured and sentenced to jail; he had died only recently, old and invalid in an alley off Chandni Chowk, according to a report in the *Express Times*. The three other men were hanged, but the man who had thrown the bomb, Rash Behari Bose, had slipped away to Japan and was never caught.

It was some months after this bombing—on March 21, 1913, according to an old British travel permit—that Yunus Ali Khan, Munir's grandfather, had arrived with his bride in Mombasa in British East Africa, where he found work as a goldsmith; a few years later he moved inland to Nairobi's Eastleigh area, where many Punjabis had settled.

Have I come a full circle, Munir thought, somewhat stunned upon reading this snippet of history; has Delhi now reclaimed me? Dada having left Delhi only three months after the "Outrage": is there a significance? And what a turn of fate that there would be a Hardinge Street in Nairobi—always pronounced "Laard Hardinge Street" in the home, in the Punjabi fashion.

But it was an older Delhi that caught his writerly fascination.

He was sitting on a bench in Sikandar Gardens, having completed his afternoon walk. He had never lived in any place where centuries spoke loudly from every direction. But then history in India came with a price, paid often with blood. Before him, on the green across the walking track, stood a large mausoleum, of the typical inlaid sandstone of such buildings, with a magnificent dome. The sun was low, the ground moist, the air effulgent. Flowers were in bloom, in every conceivable colour. He watched boys at a game of soccer in the shadow of the monument. A young, furtive couple strolled by in front of him, murmuring to themselves. He heard a woman's high-pitched voice, and looked up to see a noisy group walking organically together like some multi-legged animal, in the middle of which was the man in white, Jetha Lal, whom Mohini had pointed out in the cafeteria as "the Purifier." He was of medium height, somewhat stocky, and bald, with a sparse ring of white hair on his head and a smooth, radiant face. As before, he wore a folded blue shawl on one shoulder that was a sign of status, Munir guessed.

They disappeared round a bend, and Munir nodded off, until he felt his phone buzzing against his thigh. His excitement as he shoved his hand into his pocket and clumsily brought out the phone was, in his own words to himself later, purely juvenile. It was Mohini calling, of course.

"Where have you run off to? I'm at DRC, but you're not here. I thought you might have left."

"I'm at Sikandar Gardens. I've just finished my walk and am catching my breath."

"I'll come and join you."

"I missed you."

"Sure you did."

She took ten minutes to get there. The park had fairly filled up, he observed, watching her approach on the track from the left. She was wearing a pink salwar and a white kameez, and her controlled smile as she neared brought dimples to her flushed cheeks.

"You've discovered Sikandar Gardens. Good. It's wonderful, isn't it, all this greenery. Can you believe it, we are actually sitting here in the middle of Delhi?"

He told her what he'd been up to the last few days, and she was surprised by his adventures. Not only had he been to the tomb of the Mughal Humayun, he had also gone to the top of the old, abandoned city of Tughlaqabad. And he had returned to Old Delhi by metro and walked around.

"I'm impressed. I guess as a well-travelled man you are used to exploring places by yourself. I must have been a burden the other day."

"Not at all. It's always nice to have a local guide. Without your initiative, I might not even have ventured out."

How craven! She was flattered, smiled her appreciation. They discussed the various cities of Delhi and their sultans, which he was reading about and found exciting, and which she recalled only vaguely from her history courses.

"I read that until not long ago, between the various cities of Delhi there used to be only vegetation," he said.

"You'll soon become an expert," she said, tilting her head to squint and smile at him, revealing a few thin lines at the edges of her eyes. "You're already telling me things that I don't know. But what does a writer do with all that knowledge about the past? Does it help in your writing? Give you ideas?"

"A writer doesn't ask himself that. Or herself. It's simply there, the knowledge and the experience . . . and whatever. It comes out whenever, in its own way . . ."

"You're an odd one."

"How?"

"No . . . I meant, the other day in the old city. You were hardly impressed by the great mosque—ho-hum, your face said. No—wait a minute! And then all that interest in Dariba Kalan—jewellery!"

"Yes. Well the mosque is grand, but there are many grand buildings in the world, aren't there? But Dariba . . ."

"Dariba Kalan."

"Yes. I should have told you. My grandfather came from Delhi. And he was a goldsmith."

No need to say more. She took a deep breath.

"So you *are* a Delhi-ite after all! It's karma only, I tell you! Your dada left Delhi, and now you've returned. Why didn't you say before? It's so *exciting!*"

"I was waiting for the right moment."

They walked back to the Club through the parking lot. The stray dogs were annoying; cars hovered around in frustration waiting for spaces, guided by an attendant. He helped her over a puddle, quickly withdrew his hand, and she threw him a glance. She shooed away a bothersome canine he didn't know how to handle. They entered through the side gate, went through the library building and arrived at the front garden. It was dusk by now, the pole lamps had come on, and there were no men with guns to be seen. By this time the bar was open, but she preferred the cafeteria, which was deserted. They began their tea in a silence that felt rather conspiratorial, aware of the servers who knew them both. Finally she got up to go, and he walked her to the driveway.

"I'll call you," she said softly, as she got into her taxi.

And he knew from that last lingering look that something significant had happened.

He took an auto rickshaw to the shrine of the Sufi Nizamuddin and was dropped off on a busy highway at the entrance to a metro station. He crossed underground and emerged into an unpaved, potholed alley—a world unto itself, crowded and noisy. Beards, hijabs, skullcaps; dhotis, long shirts hanging out. Beggars and touts rushed at him as he proceeded alongside a wall of loud Islamic-themed paintings and hangings, the artists sitting idly beside them on the ground. When he inquired about the shrine, he was encouraged to keep walking. All the while his train of hopeful beggars following him, goading him to walk faster. *Aage chalo, sahab . . . this way, sir!* The road took a bend, leaning towards a narrow, covered corridor to his right. Men called out, welcoming him as though he had been expected. He entered into a passage that was hectic and festive, and dizzyingly colourful. Vocal music blared out from every stall, religious videos flickering on small TVs along the way. The smell of spice and food. There were stalls for keeping your shoes and for buying roses and sweets to take to the shrine; restaurants cried out for money to feed the poor. Fifty rupees per beggar. All along, men gesturing and calling out. Finally, after several twists of the path, he came to an open doorway where it seemed right to take off his shoes. A man sitting on the ground nearby accepted them; another man in a window above sold him a tray of roses. He declined sweets and entered into a blaze of sunlight.

He was in a paved yard quietly crowded with people and found himself gazing up at a rather awesomely oversized structure, glittering with blue miniature tiles, topped by a dome. This was the mausoleum of Nizamuddin Auliya, the Sufi mystic who had defied both sultans, Alauddin and Tughlaq. Still present in human hearts, seven hundred years later. Remembered even in Nairobi, he recalled. The building itself looked ancient yet new, beautiful yet makeshift. A tall, overweight man in white shirt and pyjamas immediately stepped over and casually greeted him, and advised him to place a handkerchief over his head. Fortunately he had one. Nizamuddin Dargah, the man said, lifting a hand, Come, and guided him through the crowd. A wide veranda went around the building, enclosed by a white latticework railing on three sides and open at the front. Munir took a step up to the veranda and his guide gently shoved him towards the door to the inner sanctum, into which a stream of men were proceeding. Munir joined them with his tray, threw his roses onto the grave, circumambulated around it and came out again into the brightness. Outside, the man was waiting for him with a register and took down Munir's name and address and accepted a donation. Then he guided Munir to the second mausoleum on the site, further up, that of the poet Amir Khusrau, a close disciple of Nizamuddin. Somehow a poet was a kindred spirit. Khusrau was a historian and a musician as well, whose compositions were still popular.

"I understand there is the grave of the historian Ziauddin Barani here," Munir told his guide. "I've recently read about it . . ."

Barani was the historian of Alauddin's period whose vivid lives of the sultans and their times had gripped Munir's imagination in the library. Without Barani, Delhi's history would have been a lot poorer. In his introduction he had rather touchingly complained about his contemporaries' ignorance of their past; it was an observation, Munir thought, that applied even today.

"Come." The man led him to a small unmarked grave, opposite Nizamuddin's mausoleum, on which had been placed a single rose.

Thus the historian. And thus fate. Next time he would bring a fresh rose for Ziauddin Barani.

He felt a mix of emotions. The spiritual atmosphere, the attendants hustling for funds, the piety on the faces, the desperation in the women who were not allowed inside the sanctum but had surrendered their desperation to the ribbons they had tied on the interstices of the railings. He imagined his dada coming here for one last time to seek blessings for his voyage to Kenya and the new life he was to begin there. He would never see Delhi again, would always remember it. Certainly the name of Nizamuddin Auliya was familiar from Munir's childhood; he had never known what it signified, until now.

He put on his shoes and departed. As he emerged into the dirt alley leading out to the road, desperate beggar women chased after him, some holding up their babies. He was horrified, embarrassed. Were they sincere, were the babies theirs, was there a godfather using them—but what did that matter? Hurriedly getting into an auto, he put some money into the hands of two women and received their blessings. "God help you. God give you a son."

"I have a daughter," he murmured. "And I love her."

The auto driver chuckled.

"You are a good man, sahab," he said.

He called Mohini later that day.

"You said you would call," he chided gently.

"*You* could have called."

Again the sparring. He was patient.

"You promised, so I waited. I didn't want to embarrass you by calling at an awkward moment. Is this a good time?"

"Yes, it's a good time. I'm sorry . . . I do tend to scold you, don't I? You take it so well. I'm still at the college. What have you been doing these past few days?"

"This morning I visited Nizamuddin Dargah. It was a moving experience. I can't get over the fact that it's been there almost seven hundred years."

"I could have come with you . . . It's been a long time since I visited the Dargah."

He had been better off going alone; some things should be experienced in solitude. He didn't tell her that, but reminded her that he was scheduled to fly back to Toronto in a couple of days. She said she would come to meet him next morning, there was a place she wanted to show him.

"What is it?"

"Wait and see."

The next morning she called and told him to wait for her outside the front gate at ten, and he duly obeyed. To his surprise, an auto stopped beside him on the road and she peeped out and told him to hop in.

"What, no car and driver today?"

"No. The car was needed today." She paused, then murmured, "And these drivers talk sometimes."

"What is there to talk about?"

"You don't understand. You are from there."

He thought he understood; he was not totally alien to the culture. She saw this on his face and smiled. "I wanted to spend some time with you alone . . . do you . . . remember how disappointed you were the other day to see my driver?"

"I didn't think you'd noticed."

They were visiting Safdarjung Tomb, she said, leaning forward to instruct the auto driver, straining her green bodice, revealing her pale skin. He looked away. They turned right at the first crossroad, zoomed along the wide Lodi Road and very shortly stopped behind the busy bus-stand at its end. They stepped off onto a clear, unpaved stretch of ground where a few vendors had spread out mangoes. Before them stretched an ancient wall, having reposed there for how many centuries, Munir wondered, staring up at it. He was aware that he was half holding his breath, waiting for the surprise she had promised; his eyes were wide open. They bought their tickets and entered through the gate. In Delhi you could walk through gates and doors into entire worlds and histories. This one was a large and lush garden, at the centre of which rose a discoloured mausoleum. Two young couples— on an escapade, Munir guessed—strolling on the grass; a young man stretched out, a book in his hand. No one else. The mausoleum was large but plain; the dome was weathered, with no ornamentation left. A Mughal official named Safdarjung was buried here. The grave was a raised platform under the dome. They approached and went up the wide steps at the sides. Looking out from the high veranda that went around the structure, Munir was struck by the proportion and harmony of the entire site, its awed silence, when just beyond the walls lay all the tumult of the modern city. What kind of mind would contemplate, create this sense of beauty and grace? It seemed as if an alien race had descended here a long time ago and built this memorial to its presence.

They strolled in the park and came to rest under a small tree. They had not said much during their inspection, now she said, "You don't get much privacy in India, but this is one of those places where you can find it. I guess that's because it's not as popular as other sites."

"You've come here often?"

"No, and not in a long time. Soon after my marriage I would come here with a friend, when we wanted to get away."

He watched her. The sun fell warm and slanting upon them and caught part of her shape in its light. I should have been a painter, he thought inanely. The worry lines on her face took away from it, but he had observed the effect of its magnetism on others, especially the man she contemptuously called the Purifier, Jetha Lal. Those deep eyes. Her braid came down almost to the waist. The bodice was tight and exposed a band of midriff.

"What?" she said, meeting his eyes.

"I've grown very fond of you. It's silly, isn't it. I'm sorry."

"It's not silly. Please don't say you're sorry. I've grown fond of you too—even though you are something of a mystery. Maybe that's good . . ."

"Then you think it's okay for us to be fond of each other?"

"Yes," in a lower voice this time. Again those haunting eyes.

They talked long and with intensity, drawing closer indelibly, desperately clinging to each other through the words they exchanged. It was as though, if the moment were not grasped and held, it would slip away forever; this magic and its forbidden possibilities would vanish into mundane, guilt-free reality. That must not happen. Whatever the consequences. Whatever? He was going away. She was married. Time heals. It must not.

He took hold of her braid, tenderly, safely, and she caught hold of his hand, to push it away, but then held on to it. He squeezed it hard.

"You are going away," she said.

"Yes."

"But you'll come back soon. Will you?"

He took a deep breath, then said, "Yes. Of course I will. And then?"

"And then."

He took her hand and placed it into his and played with her slim, tender fingers for a moment. They got up, dusted themselves, and came out of the park together.

Mohini Singh

"THERE WAS THIS interesting writer at the DRC bar—where were you, anyway? Did you get my texts? I had to sit at this man's table—complete stranger—for a full half hour! But he turned out to be very nice."

Ravi looked up from his paper and smiled. He put it down on his lap. The television was on but neither of them paid attention. Another overheated panel discussion, an incoherent shouting match. Ravi said, "I was at the door, about to enter, when I saw that group—Venkat and the others—sitting on the patio outside. I joined them for a bit. That Gujarati fellow Jetha Lal was there."

"Those fellows practically live at DRC. It's a progressive establishment, what business do they have there?"

"Well, we had an interesting discussion. You would have enjoyed it. They were saying that with our new prime minister, India has finally found itself. Gone back to its ancient roots."

"Poppycock. India has always been tied to its roots. That's been the problem all along. I tell you, the crazies have crept out of the woodwork."

"Well."

"Jetha Lal said this thing about ancient roots?"

"Ram-rajya has arrived."

"More like Gau-rajya, the Kingdom of the Cow, the way they are going on."

"It's only a metaphor."

"It's not a metaphor!"

"Well, I've not been trained like you in English. They mean a nation with Hindu values. Restoration of Hindu pride."

He threw a glance at her, but she didn't respond and he picked up his paper; he hesitated before going back to it and asked, "What about this man—you were saying?"

"He turned out to be an author from Canada."

"Canada." He went back to his paper. "A good country. Quiet."

She had done her duty. Should she tell him she had promised to show Munir around Delhi? Why, if he wasn't interested?

She watched him as he read, exclaiming softly when something caught his interest. Politics or cricket. What else was there in this country. Bollywood, but that interested neither of them, though she kept her eye on it for her columns. His hair had a buzz cut, dyed brown to hide the years, but the emaciated face had lost its Kashmiri glow, giving the game away, partly. He had been handsome once, was still good-looking. Slim and still fairly tall, straight-backed. How would she herself fare, putting on weight when she was not careful, already puffing when she climbed up two flights? And that tumour. Benign, but it had given her a scare. She didn't tell him about it. Hide the chinks in your armour.

"This Canadian at the DRC . . ."

She looked towards him, surprised at the sudden interest.

"... French? They want an independent country, I understand.
We keep an eye on them. In case our own people get ideas."

"No, he's Indian."

"Indian?"

"From Kenya—he's at the DRC for two weeks. We can see
him when we go there."

He sat back and they watched the news. Politics drew them
together, and he always had his dry comments to add to the
day's headlines from his own inside knowledge of government.
He could not tell her everything, obviously, but often she was
privy to stuff that was not widely known or became public
only later. The prime minister's projected visit somewhere, for
example, or an upcoming statement—or lack of it—on something of concern such as another incidence of lynching. And
then there was the gossip about the political bigwigs.

Asha lumbered in in her pyjamas, sat down partially on her
father's lap, watched the television with disinterest.

"Finished homework, beti?" he asked.

"Mum . . . I need help. Come."

"At this time you tell me?"

Mohini got up and followed Asha to the dining room table.
When will this end, the constant oversight? she wondered. She
stood over the girl, ruffling her curls, and bent to look more
closely at the homework.

"Asha, you know I can't do this differential stuff. It was a night-
mare for me, and now it's even more advanced. Couldn't you
have called your tutor? What are we paying this Bhagat chap for?"

"I was doing English. Mamma, what will I do? . . ."

The girl's despair was greater than Mohini's. The final exams
were twelve months away, and she was not going to be ready.

"Do the best you can for now, Asha," Mohini said. She should have been on the girl's case earlier. Only she was to blame, like all mothers. But how much can you give of yourself?

"What will become of her?" she asked Ravi, returning to the living room. "She's behind in her maths and just can't cope. I thought the tutor would help."

He looked up, unconcerned. He was an optimist, and he could pull strings to get his daughter admitted to some college. Influence was a blessing. Power was.

"We can send her away—to Canada," he said with a smile. "Why not? A foot outside the country, not a bad idea."

"I hope you are not serious. My daughter is not a foot. I don't want to send her somewhere far away."

He smiled. She stared at him in his equanimity. Nothing seemed to bother him, at home at least. Politics and their daughters, that's what they could talk about, nothing else. When was the last tender word from him? Yes, during the holiday on the Andaman Islands, when he was quite rampant. Did he have other women? Likely, she believed, with all the travelling he did. That sweater. She had not confronted him about it. Blue with thin red stripes, she had definitely not bought it. The label was not Indian. He could always say he had bought it in Chennai, or somewhere. But he did not go around buying sweaters for himself.

He turned the TV off.

"That Waqar," he told her in his peculiarly dry voice, always inflected high. "He's talking, finally. They were planning to suicide-bomb during the PM's visit to Ahmedabad last June. You'll read about it in tomorrow's paper." He gave a smile.

"He admitted that?"

He stared at her.

"Oh, they can be convinced it's in their best interest to talk . . . there are ways. These people, when will they learn? They should all have left in 'forty-seven . . ."

"Then we would have had more problems in the south," she said, staring after him as he walked off to the bedroom at his even pace. He still marched, she thought with amusement. Did he too yearn for that Celestial Kingdom? He was too sophisticated for that.

Should she have told him about her plan to show the visitor around Delhi? What did it matter, he hardly took interest in her activities. And what if she asked him, and he said no? Someone with the surname Khan? Definitely a no-no. She had not committed to Munir Khan; she should probably not go. Forget about it. He was a stranger, an alien, and of the wrong kind . . . Mamma, you are a bigot. That's what Priya, the older one, had said to her, using a new word. "If I'm a bigot, it's what the world has made me," Mohini had replied, very much irritated. "My parents come from Pakistan; they were refugees escaping murderous Muslim hordes during the Partition." For a few weeks Priya had been speaking about a special friend, and they had all teased her about him. All innocent, but also not quite so. She was sixteen then. And nowadays girls had boyfriends. This friend was a scientist's son, well travelled. He was brilliant in school. He played cricket. So what doesn't he do, this friend of yours, they asked. Bring him home, one day. And he came home. His name was Aarif Sheikh. They had to do their all to persuade the girl to cool the friendship. "This kind of thing is not done." "It's the times we live in, it's our culture, which is ancient and different." Out came the angry retort, "Isn't Shah Rukh Khan married to Gauri, isn't Aamir Khan married to Kiran?" "They are Bollywood people, they live differently from us," Mohini had replied, with a glance at her husband. "Didn't Indira Gandhi marry a Parsi?" To which Ravi contributed, "Muslims are more different than Parsis."

The next morning Mohini finally told Ravi about her plans, but only when he prompted her.

"No teaching today—so what do you plan to do?"

"I'll work on my column. Then I thought I would show that author around—you know, the one I met at the Club . . ."

"The Canadian. Good."

He didn't ask for the name, she didn't elaborate.

After her sojourn in Old Delhi with Munir Khan, summarily dismissing him afterwards, she had gone and sat down in the Club's crowded tea lounge to wait for Ravi. She had enjoyed herself; it had been years since she'd been to Old Delhi. She'd felt a sense of freedom in the midst of the crowds, away from the prying eyes of her society. At the same time she couldn't help that nagging twinge of doubt, a little guilt. She was a married woman, there were proprieties. Sitting close-packed with a man in a bumpy cycle rickshaw . . . Was she blushing now? People saw, and they talked. Her driver could talk. Which was why she had called Ravi from the car on the way back and arranged to have dinner with him. She would be seen with her husband.

Munir Khan was a puzzle. How could a person not *believe*? Certainly he believed in a philosophy of living, in right and wrong. But that was all too abstract. She believed in God; and the gods. It was the same thing, logic didn't come into it. You just believed, you did puja to the idols, you asked them for favours and guidance. Occasionally you visited a temple or got hold of a Brahmin to perform certain rituals. You went to a guru and sat at his feet. All that embedded you in a way of being called Hinduism. You were like any other Indian. Any other Hindu, at least. Was that quite accurate? . . .

She felt a little sorry for him. Such a floater. Without an anchor. But likeable . . . perhaps because of that? There were no hard edges to him. He had not tried to take advantage of her, as other men would have, he had treated her with respect. What else was there to him? she wondered; he positively intrigued her. The absolute delight on his face in the jewellery market. Guilelessly he had stood beside her and joined his hands in the temple. And he had positively flirted with her that night at the DRC bar, giving her that line about an Indian film star! A former film star—which one? Madhubala? Nutan? She had feigned annoyance but was actually flattered. She smiled.

She glanced around the lounge from her vantage point at the back. The clientele here, members all, looked older by the day. They dragged themselves in; some had to be assisted. Soon they'd come on stretchers. But you couldn't begrudge them their afternoon outing—where else could they go? We look after our old people here, unlike the West. We respect the elderly. So far. An idea for a column? And then there were the politicos and the fawning journalists. The occasional visitor from abroad, looking lost, or surrounded by local admirers.

Her eye fell on Jetha Lal, sitting midway in the room at his usual table against the misted glass wall. He joined his hands briefly to her, and she returned a smile but inwardly shuddered.

She had first met him in Ahmedabad when she accompanied Ravi on an official trip. Jetha Lal had volunteered his group of acolytes as a second line of defence for the PM's security. He's a bit fanatical, Ravi told her, but sometimes you need them, they are the only ones who are consistent. They cannot be bribed.

Munir was standing at the door, casting his eyes about for a place to sit. Without thinking, she waved him over. When he thanked her once more for taking him to the old city, she offered to show him some more of Delhi. Perhaps one or two of her favourite spots. What got into her? That was brash. Irresponsible. He was delighted. While they were chatting, a waiter came over with the tea which he had ordered and a summons to her from her husband, and she left to join Ravi at his table. No, she wouldn't introduce the two men. But she saw them exchange a glance. She didn't see Jetha Lal's curious eyes following her from one table to the other.

As she arrived at her husband's table, one of the men, wearing a scruffy beard with his white kurta and pyjama, stood up and joined his hands in an exaggerated greeting. He was called Kamleshwar, a professor at JNU, a man in his fifties. The other man was older, a former minister of foreign affairs, and he too joined his hands but didn't stand up. Kamleshwar had just finished an impassioned spiel, having counted votes on his fingers, with the pronouncement that were a national election to take place in the next few weeks, there was no way the Nationalist party could win a majority.

The minister, who was Liberal, grinned happily. But Ravi would have none of it. He spoke calmly, his voice measured.

"Do your counting, Professor, but come the next elections the Liberals will lose again; I see the signs everywhere I go. The Liberals ruled for far too many years, and the people are fed up."

Kamleshwar's passion was not to be quelled. "I travel around too, Ravi Sahab, and unlike you, forgive me, I travel by train and put up in guest houses"— he abruptly sat up and with a patronizing smile at Mohini, announced, "But let's set politics aside, we have a lady with us—a journalist! May I say, Mrs. Singh, I enjoy your columns immensely."

Mohini thanked him. The men went on with their argument, debating the current prime minister's possible length of tenure, and Mohini looked around, waved at a few people. The "Mrs. Singh" part always irked her; it put her in her place. Chapatti-maker. She watched Munir depart through the door. Jetha Lal passed by, in the middle of his group like a man carried away on a boat, and bowed a greeting to their table, baring his white teeth again. Ravi turned around and responded briefly.

"There's a happy man," he said, turning back. "If only one could have that certainty."

"Dangerous man," opined the minister.

"It's not as if your party doesn't have them."

"True."

It's always the same, Mohini thought. The same topics till doomsday. Politics and cricket. Doesn't anything else happen in this country?

The three men proposed to head over to the bar before going for dinner at the restaurant. Mohini said she must return home and help Asha with her homework. Bahadur, the driver, would take her, and the minister would drop off Ravi later in the evening.

She arrived home, Bahadur seeing her to the door, and saw Asha curled up on the sofa with a bag of crisps, watching the television. "What, no homework?" she exclaimed. "I'm stuck. I was waiting for you, Mamma," the girl replied. There was that guilty, helpless look as she sat up.

"I'll make some chapattis, you set the table now. Did Rukmini come?"

Rukmini, the part-time maid, had come and cooked the curry, daal, and rice. Mohini set about making chapattis. And then she and Asha had dinner. Afterwards, as the girl did her homework, she sat beside her and corrected her essay, and even called, deaf to her protests, Bhagat the maths and physics tutor and gave him an ultimatum.

"Look, Bhagat, we hired you to help improve Asha's marks. I must tell you that if they don't improve within a month, I'll have to fire you. Is that understood?"

Bhagat, an engineering student from a modest family who needed the extra cash, stammered, "Yes, ma'am, I'll do my level best. I promise. I'll spend twice the time with her. But ma'am—please make sure she does the homework I give her . . . it's well within her capabilities."

Mohini agreed and gave Asha the message. Asha said good-night and ambled off to her room with a look of relief. Mohini went to her room, changed, and got into bed. She couldn't sleep, and in the darkness she sat up for a long time, leaning against the headboard.

That first evening at the bar of DRC, when he'd introduced himself as Munir Aslam Khan, the tiniest shiver had shot through her. She called herself an educated, liberal Hindu woman of the generation after Independence. Yet she had known no Muslims.

There were no Muslims in her neighbourhood and schools when she was growing up; there were only a handful at her university. There were two Muslim girls in the class she taught currently, who always were together. At the Club she saw one or two sometimes. They were always "they . . ." And yet Munir was no different from anyone else. He could be a Malhotra. But what did she expect? Henna in his hair? A beard—a trim one like those Saudis had? A full, bushy one like those Taliban?

A picture came to her mind. The deep forehead, the soft face, that curious, bemused look. She gave herself a dopey smile. She liked him.

She was asleep when Ravi returned. He was in a good mood and affectionate, and he woke her up and wanted his bit.

The following morning she stayed home and wrote her column. "Love Letters in the Cloud." Tongue-in-cheek, to be sure. Valentine's Day was approaching. Smart, witty, and liberal, that was her style. The reference was to *Meghadootam*, the Sanskrit long poem by Kalidasa, in which a lover tells a passing cloud to take his message to his beloved who is far away. "The printed card is a nice but quaint tradition. Who has the time these days? Like Kalidasa, many of us now will use the cloud to send messages to our Valentines. Electronic, of course!" She looked up from the screen, pleased with herself. A sudden thought came; she quickly dismissed it.

All that morning she had debated intermittently, Shall I call him? I promised to take him out, but I can't. What will he think of me? He'll understand, probably prefers it that way. He's a private man. An author who's come to be by himself, to see his ancestral country. Didn't he say he wasn't writing any more, just toying around with ideas, how did he put it—"Kidding myself—it's a way to stay alive." Perhaps this visit to Delhi will revive him.

The day passed, with guilt and justifications, and similarly the next. On the afternoon of the third day, she went to teach her class in English literature at Lady Bhishmji College. After the class she met her dean and put it to her, "Professor Leelawati, here's a suggestion. Why don't we teach some Canadian novels? Why do we lay so much emphasis on British literature! The Raj is long gone."

Professor Leelawati, a plump, rosy-cheeked woman, wrinkled her nose.

"But the British have written the best literature."

Before the professor could trot out the holy name of Shakespeare, Mohini asked her, "There's a Canadian NRI writer visiting in Delhi, why don't we invite him to give a lecture?"

"Canadian NRI? Who is he?"

"Have you heard of Munir Khan?"

"Munir Khan? Sounds Pakistani."

"He's Indian. From Kenya, originally . . ."

"Let me think about it. You know these kids don't like anything extra outside the set syllabus."

Mohini knew that the dean would not take even a moment to think about it. Aruna Leelawati was there, courtesy of some politico, simply to warm a seat with that plump bottom of hers. She would not take an initiative unless there was money in it, or she got a foreign trip out of it. And even then, she would let others do the work.

From the college Mohini went to DRC, where she paid her bill and picked up an events schedule. But that was not why she had really come. She searched the lounge and the library, then stood outside near the driveway and called Munir. To her surprise he turned out to be at the park. She went to meet him. He was sitting on a bench looking anxious and broke into a wide smile upon seeing her approach. Those were sweet moments. They chatted casually, revealingly; at times she held back. She learned about his roots in Delhi, and told him about hers in Sargodha. They were both Delhi-ites. An hour passed; when they got up, it was almost dusk, and she had the feeling that something inside her had given way. She liked this man a lot, and she was glad she had sought him out today. While they walked back to the Club he took her hand to help her step over a puddle, and she sent off a bothersome stray dog that had taken a liking to him.

That evening Mohini again sat with Asha to help with her homework. And when her daughter went for a shower, Mohini went to the kitchen to make chapattis. Rukmini had prepared a chicken curry, which Asha and Ravi would eat, a vegetable curry, and daal. Twice Mohini almost picked up her phone, and once when it rang, her heart raced with anticipation and some fear. It was a solicitor.

The next morning, unasked, she told Ravi she was staying home again. As soon as he left with Bahadur, she went out to the street and hailed an auto. As she approached the Club, she rang up Munir. She was on her way and could he come down.

Had she misled her husband before? Of course she had. But not in this way.

She had come to Safdarjung Tomb first with her friend Surjeet, while on a school trip from Shimla. They'd had to write an essay on one of Delhi's monuments, and they picked this one, away from all the others. It was unimpressive, there was scant information about it, and it was not well preserved at all. There were hardly any people there. So they had walked around the garden, exchanging secrets, singing film songs to each other, talking about actors. A lot of giggling. Rajesh Khanna was the idol then. When, after her marriage, she moved to Delhi, Surjeet did so too, and a few times they had returned here. They stopped coming when they were noticed by some young men and teased. And then they both had children. She had not heard from Surjeet in a long time, did not know where she was.

As she was strolling in the park with Munir, those carefree days came back to her. It was still so quiet here, and green. And private. A forgotten haven. It was hard to find privacy in India, at home or at work—everywhere you felt crowded and jostled, subjected to curious looks and judgements. But here was one place where you could steal some time for yourself. Where you could come and simply be.

"What are you thinking?" he asked. They had come to sit on the grass under a small tree. It looked like almond, the leaves light green and broad, shimmering like tinsel in the sunlight.

"Oh, nothing. Nothing, really—I don't want to think anything at this moment—of responsibilities, cares—whatever! There will be time for that later." *There will be time* . . . who said that? She shook the thought away, the braid went flying across her curved back, and she smiled at him.

"Your hands are clasped tight . . ."

So that they don't stray. She felt a tingle run up her spine as she let him take her hand, play with it.

"It's blanched. You are very fair . . ."

"They say Shimla girls are fair . . . and beautiful." A mischievous smile came over her. "But I'm a Delhi girl, actually. Have you seen the film *Love in Simla*?"

"No. Though I might have heard of it. Long ago."

"Yes."

They came out of the gate and, not finding an auto, walked along Lodi Road. She felt awkward in her shoes; a cool breeze blew, though the sun was blinding. An auto soon came by and picked them up. He got off at the Club and she headed home, refusing his offer to escort her back.

They met again two days later in the afternoon. He was departing late that night and said he was packed. They had tea outside on the veranda of the cafeteria, facing the back garden with its lotus pond. The fountain in the middle was off. Beyond the wire fence on the left were the Sikandar Gardens, where in between the thick foliage walkers were visible hurrying along the track with purpose. She did her two days of yoga a week, but she thought she should seriously consider a walking regimen. She turned to look at him, saw him watching her.

"Don't forget about us, when you go back to your Canada!"

"How could I?" he protested gently.

"What will you do back in Toronto?"

"A little bit of writing, I suppose. I volunteer at a hospital, that keeps the mind occupied. One has to give back. And in two weeks I'll go to New York to see Razia, my daughter."

She imagined him with his daughter. What were they like together?

"Have the bhel," she said, pushing the plate closer to him. "You won't find it in Toronto."

"But nowadays you can find anything Indian in Toronto," he replied.

They went outside and he said he preferred to sit on the lawn, in the sun. They pulled two chairs together and sat down. In full view of everybody, but so what, it was his last day. He told her more about himself and she listened, with interest initially but then just to the voice. She imagined vaguely a dozen pairs of eyes upon them. Suddenly she heard him say, heard her name,

"Mohini—can I write to you from there?"

She laughed. "Don't act the Mr. Darcy!—you don't need permission to write!" But she knew what he meant. "Text me, but only when I tell you." She didn't elaborate.

Finally Ravi called, having arrived home, and she told him she had been delayed, she would be home soon in a taxi. Munir escorted her to the driveway. As they shook hands, she let his hand linger on hers, for an extra moment, they stared at each other in silence, and he said, "Till next time, then. I'll write."

Munir Khan

"DAD," RAZIA SAID, "there's a change in you. I've not seen you look so relaxed in months—since—" She paused. "Must be the holiday you took!"

He gave her a guilty smile. She had come to see him this weekend, instead of him going down to see her in New York. That's how she wanted it.

"I guess it did me good. The house felt empty . . . I had to get away. You can be philosophical about death and loss, but you can't escape its real effects. The day-to-day . . ."

Like coming downstairs and seeing a ghost on the wing chair . . . hearing a familiar clatter at the kitchen sink . . . talking to yourself. It had been so sudden. It often is, isn't it?

The girl had sat down on the chair now, in front of the bay window, to face him. She always preferred that seat, always liked to simply plump down on it. To her mother's annoyance.

"Have you met someone?"

A sudden silence.

"You're blushing!—you have!"

"Well . . ." he couldn't control himself. Better to have clamped his lips tight.

"Where? Do I know her? Wait a minute—did you meet her in India?"

"Look . . . let's not discuss this now."

It's not so easy, or even definite, there's a Himalayan obstacle in front of this relationship, still embryonic in any case, it's a fantasy only, and so on—, but this time he controlled the instinct to reply.

"All right. I'm sorry. I just want you to be happy, Dad."

"I know. I appreciate that. I am happy."

She went away and made tea, pointedly using the leaves he had brought from Delhi, Mohini's parting gift for him. Darjeeling. He could recall every detail of that scene in the Club garden, the catch in his throat when he said goodbye. That pleading look in those soft brown eyes.

There was a certain jauntiness to his daughter now, a fully developed personality, opinions—too many, but she was young. Politically conservative. He watched her sitting across from him, legs crossed. The open cashmere sweater, the hair short, with a streak of red. The very stylish creased white pants. Very modern. Had she become an American, in her identity? He asked her.

"I don't know," she said. "Does it matter?"

"If you vote, it does. And if you're poor, perhaps it's easier here. But you're not."

She had never been poor, not gone to Goodwill for her clothes or the Salvation Army to get a mattress. She was eyeing him with a smile, aware of his thoughts. He smiled back at her. Yes, we walked miles to school, uphill both ways . . . Why had she gone away, against her mother's pleas?

"Were you happy, Dad—with Mom? I know it's not fair . . ."

The Grand Inquisition, but her question was almost a plea. *I have to know.*

Why? How does it help?

"Well—marriage is a relationship, it's daily—or frequent—negotiation. It's hard to explain. It's not one thing, you see. It's a relationship that goes on all the time . . . there's pain and there's joy . . ."

Why did he say *pain* first? She must have noticed.

"Did you love her, Dad?"

There was a long silence.

"Well?"

"I no longer know what love is. How do you define love? In a relationship, if you give it time, there evolves mutual respect and appreciation . . . something deep and binding. There is care and there are moments of true affection. There are conflicts, inevitably. But on the whole we were happy to be with each other. You could call it love, I suppose."

"No passion, then?"

"That's for the young—when it's all or nothing."

Was this the right thing to say to your child? But what could he have said?

"But you're still young," he added. "And you—any love in your life yet—passion?"

"From what you're saying—"

"That's just me. Anyway, if there's passion in your life, then from what one has read, you don't need anyone's opinion."

They used to say about passionate love, in his youth, If your heart is set on a donkey, what's an angel to you?

"What're you smiling about? And so widely! Come on, Dad—give!"

He repeated the quote to her. She laughed.

"You *have* changed. I told you. Something's happened."

Something he had no control over. In the vacuum that was absence, there had emerged a longing to hear again that voice, observe that chirpiness, and the tenderness behind it, see that face that was his last sight of her, the large eyes trying to say something, engulfing him, the feel of her hand, her delicate fingers in his, ever so light. Not passion, but something adult, laced with the bitter knowledge of futility, pain.

His daughter was watching him.

"You two did not look happy to me," she blurted out, and it came as a bombshell. "That's why I chose to go away."

She had chosen to hurt him, puncture that new condition she had applauded in him only moments ago.

"Every marriage has its bad moments. Sporadic arguments don't make for an unhappy life together."

"I saw a coldness, a frigidity in the air between you two."

"A temporary condition. I'm sorry. We should have shielded you better."

"A sibling would have helped. I longed for a brother. Did you ever think of that?"

"It wasn't possible."

Aileen McKellar had been on the panel that interviewed Munir Khan for his job at the bank. Slim with short brown hair, in a fitted yet conservative green dress. There were three men and her, a junior, who asked him only one question, why his interest in working for a bank. Later, when he stayed late at work, she would be there and would come over to chat. Hardly the start to a passion. No, he was lonely, away from home, she rebounding from a wound—twenty-five years together was enough to bring on this realization—but they'd managed as contented a life together as any couple in their stable, middle-class neighbour-hood with plenty of kids who had now all grown up and gone away. They liked and cared for each other, the more so as they grew older—was that love? Surely yes, of a kind. There were accommodations, more on his part, but he was the immigrant. He had to adjust to her punctiliousness—everything about her was tidy and exact. Their house was like a hotel, he would com-plain, not the tiniest rumple on a cushion, not a wayward pleat on a curtain, the table laid with geometric precision; but it was always pleasant. She was on the bank's curling team, he went away to play tennis. She had choir and went occasionally to church, he went to his room to write. She grew to enjoy curry, though admittedly when much of Toronto had also learned to do so. The Cricket Club put a brand on their solidity. One child was necessary, she said, another one was not. Okay, he said.

Now she was gone and he was sitting in front of that neces-sary child, having justified that relationship. The cushions looked rumpled on the long sofa where Razia had stretched out last night. He would attend to that. He liked to keep the house ordered, as much as possible, in Aileen's memory. And because he was now used to having it that way. He missed her. Pathan and Scot, they'd called themselves. On the map of India, recently, he had seen a city name that sounded just like that: Pathankot.

Razia's voice, sounding far away, brought him back to the present. "Yes?" he asked.

"I've met someone."

"Oh. That's nice. What's his name?"

Those eyes at him. That guilty smile he remembered, before a confession.

"Dad..."

"Well?" he asked, getting anxious. "Is it a secret?"

"Actually, I got married."

"Really? And—" She was not joking. "You're not ... you can't—"

"Dad, we thought we'd go it alone initially, without family... and follow with a big reception with ceremonies later."

What do you say to that, Aileen? What would you have done? Is it me?—our darling would not have gone off and got married without telling, had you been around. For a long while he did not speak.

"All right..." he said.

"You didn't care for rituals yourself."

Did I ever say that? But we gave you birthday parties, with clowns and jugglers, and we gave you Christmas trees and the tooth fairy, those were rituals...

"You're hurt."

"What's his name, this lucky fellow?"

"His name is Mark Goldstein. And he's a philosophy professor." She burst out laughing. "Imagine me marrying a professional philosopher! You should have seen how we met. But we love each other. Passionately."

"And does he walk about with frazzled hair, looking dreamy..."

"Sometimes." She laughed lightly this time, delighted just to recall her guy.

"I'm happy for you, Razia." He got up and took her in his arms. "Will I meet him—or isn't that necessary?"

"We'd like you to come to New York and meet him."

"I'd love to. But now, let's have lunch . . ." He quickly brushed his wet eyes and went to smooth the rumpled cushions. "To remember her," he explained unnecessarily. "She'd have been delighted at your news."

She smiled her thanks at him. "And Dad—I can't have lunch with you, I'm meeting a few friends from school downtown. But shall we go out for dinner, you and I?"

"Of course, and don't worry about me."

"I won't," she said, then kissed him on the cheek and went off, beaming.

He watched her back out and drive off, and then himself went out for his walk.

She's got married, surely that's significant. So casual? Her friends had large weddings, destination weddings in exotic places, and his own daughter, his one and only, just walks to a judge with her philosopher boyfriend and gets married? And then wants a big ceremony afterwards. What?—a mullah and a nikah, a mukhi and a rabbi? A sibling would have helped, are you listening up there, Aileen, your daughter has gotten married. And I'm aching.

He passed the young Indian couple's house. Their Audi was in the driveway, they must be in. Just then a mature woman (time to use that term) emerged and closed the door behind her. She was rather heavy-set and wore ill-advised pants with a blouse. One of the mothers, he surmised. As they passed, impulsively he said, "Namaste!" She looked up, startled, then responded likewise and smiled warmly.

Back home, his mood lifted by that act of spontaneity, he sat down and turned the TV on, went to the multicultural channel. An Indian film was on, as he expected, and he watched what remained of it, a good two hours. It was a silly movie, but he enjoyed it nonetheless. He had started watching these Saturday features only recently. He had watched a very few as a child, but these newer ones were colourful and often violent and risqué, he'd noticed with surprise, though in the end all got reconciled in front of the gods and the evil ones received their just dues.

He felt a pull. Should he call her. But it would be well past midnight there. And there was the husband. It was time to nip it in the bud, this fantasy, this impossibility. It could only cause pain. And yet how could he forget her, the promise they had made. Shall I write to you? Of course you can! Don't act the Mr. Darcy! He had written her a longish email letter, compromising, juvenile, bathetic. And she had replied. I miss you. I think of you all the time. Who had written that? Both of them, probably. After that, a few texts, one hurried phone call.

He was aware that something else had happened to him in Delhi. Something had awakened in him. The historian. The poet. The Sufi, the sultan. All calling to him. Saying what? Write.

He went up to his study. Outside it, next to the door, was a pile of books he had ordered on the internet, which Razia had unpacked for him and neatly arranged. He picked them up. A history of the Delhi sultanate by Ziauddin Barani, whose grave lay at the Sufi shrine with a solitary rose upon it. An anthology of the works of Amir Khusrau— the poet whose lavish mausoleum lay next to his Sufi master's, outside which musicians sang ecstatically from his works. And the life and times of the sheikh, Sufi Nizamuddin himself. All Indian editions. He sat

down to look at them. After his first novel was published, Aileen
had turned the room into a proper study for him, with a desk and
chair, a leather armchair, where he now sat, a flexi-lamp, and
two walls of shelves. But he'd produced only two further works
here, a short novel and a story collection, and then stopped. He
could see no relevance to anything around him in his work.
Inspiration dried up, and he became a disappointment.

He picked up the Barani, flipped through it, returned to the
introduction and the lines that had particularly unsettled him.
Muslim kings, the historian wrote, "should not spare any effort
in humiliating, degrading, and insulting the idolatrous and
polytheist Hindus." So startling in its bluntness. But this was
seven hundred years ago and the opinion of one man. Two hundred years after that they were burning heretics at the stakes in
Europe, and soon after, Muslims and Jews were expelled from
Spain. Still, it bothered him, a jingoist statement from someone
so passionate about the science of history.

He had read that the term "Hindu," derived from the name of
the river Indus, originally referred to the natives of that area.
That included those who had opted to follow Islam. Only later
had it begun to acquire its rigid exclusivity. The population of
Afghanistan, where his paternal ancestors came from, had been
mainly Buddhist originally. His mother's people came from
Gujarat, where the current prime minister of India was from.
What was Munir Khan, then? "Asian" had been good enough in
Nairobi. Now art moved him; music and literature. That was his
worship, there lay his gods. He had been happily, willingly derac-
inated. Now, with a visit to Delhi, his grandfather's city, he was
saddled with this question: was he a Muslim? But did that—
whatever it meant—matter? It seemed to matter very much in

India. Everyone had a brand, and that indelible brand carried a violent history from the time of Barani that still mattered centuries later. *Your people ruled us for seven centuries,* as Mohini had said so casually. It was a troubling reminder. My people were goldsmiths, they ruled nobody, just created beautiful objects working with their hands, using their imagination.

Six weeks after Razia left, Munir visited New York to meet his son-in-law. Razia had insisted she would pay for his hotel in Manhattan, and he had to yield. This was her show. His room overlooked Broadway and he was a block away from Lincoln Center, where a few enticing musical programs were on offer that weekend. Razia had made reservations at a French restaurant nearby where they would have dinner and he would meet her young man the philosopher. Before that, at six, he and Razia sat in the hotel bar downstairs to chat. She wanted to know about their family, at least the essentials, as she put it. Not that it mattered much to her or Mark, but his family were curious. So was she, now. She had already been to Glasgow during a visit to the UK and met Aileen's folks on her mother's side. It had not been a happy experience; she'd been a teenager and she found her relatives uncouth. From her descriptions, Munir had understood that the family was working class, and the privileged girl from Toronto was not used to such a life. One of her cousins called her names. They drank a lot. To top that, she had a hard time understanding their speech.

Munir had never met the McKellars himself, Aileen preferring they keep their families at a distance. He had, however, once met a cousin of Aileen's in Toronto. His own elder sister, Khadija, was also in Toronto.

Munir informed his daughter that his Dada, his grandfather Yunus Ali Khan, came from Delhi, but the family was originally from Peshawar, which was now in Pakistan. After their marriage, Dada and Dadi had emigrated to Kenya under somewhat mysterious circumstances. Dada was a goldsmith and owned a jewellery store in Nairobi. Munir's father, Jehangir, had dropped out of architecture school and helped to run the family business. His mother's family was from a city called Jamnagar in India. As for religion—both his grandparents were devout, but not his father. His mother came from a Shia community and went to her prayer house once a month. In spite of its humble origins, his family's life in the British colony when he was a boy had been rather privileged.

"There it is. But you need carry no baggage from the past."

"It's good to know. I'm often asked where I am from, what I am, and I find myself at a loss."

"Now you know."

"But what about you, Dad. Does Kenya mean anything to you now?"

"One never forgets one's childhood home."

"But you rarely mentioned it when I was young. I wish you had."

"I was making a new life, with your mother and you. It seemed best not to dwell on the past. Though I did dwell on it in my books—which you never read."

She smiled. "I promise, I will. Still, you could have spoken about your early life. And India? Does it mean anything to you?"

He paused, then said, "It does, now that I've visited it . . ."

He realized that she was waiting for more, and ventured, "It was always that mysterious place in the past, where things had happened . . . where my grandfather came from. We saw it as a poor, backward place."

Munir and his siblings had been told that it was economic opportunity that brought their grandfather to Kenya. Yet they were aware there was something else too: those sudden odd looks between Dada and Dadi, and the pauses mid-sentence when "Laard Hardinge Street" happened to be mentioned.

They got up and crossed the road to the restaurant. Mark was already seated at their table midway in the room, eyes fixed on the entrance. He stood up—lanky and professorial with grey eyes and a head of curls, the curious father-in-law observed— and greeted Munir with a shake of hands and "Delighted to meet you, sir." They sat down and Munir found himself facing the young pair. *Passion*, she had said, *love*. He didn't want to speculate on the relationship, put it through the cynical lens of adult experience. She was happy now, and that's what mattered. He felt happy seeing her this way, and was moved as only a parent can be at seeing a child at a significant crossroads, venturing out.

He was called upon to describe Razia when she was young, and he told them how until she was three she would prefer to speak Tagalog to them, having picked it up from her nanny, Ophelia, and how in protest at having to practice piano she would go downstairs in the middle of the night and play the scales and arpeggios. There were many incidents, all delightful in retrospect. They discussed the upcoming wedding reception, for which the couple had picked early fall as the time. It was then that Munir wondered if the civic wedding had not been undertaken because Razia was already pregnant. He did not ask.

What did he want to do tomorrow, they asked. He would go to MOMA, he said, and then the opera if there were tickets.

Werther was on and he was rather keen. Mark said he would inquire about complimentary tickets from a friend who worked at one of the investment banks. She would call in the morning, Razia said.

It was a brisk early-spring night, the streets were crowded, taxis sped by, all occupied and ignoring the raised arms at the sidewalks. He crossed the road to his hotel. In his room it felt suddenly very quiet and calm, and he went to his laptop. He stared at the screen, at his current unfinished project whose nature he had yet to determine, and after a minute or two of stillness he closed the top. He undressed and got into bed with Barani's history, which he had brought with him. He read a few paragraphs about the grim death of Sultan Alauddin in 1296 and the truly horrific murder of his son Khizr Khan; he mused about the two lovers, the prince Khizr and the Gujarati princess Deval. He set aside the book, turned off the reading light and fell instantly asleep.

He was in India. A man was sitting on his haunches, his legs folded under him, and he wore a cotton kurta embroidered at the neck. He had a rich black beard on his round, beaming face, and he had a round turban on his head. Incongruous even in dream, he wore a pair of rimless glasses. There was a large book in front of him with hand-written pages.

"What have you written in that book, Sheikh?" Munir asked.

"I have written a secret history of Delhi in the time of Sultan Alauddin Khilji, the Second Alexander."

"What have you called it?"

"I have called it 'A Chronicle of the Last Days of Delhi.'"

" . . ."

"Read," the sheikh said to Munir. "Read this history, in the name of God the Merciful, and tell the world about it."

Munir woke up with a start, not sure where he was, then heard the sound of a truck on Broadway. His pulse was racing. What had he been about to say to the sheikh? In what language?

The next morning Razia called and asked him how he slept. She had some work and surely he didn't need her to distract him at the museum, and he said no, he would manage. They would meet later anyway, and perhaps Mark would have found tickets for the opera; then they should have dinner together. He spent a good two hours wandering about in the museum, then made use of the dining lounge, where she called him again. Could they meet outside Lincoln Center at six? Apparently Mark had found tickets. Munir was elated.

At six, dressed for the occasion, he wandered about the plaza at the Center until he saw them approaching, hand in hand. A handsome couple. Were we as beautiful as the young ones of today? She wore the black shawl he had brought for her from India and a dark red dress. Dark always suited her. Mark was fashionably casual, a blazer over jeans. And as before his hair looked ruffled. A philosopher, after all.

They reached him and she handed him his ticket.

"Dad, we can't come with you. But this is a good seat. Enjoy yourself."

"There was no need, if you couldn't come. Opera was just one option—"

"We have to meet friends—a prior engagement." She eyed him for his understanding, before adding, "It has to do with Mark's work."

"Will you be free for coffee afterwards?"

"I'm afraid not, Dad. But you have a good time. Why don't we meet for coffee tomorrow before you leave?"

He was deeply disappointed. He could have left this morning. He had come for her, not *Werther*—though that wasn't a bad prospect. He had come to see her, and his son-in-law. They could have got to know each other.

The show was sold out and he was grateful for his ticket. The sensibility of the story, the impossible love around which it pivoted, was alien in its setting and time, and Werther's death was inevitable, but it was performed so beautifully as to be truly moving. But the thought came, also inevitably, as he walked out: Was it to see the fatefully impossible love enacted that he'd been especially keen to see the opera? He dismissed that as too simple.

Afterwards he sat at the hotel bar brooding, having shunned two advances, one from a man, the other from a woman. Should he leave Razia a message to say that he was leaving early in the morning? He couldn't. Part of being a parent is to allow your children to hurt you. But she was not a young child. If she could be a modern, independent daughter, he was a modern father.

He was packed and downstairs with his luggage when they met at eleven in the lounge. She looked smart in a black office suit and had a briefcase with her.

"You're quiet, Dad."

"I feel quiet," he replied with a smile. He looked around, and said, "Everybody seems quiet. It's a work day."

"Did you like Mark?"

"Yes, very much. He seems a nice young man. I'm sure you'll be happy."

How meaninglessly we speak sometimes. I don't know the young man. I hardly know my daughter anymore.

"I neglected you, Dad."

He thought for a moment. "Yes, you did."

Can't you just tell a lie? Aileen would have chided.

"I'm sorry, Dad."

"It doesn't matter. I shouldn't have said that—I was being selfish. I know you have a busy life . . . a new life—"

"It won't happen again, Dad. I promise you."

She was in tears.

Mohini

IF HE HAD NOT PAUSED to chat outside the DRC bar, she would not be in this quandary. *He.* She still found it easier to refer to her husband as *he.* The traditional way, you did not name your husband—in case a spirit overheard it and used it to cast a spell on him. Wives didn't matter. She often called him by name, Ravi, she was not backward, but there was always just the tiniest of hesitation. She couldn't help it. It was embarrassing; sometimes her friends caught her short when she said *he.* But, if he had come inside the bar, instead of gup-shupping outside with those loonies discussing the cow kingdom, they would have shared the table with the stranger. Life would have been different. Would she have wanted that? Yes, please, it was too painful this other way. The tension, the thrill. The risk. Like on a precipice.

He, speaking of Munir now, had written her a lengthy email from Toronto. She had printed it out, for a keepsake, she'd been so touched, then deleted it from the laptop. She had written back, Thank you for the lovely email, but please, it's not a good idea. Send a text, but only when I prompt you. Her email account had been set up by Ravi when they purchased the laptop, and she dared not change the password. And he used the account to email common friends, and their daughter Priya in Hyderabad. And so she was reduced to sending texts from the toilet or someplace like that. A couple of times she told Bahadur to park and go buy some vegetables from a street vendor, then quickly texted Munir, and he replied. Both texts she later deleted. *He* sometimes used her phone too.

Their texts were silly and embarrassing. Not worth repeating. Who would imagine she was the same person who wrote those smart, provocative columns on the Kingdom of the Cow (which had received a few thousand hate mails), care for the elderly (love mail), Valentine's Day (love mail from the young), and love jihad (mixed response)? The last one was against the right-wing group that claimed to have collected the names of all Muslim young men in Delhi and warned that they would watch them on Valentine's Day in case they way-laid Hindu girls. She loved her country, the craziness too, but it was the fanaticism of the Hindu jihadis that was simply unbearable.

What was it in him that had so unhinged her? Did there have to be a reason? Not loving your husband—let's admit it, was there ever love?—does not mean you go flying into the arms of another man. A foreigner. One of them. A marriage was for-ever. Forever? Where was this leading to? What madness had overtaken her? A Punjabi Hindu woman, from an ancient tradi-tion that extolled the wifely virtue of Sita—who would rather that the earth under her feet open and swallow her than her innocence be doubted—and from a respectable conservative family of Partition victims, who had to leave their homes merely because they were Hindus.

Munir Khan was a good person. But what did that mean? His wife or daughter might have a different story. God, no. Don't let that be. His daughter Razia had sprung a surprise on him, he'd written. She got married without telling him. It's their life, their decision, he had glossed, but that must have hurt.

They had laughed together. They had shared stories. Sometimes he had pronounced words the British way, sometimes like an American—or Canadian?—and sometimes like an African. One time he pronounced "liar" for "lawyer," the good old Punjabi way, and what a laugh they'd had. "See what you've done to me," he'd said ruefully. He liked history, enjoyed finding out about the past, yet he was so free of it himself. It was liberating to know a person without handicaps, yet she had sensed that he felt rootless and sometimes lost. Delhi had given him his history, himself. He'd said, I didn't realize how Indian I was, even though Aileen kept reminding me. She couldn't tolerate spicy food. It was her digestive system. Sometimes I would get a craving and go away somewhere and treat myself to a kebab. Or chana. She laughed. But she'd thought—though she didn't tell him—that Aileen should have tried harder to get used to Indian cuisine. She simply had not been interested.

So desperately want to come and see you again, he had texted. *Why don't you?* she wrote back. *Are you sure you want me to come? Yes, I'm sure.* The next thing she knew, he'd made a reservation.

But she wasn't sure. And she was.

Munir

FOR HIS RETURN VISIT to Delhi, Mohini had booked him at
the Sheth Rustomji Jamshedji Guest House on Bahadur Shah
Zafar Road just outside "his" (as she called it in her email)
Shahjahanabad, or Old Delhi, and that's where he proceeded by
prepaid taxi from the airport. It was well past midnight, the air
warm and thick with mist. The streets were empty but for the
odd motor vehicle. It felt different returning to Delhi six months
later; this time he had a definite purpose, to see Mohini again.
But it had begun to seem like a mad, reckless venture as soon
as he boarded his plane.

Razia was thrilled when he told her of his decision to visit
India again. To Delhi, yes.

"Wow, Dad. I'm so happy for you. Go for it!"

"It's a bit complicated."

"How?"

"I'll explain later."

"Do you have a photo . . . of her?"

"No," he lied.

There was a selfie they'd taken at Safdarjung. A daring move. They shouldn't have, but Mohini had insisted. On his phone. A memento. A piece of evidence.

"Shall I send her a present, Dad?"

"It's too soon, I think."

"Go and get her, Dad."

It was not a question of going to get her, but just to see her again. Sit next to her, be with her again.

But more and more this seemed like a terrible mistake, a delusion. He had toyed with this feeling throughout the long flight, but then that face—that last gaze. The promise. The feel of her hand, her hair. Over the past months he had called her twice; each time she had seemed nervous and they had spoken so briefly that he was disheartened. Their emails were short and oblique, as though someone were watching. The last couple had been especially distant. A few times he had visited the *Express Times* website and read her columns—to feel close to her—but in them she was different, engaged with issues. Are you sure it's a good idea for me to come? he had asked finally. Yes, you should come. You need to do your research, don't you?

On the way, he recalled the people he had become familiar with on the previous visit. The straight-backed Ravi with the dyed crewcut. The husband. The distraction—Munir had simply thought past him in his mind, until now. Who would blame him for taking a hatchet to Munir? Silly Munir, he would only have himself to blame. The servers at the lounge and the dining room, the reception clerks, the uniformed guard who called taxis for him with a smart salute, they'd all become friends of sorts. That unctuous, smiling saviour of Hindu virtue, Jetha Lal, in his clean whites and blue shawl. The Purifier.

Always watching, always someone to watch. His young followers buzzing around him.

The cab driver had to stop and inquire a couple of times before he found the guest house, an old house deep in the shadows behind a large black iron gate. He knocked on the gate, without result, whereupon the driver, who had been watching, came out wearily from the car and obligingly banged loudly enough for the neighbourhood to wake up. There is no concept of too much noise in India, Munir recalled. An old watchman, awakened, appeared from the shadows and the gate opened with a loud groan. A man in pyjamas floated behind like a ghost and spoke to Munir, reproving him for his lateness; he had been expected earlier in the evening and could not very well be fed now. Munir explained that this was the time most flights arrived from abroad and said he did not want to eat. He should have been clearer when he telephoned to confirm his arrival, he apologized. He earned a brief smile. They went in through an open corridor into a dimly lit front hall from where the man took him up a flight of stairs to his room.

The house would have been stately once, with wooden floors, now scuffed, dirt-filled and creaking, high ceilings barely touched by the dim lighting, and arches along the corridors. Old faded prints and photos looked out from the walls, ghosts from the distant, colonial past. The white paint everywhere was faded or peeled. His room was rudimentary but large, the carpet threadbare and ancient, the ceiling damp, from where instead of the former chandelier hung a lone light bulb. There was also a bedside lamp, new and modern, as alien as a UFO in the room. He could set a ghost story here, he mused. What had Mohini been thinking? Had she even been inside this place?

The next morning, to his great relief, she called, asked how he liked his accommodation. "It's amazing, isn't it, perfect for a writer!" He was not going to quibble, it was just lovely to hear her voice again, which was all Munir could respond with. She was busy today, she said—she had to finish a column—it was on a new court ruling that audiences should stand up in the cinemas when the national anthem was played, and she was excited to write her dissenting opinion; and she had to meet Asha's new tutor, Chetan. She would see him tomorrow. What was the point of him being here, then, he thought to himself, disappointed. She certainly had the time to yammer on about her busy schedule. He smiled at his reaction. And this Wuthering Heights of a place? It was gloomy and depressing. Had her feelings about him changed? It would be only natural for her to have second thoughts or qualms. But then she would not have told him, unequivocally, You should come.

He went down for breakfast.

The caretaker from the previous night, white shirt hanging over white pants, eyes bleary, and a few days' stubble on his unwashed face, came over as Munir took a chair at the over-sized dining table and asked him if he would be in for lunch and supper. Munir hesitated, the man's stare demanding an immediate answer. "The cook has to know," he explained.

"I'll have supper here," Munir decided. "Lunch I'll take outside."

Almost by instinct, he rolled his head side to side in the Indian way to elicit approval, and the caretaker did likewise, and all was settled. Munir already felt better. By this time there were two other guests at the table, having their breakfasts in silence. A young man in a grey cotton suit that needed pressing, wearing glasses, and a stocky older man in a bush shirt, also in glasses. Munir's breakfast arrived immediately after the caretaker left, two crisply fried parathas with yogurt, which he found more than satisfying. He refused an omelette to follow that.

His map discreetly in his hand—he felt reluctant to fetch out his smartphone in the crowds—he came out of the pedestrian entrance beside the front gate into the wide thoroughfare now chocked with screaming traffic. The old city was on the left, the watchman had indicated, ten minutes away, and that's where Munir headed. Across the street was Gandhi's memorial, where his ashes were kept. A place to visit, Munir reminded himself. It was already hot and muggy, the sun brilliant and blinding. Munir wrapped his handkerchief under his collar and round his neck to soak up the sweat and started walking. He reached an intersection, watched the traffic whizzing past without let-up. Crossing would be like swimming across a rapid. He stood on the sidewalk, stunned into inaction. Finally he joined two other pedestrians and crossed with them, the traffic running past them as if they were invisible. As they parted on Asaf Ali Road, one of the men turned to give Munir a piece of advice: "When you cross a road, sir, don't look at the cars—just keep walking, and the cars will take care of themselves." Easy to say, but Munir thanked him.

He continued walking on the main road for a while, and then on an impulse he took a side road. The map said Chitli Qabar Bazar. He felt a rising thrill. He was back! Soon he reached the tumultuous Chawri Bazar, which he recognized from his previous visit. Was he actually smiling? So much life, so much humanity. A cart creaked along, pulled by a boy in front and pushed from behind, heaped with paper; another passed carrying paper and plastic decorations. No wedding preparations are complete without a visit to Old Delhi, she'd told him. The second floor of a building was under precarious repair, with banging and shouting. The impulse was to linger on everything, not let it pass away. Crooked alleys led off mysteriously into the gut of this ancient city, enticing.

He walked into an alley, then another, following the crooked paths, hopefully keeping course. The little streets were more residential and quiet, though the ground floors were busy with all sorts of industry—hand-printing, sewing, garland-making, metalwork. He could not find his way back to the main road but arrived at the great mosque on another one. All the long roads seemed to converge to this one focal point, where once the entire neighbourhood would have dropped all business to come and pray. Where his grandfather came to kneel one last time to Allah before setting off for Kenya. Since his previous visit to Delhi, Munir had realized that Dada had become an actual presence in his consciousness: he was now a person from a certain place, with a story of his own. The old man in the armchair, wearing a white skullcap, reminiscing with his wife about Dariba Kalan.

Without thinking, Munir went up the wide steps of the mosque and entered the courtyard, carrying his shoes in one hand; he walked around from side to side, taking quick steps over the hot floor where there was no matting, looking over the walls at the different vistas, then to the fountain in the centre and the prayer hall before it, on the fourth side. People were knelt in prayer, in the midst of curious tourists inspecting the carved calligraphy on the wall. Munir turned and walked to the arcade along one of the sides and sat down to rest on a bench beside a woman, keeping a respectful space between them. The sun was beating down, the open space before him burned like a furnace. The walk had been long, he should have brought a bottle of water, he would buy one as soon as he came out. What had brought him back here? The mosque was like a pole of a magnet, pulling you in. The woman beside him was inspecting him with a mixture of commiseration and amusement. He smiled at her, noticing that her clothes were old and faded, and in several layers, despite the heat; her feet, outside of her worn-out rubber slippers, were cracked and dirty. He noticed the faded henna on her heel arches and the broken toenails.

He took out his notebook and made some notes. He didn't like becoming conspicuous, but the alternative was to forget. His clothes betrayed him, anyway, now that he was no longer in the thick of a jostling crowd. And his face. His manner. Having finished, he consulted his map, then gazed around the courtyard, now more crowded with visitors. He felt pleasantly at ease. He had a bond with this city, a historical connection, vague but real. He had to hand it to Mohini, the guest house had drawn him out. And she was his other connection to Delhi.

I think of you all the time. Sappy but true. He imagined Aileen's face, if she heard him say it. Her wry expression and acerbic comment with too true an observation, bringing him back to earth.

He hardly knew Mohini. She had a husband and family. A history. The moral dimension to this relationship had not touched him, he was surprised at himself. He had lived a detached, secular life, an individualistic and empirical existence, but with a firm sense of right and wrong. All that high-mindedness had been washed away by this primitive obsession. Heaven sends us habit in place of passion, he had read somewhere. Now he was in the grip of a passion; habit was what he'd had with Aileen.

He stood up with a nod to the woman next to him, who had not stopped staring at him, and went out and down the wide steps of the mosque and past the police barricades into the street. He walked to Chandni Chowk, the promenade that began opposite the Red Fort, passed the Sis Ganj gurudwara, where a prominent notice proclaimed it to be the site where a Sikh guru had been beheaded by a certain Mughal emperor. A pamphlet appeared in his hand, proclaiming the anniversary of a Sikh massacre in Delhi in 1984. Further along on the sidewalk, in the midst of passing crowds, a mendicant sat before a fat, coiled snake inside a basket, into the open lid of which the occasional passerby dropped a coin. Munir couldn't resist doing the same. Finally he turned a corner and arrived at the street he was looking for. Dariba Kalan, the glittering jewellery market that was never-never land.

Today was Saturday and the street was packed with shoppers, many of them well-dressed, well-filled women from the suburbs. He walked up and down the street, then somewhat tentatively entered an alley; at the back sat three women on low stools, in various stages of food preparation, one of them before a fire; they hastily covered their heads and Munir said, "Sorry," and turned around.

Looking for a place to eat, he came upon an eatery at a corner, open on two sides and overflowing with people; he was about to pass it when the manager, catching his eye, motioned him to come inside. He made a place for Munir at a small table near the doorway, had it wiped, and without taking his order put a large vegetable paratha before him, with a bowl of yogurt. "Very good," he added with a nod.

Munir helped himself. When he finished, he asked for tea, not realizing that tea was not served at lunchtime; nevertheless, it was brought for him from a neighbouring establishment, and sipping it he watched the crowds outside. At length, he asked for the bill, paid extra, and departed, taking a cycle rickshaw back to the guest house, where a new man was on duty, young and clean-shaven, in black trousers and white shirt. His name was Naren and he took away the jug of filtered water to refresh it.

In his room, Munir immediately went to his computer. It had been shifted towards a corner of the table, he noticed, when he'd left it right in front of the chair. When he pushed back the lid, it opened straight to his email page. This was not how he had left it. Someone had fiddled with it. When Naren returned, Munir complained. Naren was silent, stared uncomfortably at him.

"Did you play with this computer?" Munir asked half seriously. Naren looked too simple to know what to do with a laptop.

"Sahab, some police people were here, asking questions."

"About what?"

"They come looking for terrorists, sometimes."

"Do I look like a terrorist to you?" Munir asked with a smile. But he was bothered. Couldn't the cops have waited for him to return? What did they expect to find, what had they found?

"I don't know about these things, sahab," Naren replied and grinned foolishly.

"All right. It doesn't matter."

Munir changed all his passwords, then lay down in bed. He fell instantly asleep.

He was woken up by a phone call from Mohini.

"I'm sorry I didn't call earlier. It's been really busy. Were you lonely, what did you do today?"

He told her.

"Oh, wonderful! I knew you'd like it there. How do you find the place?"

"Modest. Rudimentary. And I think I just slept through suppertime."

"I'm sorry . . . they'll fix you something. Did you miss me?"

"I came all the way to be with you."

"I told you, this is how it is in India . . . I can come tomorrow to see you for a few moments . . ."

A few moments each time, is this all it was going to be . . .

"Something strange happened," he said.

"What?"

He told her about his computer. She became silent, then said, "These things happen, particularly in those areas . . . There are always threats. Those must have been security people. You should move to DRC soon."

"I've already made a reservation. I'm moving there Monday morning. Can we meet at Safdarjung in the afternoon?"

"Let's meet at the Gandhi Smriti—Birla House. It's where Gandhi was shot and is now a museum. Quite close to the Club. You can even walk there. Gandhi's been in the news lately, and I've been thinking about him."

"All right."

He had a shower and went downstairs with the purpose of going for a walk; on the way out Naren intercepted him to tell him his supper was ready. Grateful, Munir went to the dining room and sat down at the large table, where his dinner was laid out, simple vegetarian but substantial. Munir asked for tea and it was brought to him. Then he went out for a stroll, the man at the gate advising him not to wander too far. He walked for ten minutes and returned to his room.

The feeling of having been touched by an invisible hand remained with him as he tried to sleep.

———

The next day was Sunday; in the morning he again wandered through the old city. After some effort, making a lot of inquiries, he found the little temple of the eighty-four bells where he had come with Mohini. It was open but there was no one inside, not even the priest. The floor was wet, looking recently washed but not dried. Munir paused some moments to pay his respects at the idol in its glowing niche at the far end. He came out and, hailing a rickshaw, visited the house where Ghalib, the great Urdu poet, had lived in the nineteenth century. Ghalib, who apparently had a lover next door, their impossible relationship the subject of a well-known poem, had described in pithy detail the devastated condition of Delhi after the failure of the 1857 Mutiny—the First War of Independence, as Mohini called it. The great mosque had narrowly escaped destruction at the hands of the East India Company. He wondered if his grandfather's family were in Delhi then, and what they would have seen. He noticed that, having embedded himself inside Delhi, this old ancestral Delhi, he couldn't help extrapolating Nairobi's Eastleigh back to these streets. The poet's house was now a rudimentary museum, with manuscripts and objects from his period. A few stores down was a tea place where he entered somewhat hesitantly and sat down at a rickety table. A gang of three boys next to him had ordered paya—the spicy curry of goat's trotters—which had Munir's taste buds running. Paya day had been a big event in his house growing up. The trotters would be bought with the skin still on, and the first order of business was to burn it off on glowing charcoal. The trotters were boiled overnight and the remaining skin removed. Only then was the curry made. Sticky, spicy, and hot, consumed with steaming naan.

Throwing health warnings aside, Munir ordered a plate. As his paya came, with naan, one of the two boys voiced something to him. At Munir's confusion, he spoke again, but in a thickly accented English. "Sir—you from Foreign?" They all became excited and greatly interested when he told them where he was from. He politely refused their offers to show him around, and washing his sticky hands with lemon water and soap, he left, feeling intensely pleased with himself.

A cycle rickshaw took him back to the guest house. And the next morning he checked in at DRC.

He stood for some moments on the porch steps of Birla House, a dignified white bungalow on a quiet residential street, contemplating its garden, its understated elegance. As was expected of any visitor here, he traced the path Gandhi had taken to the spot of his assassination, from the porch steps down to the lawn, the mahatma's hands supported on the shoulders of two young women. Munir was familiar with the scene from the Attenborough film. This was the house, owned by an industrial magnate, where Gandhi had undertaken his "fast unto death," which he broke only when Delhi's influential citizens had signed a written promise to resist any outbreaks of communal violence in the city. It was the aftermath of the Partition. Behind the frail old man had been a small crowd of people; in front and on both sides many more. From the frantic crowd at the front, before the prayers could begin, the assassin appeared, did a namaste in greeting, and shot Gandhi, who uttered "Hé Ram" as he fell. Oh God. What more satisfying death for him.

The city's violence would have affected his grandfather's family—those who had been living in Delhi—had they stayed on in the city during Partition. Perhaps they had already gone away on one of those trains bearing refugees to Pakistan. Only now did it occur to him that the Partition was never mentioned in their home in Kenya. He only knew that there were two countries, India and Pakistan, in place of one, and they had gone to war when he was still a young boy. His father Jehangir had friends from all Indian backgrounds; on Saturday afternoons they would gather at the Nairobi Club to play snooker and drink whiskey. He knew nothing about his Dadi Amina's background; his grandmother had been a busy woman in their household, providing food and comfort, and open arms to rush into when the world became unjust. On Eid days she gave him money with a smile and a pat on the head. He could recall clearly her death one August night during school holidays. It happened very fast, from an attack of meningitis, as he learned later. Their doctor had been away that night. He remembered her body lying on the living room floor, the female mourners sitting before it, crying. His grandfather developed Parkinson's and died some years later.

A shadow fell before him and he looked up. It was Mohini. That same pale face with pointed chin, the long braid; the large moon-eyes and the forehead dot. "Mohini . . ." he uttered, as though not believing.

"You're standing where Gandhi-ji stood when he was shot."

"Yes."

"How are you?" she asked and he caught her hand furtively, before she quickly pulled it away, with, "Careful, you!"

There was mischief in the tone, he thought, and a hint of pleasure. He suggested they go to Khan Market for coffee or tea, and she said why not the Club. That would have been his first choice anyway, and they hailed an auto.

"Didn't you like the guest house I chose for you, near Old Delhi?"

"It was well located, but hardly the height of comfort. And how would you have reached me?"

"I would have taken an auto."

"With a guard at the gate? And a bunch of curious and sombre-looking seniors on the scene?"

She laughed.

"And the security people searching for a terrorist in my room?"

The club cafeteria was not crowded, and as always they elected to take a table at the back, facing the door. The adjacent tables were not occupied, which gave them some freedom. They ordered tea and he told her about his adventures.

"I would have loved to eat paya!"

"Wouldn't have been healthy for you . . ."

"And I suppose it was okay for you, a foreigner?"

She said she hadn't been to Ghalib's house in years, and then recited the famous lines in Urdu and translated, "*It was not to be—it was not our fate—this relationship should happen* . . . something like that."

"I hope that's not a foretelling."

She blushed, said softly, "No." They both waited. "What are your plans for today?" she asked then.

"I think I'll go to the Nizamuddin place."

"Amir Khusrau?"

He nodded. "And Ziauddin Barani. Perhaps I'll get inspired." He told her the story of Khizr Khan and Deval Rani as related by Amir Khusrau in the poem he had recently read.

Deval was the beautiful Gujarati princess who was brought to the Delhi court of Alauddin as a favour to one of his queens, Kamla Devi, who was also Deval's mother. Kamla herself had been captured and separated from her daughter and husband some years before, when her kingdom of Gujarat was conquered by Alauddin's forces. She was war booty, but a queen now. In Delhi, Alauddin's son Khizr Khan and Kamla's daughter Deval Devi fell in love. The ending was tragic.

Mohini knew the story, if only vaguely, but she had an opinion. A strong one.

"But it's not true, that story," she said flatly.

"Perhaps not exactly. Khusrau must have embellished it. Poetic licence, surely?"

"Embellished! Can you imagine a Hindu queen like Kamla Devi asking for her daughter to be brought to the harem? It's not possible! Amir Khusrau made it up. A Muslim's fantasy."

"A Turkish Indian poet who happened to be a Muslim, you mean."

That caught her short.

"You're right . . . how silly of me. I'm sorry."

"And you, are you my fantasy?"

"Yes," she said brightly, and stood up. "Aren't I what you always imagined? A film actress of yesteryear? Let's go."

The cafeteria was already filling up. Outside, at the crowded driveway where she waited for her car, he asked, "When?"

She paused a moment, then said, "Tomorrow at four. Safdarjung. Bye."

He watched her taxi leave towards the gate, trailed by a few others. He turned around, pulled up a chair on the lawn, and sat down. There had not been a private moment between them yet, but there had been enough to fill his heart. Then why did he feel unsettled? Had they averted a quarrel? *A Muslim's fantasy.* The words echoed in his mind. There's a minefield here, he said to himself.

Jetha Lal was passing by and stopped.

"Namaste, sir. Haven't I seen you before?" he asked Munir.

"I was here in January—must have been then."

"Yes. And back so soon? You must like India!"

"More and more," Munir said, and regretted that.

"Good," the man said, then with a wave of the hand walked on, saying something to himself. He was soon joined by a few young followers and the gang in white made their way towards the library.

Munir wondered why the man had not asked him where he came from. He'd not even introduced himself.

He got up, went to the gate, and took an auto to Nizamuddin.

It was Thursday and the place was crowded; there were a lot of women present. On this day sacred to Muslims, Dada must have visited here as a young man. On this day, in Nairobi, Dadi and his mother had cooked sweet yellow rice, sooji halwa, and channa, and coming back from school in the afternoon he and his siblings would make a dash for the dining table.

He did his usual rounds of the two eminent mausoleums, paid his donation to the big attendant, who knew him now, and went and stood before the grave of the historian Ziauddin Barani. He had saved a portion of the flowers he had bought, and now placed them on the grave. A wry smile came upon him.

"Well, Ziauddin, what secret history did you want me to read in that dream?"

Barani sat on his haunches, just behind his grave, wearing a gold-embroidered olive coat and a red turban. "You'll find it," he said. "Where will I find it?" "Go ask Amir, he might know." "But I just saw him!" Munir protested.

Munir turned around, amused with himself. The attendant, who was called Khursheed Nizami, said to him, benignly, "They didn't know English, sir. But maybe the sheikh understood. He was a very learned man."

"Then why have you given him such a modest place to rest?"

A careless shrug in return.

The next day at a little before four, he arrived at the Safdarjung Tomb. Not a soul in sight. He walked once around the garden and then up to the mausoleum. Standing at the parapet of the terrace, he saw her arrive through the gate in a hurry. She had on a greyish sari this time, in marked contrast to the bright yellow and red of yesterday. Night versus day. A camouflage against the green of the lawn? He walked down to go meet her and presented her the pink rose he had asked the gardener at DRC to give him. It was not done, the gardener said, but still cut a branch and handed it to him with an indulgent look.

They went and sat down, away from the line of sight of the entrance, where a yellow bougainvillea tree gave them a partial shade. How serene it was here, walled in and protected from the frantic bustle of Delhi, how precious was this sheltered privacy of theirs, every terrifying moment of it, under the blind eye of the old mausoleum.

He found himself telling her about his childhood, his school years, his two sisters, perhaps repeating in parts what he had already told her before. No, they hadn't worn the chador, they were modern girls. Did it matter? Of course not, she said. She apologized again for her thoughtless remarks of the day before, when he'd told her about the romance of Khizr Khan and Deval Rani. We pick up attitudes without realizing, she said. He agreed, recalled for her the Asian racism in Nairobi. He told her they had spoken a corrupted Urdu at home in Nairobi, but that his generation spoke mostly English. He started to tell her about Aileen, and stopped. "Are you really interested?" She laughed with delight. He toyed with her fingers, long and pale, cool. "You're so beautiful," he said; "please be real." As she looked at the ground, he stroked her hair lightly. All this, because illicit, with trepidation, a tremble in the hand.

"Did you find there was a lot of adjustment to make, with your Canadian wife?"

"Her parents were from Scotland. Yes . . . she could be rather forthright, which was a little shocking at first. Very candid with her opinions—but she too adjusted, became less so. Behind that cold exterior was a gentle and caring person . . ." And he was trying too hard to find a balance, not to sound critical, not to be too complimentary, in case he drove away this woman who sat beside him.

It had taken Aileen time to warm up, to awaken to her own sensuality. She preferred a cuddle to sex. Was it his problem? And Mohini?—she was a smouldering flame.

"She was very neat and orderly—and that was a problem for us initially. I was messy." He stroked her neck, then playfully ran down the bumpy spine, lingered at the open midriff. He heard a deep breath, but otherwise she pretended not to notice.

"Tell me about messy! I am thankful I have daughters . . . though Ravi doesn't share that feeling. He would have liked one son." She gave a rueful smile.

Her bau-ji had encouraged her to go for higher education. She had studied literature, and her final paper had been on Henry James. Bau-ji himself had gone to university in Lahore, with men who went on to become famous. But Partition came and it had turned him bitter. The family had to leave their family home in Sargodha and he lost his brother.

"His brother—your uncle?"

She nodded. He didn't know what to say, came out with, "I'm sorry."

"Mohan was his younger brother. He was in college. My father's still not gotten over his loss."

"And your mother?"

"She too. They were already married when they arrived. She'd been to high school but not to college."

She suffered from depression now, and Mohini thought she would travel with her parents, take them on a few pilgrimages.

Where? he asked, idly. She named some places. Puri. Dwarka. Shirdi. She was religious, then? he inquired. Yes, she replied, looking at him, surely he knew that. But in a spiritual way. He said nothing, but recalled her visit to the eighty-four-bell temple, how she had covered her head and joined her hands in worship.

He felt a quiet thrill as they shared these confidences, these stories of their lives, these intimate parts of themselves. This was how it should be, their relationship. At this moment nothing else mattered but themselves. He watched her looking dreamy, leaning back on her hands, her feet in front of her, and wished he could lean forward and kiss those feet, that belly, those lips. She looked up and smiled at him, perhaps reading his desire.

They decided they were hungry and got up to go. Outside the entrance, at the bus stop, they caught an auto to take them to the Club. The upstairs dining hall was crowded, but as a guest on the premises he had priority, and she was known. They were given a table and they both ordered beer. She was in the mood for lamb pasanda and they ordered that with daal and naan.

A figure drifted over and stopped by them.

"Ah, Mohini-ji, how wonderful to see you!"

It was Jetha Lal with his toothy grin, and they bantered in Hindi for a while. Mohini stopped to introduce her companion: "Jetha Lal-ji, have you met him, this is Munir Aslam Khan, a famous writer from Toronto. And this is the famous Jetha Lal."

"We met yesterday, on the lawn," Munir said as he shook hands with the man.

"Indeed, we did," agreed Jetha Lal. "But you didn't tell me your name."

"Now you know."

Jetha Lal nodded, turned to Mohini. "Did I hear you sing Ghalib yesterday in the cafeteria— '*Yeh na thi . . .*' Wah! Wonderful! 'Some things are not meant to be . . .' We must remember that . . ."

And, after a quick stare at the servings on their table, and a nod, he left, humming the poem's tune.

"Likely spying on me," Mohini muttered.

They got up to go. He couldn't help noticing, on the way out, a few casual stares directed at him, the stranger in the company of a woman they knew. At the driveway, as she waited for her taxi, she asked him if he was comfortable in his room. "I haven't seen a DRC guest room, actually."

"Would you like to come and see it?"

She returned a mischievous look and left.

In his room Munir sat in front of the TV and picked a channel showing a cricket match. He had not watched a full game since he left Kenya, though there he had played for the Duke of Gloucester School for Asians. The shorter, more popular form of the game was showing now, and he noted with displeasure that in place of the classic elegant whites of before, the players wore bright, gaudy attire, and they swung wildly at any ball that came their way; cheerleaders in short skirts danced on the sides—in case the game got boring? Not cricket, he murmured to himself. But perhaps I'm getting old. He nodded off, then woke up to a light knocking on the door. He got up and went to open it.

She was standing there, a faint smile on her face. "Can I come in?"

She hurried in, and he shut the door behind her, and as she turned to him he drew her close and crushed her to his chest.

Mohini

NOW, WHENEVER THEY ARGUED, and it seemed they did so frequently, he was likely to come out with a mocking, "And I guess you find that Khan of yours perfect!" Once he said, "Still pining for that Muslim! Don't forget your parents escaped with their lives, from the other side, *his* side!" This was not usually like him, he was deliberately provoking her with these cheap communal references, and she had replied sharply, "He's not my Muslim! He was born in Kenya, his folks are from Delhi! And he is a Canadian."

"Your Canadian, then."

Asha would watch and smile in that triumphant smile of the teenager.

But he had stopped short of making the blunt accusation, You are in love with him. He is your lover!. That would mean they had crossed a threshold in their marriage. He would not go there. It would be humiliating, in his position. If he suspected something real, he would not be so flippant about it.

But she *had* crossed the line. It was like walking into a fire, and there was no turning back. It terrified her when she thought like that.

Could she back out and call this a fling? But it was not a fling, it was a commitment. A longing. A pain. Was she immoral? Was she doomed to come back as a bitch in heat in her next life? That's what the elders would say of an adulteress. Did she really believe in another life, in karma? Yes, yes, yes.

She had not hurt anybody. Not even Ravi. He was just irritated; he would feel insulted if he knew the full extent of her transgression. No heartache, he was too cold for that. His would be a slow, burning rage. Frightening. Would he kill her? Was he capable? For his honour? And yet she knew he had been with other women. She just knew. From an off-colour joke made by a colleague, a look from a woman . . . that sweater that she could never have bought for him, just because it didn't suit him the way she knew him.

And yet. Could any man—Munir—be absolutely trusted? Having given him—what?—more than which she could not give. Her promise, her bond. How old-fashioned she was. She had known of women who had casual affairs, she had seen men flirting with women at public events, she and Ravi had even talked about it, amused. How can people be like that, they'd said. . . . Suppose one day Munir stopped responding from Toronto. Forgot about her . . . more realistically, concluded that the trouble was not worth it. Found someone young and free, a divorcee or widow whom he did not have to travel thousands of miles to spend a day or two with.

He just wasn't like that. She knew. In her bones, in her heart and body. He had found Delhi, he had found her. They must have been bonded in a previous life. The gods made a mistake and separated them, but now they were united.

And yet.

They had gone to see the fortress city of Tughlaqabad. Bahadur dropped her off at DRC. Mohini watched him drive off, out of sight, then she and Munir called for a taxi, which they hired for the day. Tughlaqabad was the most isolated and private it could get, but it was far from romantic. It was forbidding, haunted by its history. The sultan Tughlaq had removed the entire population of Delhi to his new capital in the south, even if they had to be dragged out of their houses and onto the road; then he brought them back. Munir had already been here before, on his previous visit. Now they walked among the grey and brown ruins, over and around sharp, broken rocks and collapsed walls, through the bazar and past dungeons, and headed for the highest point, a flattened tower, and looked around. Down below, the busy Mehrauli Road, further along which was the Qutub Minar, site of the first Muslim sultanate. All school kids studied about it, how Muizzuddin of Afghanistan just managed to defeat the Hindu raja Prithviraj and changed history. Later came the fierce Alauddin, having treacherously murdered his good uncle, exhibiting his head on a spike. This was also the time of the Sufi Nizamuddin, the poet Khusrau, and the historian Barani. Alauddin in his turn was suffocated during an illness by his catamite and chief adviser, the evil Malik Kafur, who had been bought for a thousand dinars as a slave. Soon after came the stern Tughlaq, who died in a miraculous accident after making a vain threat to the life of the Sufi.

It calls for a Shakespeare, this history, Munir mused. There is you, meanwhile, she murmured. They watched the little village down below in the lee of this old fortress. What kind of people live there? he asked her. Would they trace their ancestries to those times? I don't know, she said. They sat and touched fingers. Held hands, like preteens. They looked around, pointing out places they knew. Everything seemed risky yet necessary. This jaunt with Munir was stolen time. Any moment *he* could come walking up, her husband, having had her followed. She sensed his shadow everywhere, more out of fear and guilt. When did she begin to think this way? Since the start of her sin? Like Lady Macbeth: *Out, out* . . . but she hadn't murdered anyone, she had only loved. For the first time.

And then—but why?—Munir read to her a passage from Barani from his notebook. The Hindus were the worst enemies of God and should be oppressed, said the historian. Why did Munir bring it up? To say that a great historian could be a bigot? To demonstrate the contradictions that could exist in a man? To test their relationship? How naive he could be . . . there were matters he just couldn't understand, emotions he couldn't plumb. He had shown foreignness. She found the passage offensive. It mattered to her. He was right, it had all happened seven hundred years ago when the world was a different place. Still, it got to her somewhere inside. At such moments she understood the demands of the Nationalist party and even the fanatical NSS, the so-called National Service Scheme. It was the NSS, after all, that had helped the Hindu refugees who had come over from the new Pakistan, among whom were her parents and grandparents. She had heard their stories, witnessed their bitterness and grief. They had not forgotten. You only had to get her bau-ji started, how at the hour of the morning prayer, four a.m., they sneaked out of their house in Sargodha, the azaan sounding out from the nearby mosque . . . *Allahu Akbar*. Bau-ji knew that azaan by heart; for some strange reason he even liked to recite it, and Ma would cut him off sharply.

How different from other men she'd known was this one sitting beside her, their hips touching, their arms squeezed against each other. Ravi had his DNA theory of Muslims. "Over the course of generations, after some centuries, the DNA changes. And so these people are different. Violence and sensuality is in their DNA, since the time of Mahmud of Ghazni and Muizzuddin Ghori, and Alauddin Khilji and Nadir Shah . . . and Babur. All mass murderers. Now they are into terrorism." And she had asked, "Then what about Delhi 1984, and Gujarat 2002, what about Ashoka and his river of blood?" "Those were responses, my dear. And Ashoka repented and became a Buddhist. But they—the Muslims—always instigate. Their blood is hot. It's the meat they love to eat."

"But you eat chicken now," she said. Caught out, he said, "Not beef."

Her father and mother had agreed wholeheartedly.

"But what about your neighbours in Sargodha, Bau-ji, weren't they your friends? Didn't they send you presents for Diwali and you sent them gifts for Eid? Didn't Ma visit the grave of a Sufi to ask for children . . . after which you had me, Ma?"

"Then you are half Muslim," Ravi joked pointedly.

Her father, the professor of statistics, responded, "Exceptions don't disprove the rule, Mohini. Statistical trends are there."

Recently, with all the talk of terrorism and Pakistan, and

memories of the Partition still alive, her parents' position had hardened. Ravi had become cruder in his prejudices. And she herself had not remained untainted by the hatred and suspicion in the air.

Now here she was next to Munir Khan. Another exception? The Sufi who begot me must be laughing in his grave.

"There's a concert at the Siri Fort," she said to him. "The Mishra brothers. They are excellent—classical vocalists. It's time you learned about Indian music."

"Yes, let's go," he said with a smile.

"I'm going with Ravi. But you should go. Hire a taxi and tell it to wait for you."

"I'll do that."

He would do anything for her, she thought. And she for him. He had brought two opera DVDs for her. She should watch *The Marriage of Figaro* first, he said. She wasn't sure she would like it, what with all that screeching, but he said why not give it a try, she would enjoy the comedy and even the singing when she got used to it. The plots of operas were like those of Bollywood. Okay, she would give it a try, she said. The other one was based on a novel by Goethe, called *Werther*. She didn't know it, but she was intrigued. A bit depressing, was his opinion.

But why had she hidden the DVDs in her drawer among her underclothes? How stupid. Where else? . . . Why had *he* been there, put his hands there? He was her husband. He had been looking for his socks and just happened to get into her undies. He smiled when he found the DVDs. "New interest . . . in music, I see."

"Mozart—we should know about that, shouldn't we?" she said. "Munir Khan gave them to me. Nice of him, wasn't it?"

He could have asked, Then what were they doing among your undies?

"We have classical music of our own," he said. "Even more ancient than the Europeans'. But I agree, we have to know about Mozart, be more broad-minded, now that we are global."

The next evening they watched the opera and both enjoyed it. The laughter seemed to bring them back together for a while, like old days. Even Asha was drawn to it and watched it till the end. It was she who commented on the obvious, that in the story the Count philanders shamelessly while the wife remains chaste. Ravi was beaming. He said to his women, "European ladies had values in those days, just like Indian ones."

At Siri the place was flooded with lights. Dust, cars hooting, the crowds. The *bheed*. The night air was thick and moist, a full moon was out. And hundreds of devoted fans filling the seats. The Mishra brothers began with a lovely thumri, a single-line love song to Krishna, repeated over and over in variations. *Kya karun sajani, aaye na baalam ... What to do, beloved, he doesn't come ...* Then a couple of khayals. A bhajan by Meera. *Paga ghungaru bandh ...* She wished he were there to share the music, for her to explain it to him.

Discreetly she had cast around for a sight of him. When Ravi stood up to walk around and chat with people he knew, she had looked with some concentration and saw him near the front. He was in a red polo shirt and white linen pants. Poor fellow, he must have come early, like a true Westerner just on time, but here nothing started on time. To wait, then sit through the Mishra brothers, listen for a few hours to a

kind of music he was not used to! He had to learn, regain at
least a part of the Indian-ness he had lost. *Kya karun sajani* . . .
A tender feeling came over her.

Ravi came over.

"I saw your friend Khan out there in front. You seem to have
had an influence on him!"

"I told him about the concert. He should learn about his
roots."

"Roots. He has no roots left here." Then he cocked an eye at
her: "You want to call him over?"

"No, let him be."

Her heart was beating fast. Where lay the trap? Did he see
through her thinly shrouded nonchalance, into her eagerness
to call him over and be near him again, hear his voice? Ask him
how he liked the music, explain it to him? In her responses to
her husband she did not know how real she was, how truthful.

The two of them were playing games now.

The next day she was hesitant about calling him, or responding
to his many calls. She did not know what to say to him. How to
proceed. She had committed herself, now what? How to behave
in such a circumstance? More lies? She had told Ravi she would
be home. There was to be delivery of a dresser, imported from
Italy. A designer was finally coming with ideas for the kitchen.
Ravi said he would come for lunch and meet the designer. Life
proceeding normally, with plans they had made, decisions to
be made.

The following morning she picked up the phone immediately
when Munir called. It was ten a.m. and Ravi was already gone.

"I'm sorry," she said.

"Are you well? I thought you might be sick . . . or your daughter. Or that you had changed your mind."

"About what?"

"About us."

"How could I? I missed you. There were things to do. I was confused . . . Did you enjoy the concert? I saw you."

"I saw you too. It was too long. I thought I was late, it turned out I was early by an hour. I'm still aching from those hard seats."

She couldn't help laughing.

He said, "I could have joined you up there, where you were sitting."

"I'm sorry. But I didn't want to share you."

"I feel the same way. Today, then? Can we meet?"

"I am so busy. I have my lecture today . . . Then I am back home to prepare dinner. And write my column. An Indian woman works three jobs, you know."

"The day after?"

"He's home and my parents will visit."

"And I am leaving the next day."

"So soon?"

"I've been here two weeks."

But you'll be back. He had to come back. For how long, this precarious arrangement? She had been in tears, but she didn't show it.

"I'll come in the morning. You are leaving at night, aren't you?"

She picked him up at twelve and Bahadur dropped them off at Khan Market nearby, where he shopped for a gift for his daughter.

She bought him a CD; he bought her earrings. They browsed through the bookstore, where she bought a new book for her father on the partition of India.

"The same thing, I know. Endless stories about the Partition. But Bau-ji will like it. He never tires comparing his story with others'."

They were having lunch at a trendy restaurant, the atmosphere there cool and fragrant, smart young business people discussing their projects.

They returned to the Club and discreetly took different routes. He went to his room via the reception entrance; she went to the lounge, went up the stairs and crossed the balcony. They met in his room and embraced with relief. They made love. She cried. They both had taken wine and fell asleep.

At about five they came down together, feeling emboldened, to go to the lounge. On the way out, they were suddenly surrounded by a swarm of noisy young men clad all in white. Jostled by this sweaty, unshaven crew that had appeared like a bunch of jackals from nowhere, they couldn't move, they couldn't hear themselves, until Mohini screamed, "Let us through, you people!" Only then the swarm parted, with good-natured pretence: "Oh, let Madam go, she's on important business!" "Sorry, Madam!" "And this gentleman, are you her driver, Sir?" "Heh-heh . . ." "Oh, excuse us!"

It was a frightening experience. As they crossed over to the lounge, he remarked, to break the silence, "What was that about?"

"No manners," she said. "Why do they admit this kind of riff-raff at the Club? Used to be so exclusive."

"It looked deliberate, that . . . swarming . . . do you think it was?"

She didn't reply.

"Do you know these people?"

"No," she told him briefly. But they looked like unwashed versions of the Purifier Jetha Lal's followers. An uncouth bunch, who needed scrubbing to clean themselves inside and out.

Ravi arrived shortly afterwards, wearing a sporty linen jacket over a purple shirt. He put a box of barfi before Munir as a parting gift. "A guest is always bid farewell with sweet memories," he said. Really, Mohini said to herself. As they sat chatting, Ravi's interest as usual Canada and its economy and politics, the young men from before came in, occupying the doorway, looking around. Mohini counted eight of them. They saw Jetha Lal and his crew at his table by the side window and went to chat with them. Ravi watched them with a twinkle in his eyes.

Ravi said, "They've just finished duty in Ayodhya, and are on their way back to Gujarat and Maharashtra. We keep an eye on them."

Mohini and Ravi explained to Munir the significance of that. Ayodhya was believed to be the birthplace of the god Ram. The first Mughal emperor, Babur, had built a mosque there, apparently on the site of a temple. The site was in contention, but in 1992 an activist mob had demolished the mosque. Now they sent volunteers to keep watch over it while the government and courts prevaricated in coming to a decision about it.

A ruckus erupted from the group, someone among them having shouted something and others responding. The young man who had been conspicuously blocking her and Munir earlier was standing up, and he again shouted out something like a toast. The others responded, "*Zindabad!*" Everyone else in the lounge was stone-silent. Then normality returned, the usual soft hum of chatter and the clatter of dishes.

Munir looked at Ravi, then Mohini, for an explanation.

"They were toasting Nathuram Godse," Mohini said bitterly.

"Who is he?"

"He was Gandhi-ji's assassin. They've started putting up statues of him all over the country. To them he was a saint."

Later they were sitting at the bar when Munir's taxi arrived. He said goodbye and left.

Her eyes boring into his, bidding him goodbye and pleading for him to come back soon.

Munir

WHAT'S BROUGHT THIS ON? A call from his agent. A long bout
with a bottle of Scotch.

The creative life runs its course, though the body that's sheltered
it keeps going. An empty shell. There's no more to say, I've passed
on like a wavelet that's risen and waned, disappeared without a
trace. Writers should know when the force is gone. At home in
Nairobi we had a set of books by the famous Indian author Mulk
Raj Anand. One was *Coolie*. Another was *Untouchable*. The author
was a distant relation of Dada's, how, I don't know. Thin, badly
produced books, easily readable and quite gripping. What's an
Untouchable?—Dada explained: no it's not a snake. But the author
in his dotage was still at it, sputtering along on empty. The American
Philip Roth, on the other hand, recently announced that he has
retired from writing. I met him once, outside a publisher's office in
New York. He stared blankly at me—or looked through me—as we
were briefly introduced at the door. Didn't know who I was. Why
should he? A Canadian Punjabi from Kenya? Triply marginal.

Munir, Munir, stop it.

———

Max North, with a chortle:

"You son of a gun, Munir, you know you can't hide! We're all waiting for it, breathless, need I say it? Publishers are eager to get their hands on it—this magnum opus that's been ten years in the making . . . Admit it, now. I was in London and Jeff from Ironsides says he can't wait to lay his hands on a new work by Munir Khan . . ."

"There's nothing, Max. I'm—"

He never listens. Warm, yes, stylish, yes, and meaning well. Boundless enthusiasm that eventually sputters out, and then, as though nothing happened, all forgotten. You leave messages, and nothing. He's on a boat somewhere, perhaps off the coast of Greece.

That's the business to be in. Let the creators agonize.

"Willie Straus is over from Frankfurt, scouting, and you know what he said, Munir?—hold your breath—'Munir Khan, you mean he's not published in Germany?' He should know. I've given him notice—'If you don't publish all of Munir Aslam Khan, you're getting nothing more from me.' I promise, Munir, within a year your whole list . . ."

"That's nice, Max. There's hardly much of a list, though."

"Willie will pass by the office tomorrow. Why don't you come around eleven—do you drink cappuccino? We have a new machine . . ."

Cappuccino? If this Willie guy were really interested they'd ask me out for lunch. I know the game, Max, I've been here long enough.

"Chapter? Introduction . . . ?"

"Sorry?"

"Anything I can look at, Munir? All right, I know, you'll wait until you're ready. But a title as yet? A paragraph? It has to enter our world catalogue in four weeks—"

"As I said, Max, there's nothing . . . yet. All I've done is scribble some notes on medieval India. Nothing will—"

"You know which writers sell the most in the world today? You got it—India. There's a book I'll send you soon . . . It's called *Raja*, simple. Sold rights in fourteen countries already. She's off to India to do research on background—elephants and temples and so forth."

"Well . . . that's wonderful. Good for her."

Elephants? God, I'm glad to be out of this business. Except for this one little idea . . . but that's between me and Ziauddin Barani of Delhi. Not you, Max. Something private I don't have to show anybody else.

Not yet. Perhaps never.

"Dad—have you been drinking?"

"Sorry—I . . ."

"It's not a good idea when you're alone. You know better, Dad."

"I just dozed off, here."

Always good to hear her voice. Someone who cares. There's something special about a child—she is yours, absolutely. She ties you to the world, gives you a stake in it like nothing else does. Not your books . . . Your books? Not even one? No, Munir. And *she?* Mohini? How can she, who belongs elsewhere? She's a happy illusion, a happy maya.

Everyone needs a maya.

"I don't know if I should tell you this now, you're not quite there."

"Of course I'm here, and of course you should tell me—what is it?"

"I can't come home this Christmas."

"You mean . . . why not? Not even for a day or two?"

He's stunned. He swallows. Can't come home? He's been looking forward for months to seeing her again. Every Christmas they've spent together, ever since she was born. Gone shopping. Exchanged presents. Christmas is the happiest time of the year, barring perhaps the first real day of summer. Everyone greets everyone else, we think of our loved ones. It's commercial, yes, but everything is, isn't it? We sit on the living room carpet together and open the presents. What joy in giving a present to a child. The look on that face, when she gets something even beyond what she thought possible. And your heart is full. And you receive a hug. What better memories? A Christian festival? Not necessarily, though a Handel concert is nice. A children's choir is divine. Why, *why* can't she come?

"You know Mark doesn't celebrate Christmas. I can't leave him alone, Dad."

"No you can't, but you should both come. And what's wrong with celebrating, call it anything—Kwanza, Kwa heri, Deepawali, what difference does that make? It's family time!"

"I can't, Dad."

"All right, I guess," he says, punctured.

"You won't mind too much?"

"No, I won't mind." Yes he minds. He minds very much. *She's leaving home, bye-bye.*

"This will be the first time—"

"I know. Don't worry."

There's always a first time, isn't there. The first grey hair, the reading glasses. Life winding down. Is that the last tie she cuts before she drifts away? Why should I complain, I cut mine when I was much younger. Never—hardly—looked back. Until now. Until Delhi.

Well, Aileen, here we are. What I can say has been said a thousand, a million times before, therefore has no meaning when spoken. You know that. But you got a good piece of real estate, I don't mind telling you that again, here under this maple tree, right in the city. A beautiful place, this . . . No, I'm not happy you're dead. Yes, there's this person in Delhi, but it's all up in the air, as I said. I could tell you you should have been careful, no need to get more sweets for Halloween, just close the door, turn off the lights, and the kids will understand. You wouldn't listen. I should have gone. But an accident's an accident . . . How do I spend my time? All I do is mull around now. A slight increase in the intake of single malt, of which it was you who gave me the taste, remember. A bit of writing, I can tell you that, though not Max North. He called the other day—after a long time— and you know what he's like, all bluster. Invited me for coffee. I didn't go. More important, Razia won't come home for Christmas this year. It's going to be lonely, just me and me, like during those student Christmases long ago. But I'll send her a present from the both of us. And I'll buy me a sweater from you. I need one. We were always practical—at least in recent years . . . Nothing more for today, Aileen. Here is a yellow rose.

I see someone's left a red one before me. A fresh one. Who could it be? A secret admirer? A not-so-secret one? You wouldn't have done that to me, would you, Aileen? But then perhaps...after twenty-five years, when boredom set in? When we stopped looking at each other closely? When you went off to meet friends at the Cricket Club? No matter. And here is a book I bought for you in India.

There was a hiatus. Time out while the heart aches, time to face the practical world. What have we done, is it too late? Yes, it's too late. He had not written or texted her—phone was out of the question—and neither had she. But finally, he couldn't resist and called. It was nighttime, his.

"It's me."

"I know."

"Is this a wrong time?"

"Yes. I'm in the kitchen, and he's around."

"Isn't it morning there?"

"I'm making parathas. I wish I could send you one."

"Just wanted to hear your voice—"

"I'll write or call—now bye."

Just that, a hurried "bye." A bye is when a ball drifts away from the batsman, untouched, unwanted. Was he a bye, a drifter?

He wrote her a text. *Thinking always of you.*

And at that moment a thought flashed. An image—that dim room at the Sheth Rustomji Guest House on frantic Bahadur Shah Zafar Road. Couldn't be. He had walked to the old city and returned to find what?—the police had been in his room. Just a routine search, the man said—his name was Naren—looking for terrorists. Munir thought his computer had been unlocked. Now he recalled that he'd also left his phone behind, in his jacket pocket in the closet. It contained the selfie he and Mohini had taken at Safdarjung.

Couldn't be. He was being paranoid.

Everybody's here for the block party, and we pretend nothing's different, Aileen could be around somewhere in one of the two rooms or in the kitchen chatting with someone. Hiya, says Andy, the host this year and the cheerful face of the block; beard's a bit scruffy, he's just retired and the kids never returned. Sitting on the porch on warm evenings he'll greet all and sundry, ready with a quip. Your beautiful daughter not visiting this holiday? No, she's staying with her husband in New York. Ah, she married an American; there's some nice Canadians, too, you know. Too late! Beryl looks cheerful and different. We all remember the day her little son died, as he was expected to, but her face broke then and never recovered; she put on weight, picked up a stoop. But they've persevered, always with a cheerful greeting, she and Jim, no other kids. Now she's returned after three months away and it seems she's had her face done, it's all smooth, and, We're going to LA, she says. We'll drive to Las Vegas from there—have you been? And Jim explains, We haven't either, but you have to see it once, I guess. Is something up, Munir wonders. I hope they're okay. Jim and Beryl and Andy and Alice are the only ones left of the old guard, been here twenty-five years or more, except for that couple whose names I still don't know, the guy making a racist remark when Aileen and I first moved, something like, Where did you find

him? Not where *you're* from, Aileen had replied, then to Munir:
Left over from the Stone Age. Not another word exchanged
in twenty-five years. But they don't speak to anyone, except,
it seems, to Beryl. Those two could be hiding dead children in
their basement, Munir once said. That's cruel, Aileen said.
When Aileen died, they pushed a sympathy card through the
mail slot. A cheap one, but still. How the demographics have
changed, his the only brown face once, now there are two
young Asian couples and an elderly Anglo-Indian who wears a
fedora, and his wife. Hi Joanna, Hi Munir, meet my daughter,
the one I spoke to you about, analyst at the Bank of Montreal.
All high achievers, Joanna's two daughters and nephews, all
gone to MIT or places like that, and her father a former university president. Razia not here? No, not this year. Well, maybe
some other occasion soon. I hope so. A significant pause. They
all remember Aileen, but nothing gets said. What do they have
in their minds, about him, he wonders. There are the inevitable,
though disinterested book questions that he instinctively
deflects with some nonsense. And then the young Indian
couple who inspired his visit to India. Should he tell them that?
No . . . Their names are Raj and Shobha and hello, she's pregnant. You must miss India. Not at all, she says. No? No, except
the family. Why is that? It's become unlivable, the corruption
and the pollution . . . they've made it impossible for young
people. No, we like it here. They're looking for a family doctor,
and he gives them some advice, and the name of his own
doctor. He wanders around. More young people. How it's
changed, this neighbourhood. The two hardware stores are
gone, so is the butcher shop, and the watchmaker and the couple
of boutiques; but now there are three Starbucks and a French

café. More flower shops and two mani-pedi places. An Indian restaurant. Who says the economy is bad? But how times have changed . . . This is home, he looks around, these are my neighbours, we accept and like each other but don't intrude . . . But it won't remain the same forever . . . some will die, others will move. Two women are introduced to him, Joanna's friends, a librarian and a teacher. An accident, their presence? Meanwhile Joanna's hurried away. How was India? Wonderful. They talk enthusiastically about India. In some strange way, it's taken me back, he finds himself saying, then keeps quiet. We all harbour worlds inside ourselves.

And then, Surprise! cries a loud chorus, and Razia makes an appearance—wine glass in hand, leaning sideways, smiling—and Munir stifles a sob. He feels the heat of all eyes upon him—"Hi, Dad!"—and they embrace. "So you made it."

"Hear, hear!" says Andy. "Three cheers for Dad! And daughter."

Yes, all the while they've harboured sympathy for him, it's his first real Christmas without Aileen.

He and Razia walk home together. It's bright outside, and there's ice on the ground, she supports him though he thinks he doesn't need it. When they are home and having coffee, she says, "We had a quarrel—Mark and I."

He stares at her.

"Don't tell me it's going to be all right."

"Of course it's going to be. He'll call you."

"You know that, do you?"

"Yes. I do. I would."

"That doesn't count, does it?"

A lovely girl like that, why wouldn't he call her? He's heart-broken and in despair already, I bet.

They say nothing for a while, and she flips the pages of a *New Yorker*.

"Dad."

"Yes . . ."

"I am so grateful you had me."

It takes a moment for that to sink in. "What a thing to say," he says softly. "We had a child and it turned out to be you. Wonderful you. Thank you for the joy you bring."

"I mean it. You are a good person. A moral person, Dad."

"Am I now. I wouldn't be sure."

"Tell me about her."

"Who?"

"Don't play innocent. India. I heard you telling those two people that you had a craving to return to India. Can't be the Taj Mahal."

He laughs. He gives her her present from Aileen and himself, from where he has placed it, where presents have always been placed before being handed out in the morning every Christmas. And he gives her his present for Mark. She's brought him a travel kit and walking shoes. They decide to visit the cemetery the next morning. And while they're discussing dinner plans, sure enough, Mark calls. It's a long call, which she takes in her room. When she returns, her face is wet and she looks happy.

"I'll go back on New Year's Eve, is that all right?"

"Of course."

"Now what were we talking about? Ms. India."

"Mrs.," he says softly. Why did that have to come out?

"Dad . . ."

She's like my mother now.

"*Dad!* . . ."

"Yes."

"Dad, don't tell me . . . she's married?"

"I can't help it. Couldn't help it. It just happened."

"That's a fine endorsement for marriage from you."

She knows that half the marriages in our part of the world end in divorce. It's a healthy alternative to the prison of a bad marriage. We just pretend when we get married that it's going to last forever. And we celebrate and bless like there's no tomorrow.

"You've got yourself into a fine pickle, Dad. She won't divorce or anything?"

"They don't do such things."

"Anything else?"

"She's a Hindu."

"That makes no difference, does it?"

"Over there it does. It's in their genes."

"Just let it go, Dad. You'll find many women here with the same values as you. No hang-ups."

He smiles at her. Inanely, as only a bout with Scotch can make you do.

She gets up, comes over to kiss him goodnight.

"Look after yourself, Dad. And talk to me."

And she goes up.

Mohini

THEY HAD LIVED IN TERROR for two days, her father Chand
would say, as mobs roamed the streets in their Minto Close
neighbourhood of Sargodha. India had declared independence,
Sargodha was in Pakistan, which would soon declare its independence, and the Hindus of the city had begun to flee. His
father Nathu Lal had declared flatly that he was not leaving.
We have lived here for generations, Nathu Lal said. Since
Mahabharata . . . my own grandfather traded in Kabul and
Peshawar. There was substantial stock in his men's clothing
store and the tailors were dependent on him. Muslim tailors.
One of whom, Hassan, had said he would take them to the railway station if they desired. I will let you know, Nathu Lal told
him, but I don't think that will be necessary. The sarkar is sending troops all across, and Gandhi-ji is exhorting the nation to
peace. Have you heard that he plans to visit our Pakistan? The
two nations will be like sisters. People will come and go. What
border, what partition? There are temples and gurudwaras
over here and mosques over there. Ajmer Sharif is in India,

Nizamuddin Dargah is in India. In vain Chand exhorted, Bau-ji, there is already violence in the streets! We have two girls in the house and your daughter-in-law, we have our mother! Chand's mother was all for packing up and going. What can Gandhi-ji do from there? she said. Let's go and at least save our lives. Would the old man but listen. Then one afternoon Hassan came back from his lunch with a long face. Things don't look good, Babu-ji, I've heard this street is next on the list, and this shop is a target. You must close it now and stay indoors. Only then did Nathu Lal relent. Post-haste the shop was closed. I will bring news for you, Babu-ji, and some food, if you don't mind. Yes, my son, you do that; and look after yours. Meanwhile complete that kurta we promised Sirtaj and that one for the English sahab that he wants to take to England. Tell Nuruddin and Afzal to complete their orders too . . . when the violence is over . . .

Hassan opened the door a wedge and slipped out into the dark. Closing the door shut, he shot the bolt, inserted the padlock, and turned the key. The resulting sound was terrifying. They were prisoners. Are you sure you trust him? Dadi asked. I trust him, Nathu Lal said. If I don't trust Hassan, who is left to trust? They sat in silence, behind the door. Their two daughters, Madhu and Suman, brought tea. They ate the stale chapattis which had been set aside for the street dogs. And then, in the distance, a few shouts in the absolute stillness; and if you breathed in deeply, the faint whiff of burning. Dadi hastened to the family shrine, praying frantically. Save us from the fiends, she prayed; save us from those murderous *mlechhas* and I promise I will visit the tirthas and the dhamas and the holy cities across the land . . .

The next morning the looting and shouting was closer, just

down the street. The screaming. Their front door broke open with a crash, and they, who were at the back of the house, escaped to the yard, then behind the storage shed against the wooden fence. Peeping out from the side, his mother tugging his arm, Chand saw looters coming away with bolts of cloth, the two mannequins, shirts and ties. His father never swore, but this time, as he saw his precious cashmere stock disappear, he swore, *kutte ki awlaad, haramkhor*. Sons of bitches, bastards.

In the evening, Hassan arrived, calling out softly, Babu-ji . . . Nathu Lal-ji . . . it is I, Hassan . . . And Nathu Lal came out into the yard, checked there was no one with Hassan, and the family emerged, dishevelled and dirty. Hunger and fatigue. Their house now only broken walls, smoke and cinders. There is a train at night, Hassan said. Delhi-bound. I will take you to the station. There are soldiers there. But meanwhile stay still. Any movement and they'll be here. Do you have money I can use to bribe? He left a bag of pakodas and some mangoes behind.

Don't ask, Mohini's father would say, don't ask how we reached the station, how we got into the train.

"It was terrible," Ravi said sympathetically. "We know your generation suffered a lot. But—we can proudly say—you've pulled yourselves up and brought us where we are now. Where the nation is."

There was a moment's silence. Bau-ji finally said, "What a price."

Ma silent, just a stream of tears on her face.

When the train had gone some distance, just outside Lahore, Mohan went down the compartment to report on the condition of the toilet. He was never seen again.

"Bau-ji," Mohini said. "No need to dwell on it. That was a long time ago, and it's over now . . ."

"Butchered," Bau-ji muttered. "A gang of Pathans had got on the train, we heard afterwards. There were many dead bodies that arrived in Delhi on that train. Not my brother."

"He's with God."

"Who knows? Maybe they kidnapped him, converted him into some Abdullah or Mohamad Khan…that happened too…"

There was a photo in their album of the two brothers, close together in what might be an actors' pose, hair slicked, wearing sports blazers. Smiling, almost laughing. Two stage comedians before a gig, perhaps.

Mohini and Ravi had come to see her parents at their flat in Gurgaon. It was a two-bedroom government flat on the ground floor. Two girls came to help part-time each day. Now, for some reason, Bau-ji was losing weight. It was a worry.

Countless times now she had heard of the family's escape from Sargodha. A wound that never healed. No point telling him that there was killing on both sides. The family whose house they came to occupy in Delhi had escaped or been murdered. It was to control such violence in Delhi that Gandhi had gone on his fast at Birla House—and paid with his life. She could not even imagine what it must be like to lose your family home and town, never to see them again.

Bau-ji never spoke more of Hassan, who had saved the family, except that shake of the head and the brief, "Not Hassan," when the subject arose. Hassan must be Bau-ji's age, somewhere in Pakistan.

She felt sick. Who had prompted Bau-ji this time? Was it Ravi, who was beaming? She was being unfair to him. He was her husband. They had tied the knot before the gods. It was her guilt that made her sick.

They were discussing the family vacation that they had been planning for a few weeks now. She said, "What do you think, Ravi? We fly to Bhubaneswar, tour the city—"

"See the temples. It's a city of temples."

"Yes. That's the whole purpose of going there in the first place. Then we take a car to Puri, visit Jagannath temple, stay the night, and go to Konark. The sun temple."

"But that's a defunct temple. Ma would not be interested."

"Ma, would you be interested in the sun temple in Konark? It is dedicated to Surya."

"I don't know—can I get prasad there?"

"Konark is a must," put in Bau-ji firmly. "How can we go to Odisha and not go to Konark?"

"And Dhauli, site of the Kalinga war," Mohini put in. "It is now a Buddhist pilgrimage site."

Bau-ji nodded. Ravi was noncommittal. Ma was blank. Her agenda was clear, an impossible itinerary of shrine visits following Puri: Varanasi, Dwarka, Somnath, Shirdi. Vaishno Devi. The last one should perhaps have been the first, the journey up the hills was so long and arduous.

"These days we can rent a helicopter to take us to Devi's shrine," Ravi said with a smile. "No need for old folks to suffer."

"No heli-beli copter for me," Ma said firmly, "if I have to see Devi, I'll go on these two legs. And with her power coursing through me, I will make it to the top!"

Everyone looked at her indulgently. Normally quiet, but when she spoke up you listened.

"Ma, now tea. I've brought dhokla. These Gujarati farsaans are all the rage now, thanks to the prime minister."

———

How easy it seemed to put him out of her mind with her daily worries, she thought, as Ravi drove them home. But he was always there, somewhere in her being. He was in the pain in the pit of her stomach, he was in her guilty heartbeat. He was her secret solace that she could turn to in the middle of the night whenever the thought occurred, Mohini, you are alone—no one to talk to, no one to confide in. But she was not alone anymore. He was an essential part of her even in his absence. She wished she could tell him about her bau-ji and Ma, how painful it was to watch them grow older and more helpless by the day. Would he understand why Bau-ji hated *them*—sometimes it was the Pathans, other times the Muslims or the Pakistanis—? He had lost his beloved younger brother. Yes, Munir would understand—not the hatred but the pain. Perhaps even the hatred.

Back home in the washroom she wrote a quick text to him: *Thinking of you.* She sent it then erased it from the phone. He couldn't resist and wrote back, *Me too.* She forced herself to erase that one too.

In bed Ravi turned frisky but she warded him off. I'm tired. But then she quizzed him about those zealots at DRC, how they had frightened her.

"They were just being rambunctious, Moi, they were excited about standing guard over the temple at Ayodhya."

"Do you think that was right? There was a mosque there, five hundred years old, which they destroyed."

"What's five hundred years? Our history, the time of Ram, goes back thousands of years. The Muslim presence is just a blemish on the surface—and can be . . ."

"Wiped off?"

"Not so easy, I've told you. Now that I have answered your question . . ." He raised himself over her, "I must have my baksheesh . . ."

She resisted mildly, but she had no choice and cried silently afterwards. She missed Munir.

In the old days, a Hindu wife joined her husband on his funeral pyre. She followed her husband from janam to janam, from one birth to the next. Sita stayed chaste even in captivity for years. Sita the ideal.

Mohini slept.

Munir

HAVING SETTLED ON THE three-legged folding stool he'd brought with him, he placed his phone on the edge of her headstone and with a little effort turned on the music, keeping it down. All around him the distorted Cartesian geometry of the headstones, uneven rows and columns, imposed upon the lush greenery of Mount Pleasant Cemetery. This is where I want to be buried, she'd said a few times when they'd passed here; she couldn't have known the time would come too soon. A few rows down from him, a pickup was parked, its back loaded with tools. Into this still life now punctured the treble of the singer, the chorus, and the ecstatic clang of percussion. Amir Khusrau rendered into song.

I thought, Aileen, you should know what's happening to me currently. This is the poet I've discovered in India. I left a book of his poems here for you last time, but it's disappeared. No doubt some vandal. I know you didn't care for Indian music or poetry, neither did I very much, I just thought to tell you of this new interest of mine in medieval Delhi. Are you surprised?

Who can tell, it could lead to something . . . fingers crossed, and so on. I know I haven't told you about what else in India; about her. What she looks like, what attracts me about her. Who exactly she is. If she's attractive, younger. Yes, she is both. And very bright. Too perfect? I'm very fond of her, Aileen. You would like to know if someone like her would have been better for me, but that question has no answer, does it? Or maybe it has, but does it matter? How do we know it would be the right answer anyway. But yes, I've been transported, recently. My heart aches for her presence . . . her voice . . . I won't say more. Passion, Razia called it, about her own love life, and I dismissed the thought. But for me this is it, I know, though muted by life's experiences. It's not that I don't also miss you . . .

Something bothers me about this poet and his friend the historian, though—

There came a step to his right and a figure loomed, startling him. It was the same man he'd run into at the gate the last time he came. Tall, with a deep brow and thin grey hair combed to a side, in a well-worn tweed jacket. Why was he here, with that expressionless face (but hardly the attire) of an undertaker?

"Hello," Munir said.

"Hello."

They became quiet, contemplating the grave, before Munir asked, "Did you know Aileen?"

"From way back."

The man bent down and placed a bouquet of roses on the grave. An awkward moment followed, then Munir said, "I was telling her about the poet I discovered in India. From the late thirteenth century. These are his poems set to music."

"Indeed."

"We were married twenty-five-odd years. A long time. Last time I came I placed a book of poems here." Munir looked inquiringly at the man. "Did you see them?"

"I imagined it was placed there as a joke. I removed it."

"I see. You threw it away?"

"I'm afraid so. I'm sorry."

"Not easy to find, those volumes."

The man said nothing. And Munir thought, Why assume it was placed there as a joke? Because the script was Urdu? What gall.

"I was just telling Aileen how the poet bothers me, when he shouldn't, really. He lived seven hundred years ago, after all. He wrote for his times."

The man smiled benignly at him. He must think I am crazy, Munir thought.

At that moment he spotted Razia, who had just walked up behind the man.

"What bothers you about the poet, Dad?"

The man turned, and Munir, happy to be rescued, said to him, "My daughter—our daughter, Aileen's and mine. Razia."

The man shook hands with Razia. "Very pleased to meet you." He introduced himself, "I'm Ian—Ian Fraser—an old acquaintance of your mother's."

With a partial nod and a partial bow, he left.

"Did you know him, Dad?"

"Never met him. Seemed rather presumptuous—as though this were more his territory than mine."

"Maybe he manages the cemetery."

Munir didn't inform her that the man had brought the expensive bouquet of roses that were on the grave. They sat in silence then, he on his folding little stool and she on the ground beside the grave. Finally they got up, Razia placed a blue lily on the roses, saying, "I love you, Mom," and they left. The girl had tears in her eyes.

"It's a nice spot you picked for her resting place, Dad," she said.

"She picked it herself. And the one next to it is mine."

"You've still got an eventful life ahead of you. Remember?"

On the way to the car, Munir asked her, "How are your friends doing? How's Lucy?"

Razia had retained most of her friends from school, and they had formed an ever-tighter group over the years. He and Aileen had known them as long, ever since kindergarten, and knew everything about them. Who went where to university, who became the lawyer, who the pediatrician, who the banker. And who had the mental breakdown and stayed at home; that was the sad part, it made you thankful for yours, who remained intact.

"They're doing great, Dad. Lucy's been promoted senior associate at her firm. June's still in graduate school at Duke."

"Meeting them later?"

"At a pub. Downtown."

"Late night?"

"Not very."

He was disappointed. She had given short notice to say she was coming to Toronto for the weekend, and he'd said, This is your home, Razia, you don't have to ask. You know I long to see you. And yet how could he expect her to sacrifice quality time with friends just to be with her old dad? It turned out he was no more than the concierge. You are acting spoilt, Munir.

———

In the evening after dinner, which he cooked for himself, he watched a movie on television, an old Western, and then sat with his drink trying to read.

Razia returned a little before midnight. She must have left the party early for his sake, he thought gratefully. There was a time when she would return at three and he had stayed awake for her, much to her annoyance. I'm an adult now. Yes you are, dear. It's just us, who are crazy worried.

"You're up late," she said.

He smiled. "I watched TV for a while, now I do my penance." He indicated the book in his hand.

"And the drink?"

That needed no answer. She went to sit across from him, legs crossed under her, an affectionate smile on her face. She had her winning ways. All his resentment had evaporated at the sight of her. He watched her, tall and angular, the black hair long down to the shoulders, the cheeks only slightly chubby, which for a long time she'd treated as a flaw inherited from him. The black Indian dress she was wearing was one that he had brought for her from Delhi.

"I'm worried about you," she said.

"No need. I'm all right. I'm used to being alone by now." He smiled his appreciation at her.

"Talking to Mom's grave? That's no cause for concern?"

"That's a nice touch, isn't it—playing music to her? I believe I was explaining my new interests to her. Perhaps I'm going crazy. But it's a nice feeling, to be able to do the odd thing now and then."

Which he wouldn't have done before. She eyed him, reading the thought.

"Do you really believe she can hear you . . . from there? Do you believe in the afterlife?"

"No. But I think she did—your mother did. That's not why I talk to her. I just feel good doing that. I just feel I'm remembering her more genuinely."

"That's nice."

"And you get used to talking to a person."

She laughed. "Don't I know that!" She turned to him: "Tell me more about her, Dad."

"You know about your mom."

"I mean *her*. That woman."

"Her name is Mohini," he said quickly. "I think I told you that."

"You didn't. I'm sorry. Tell me about Mohini, then."

He told her how they had met and how she had shown him around Delhi. He told her about the great mosque and the Dariba Kalan jewellery market—that was where his grandfather probably came from, and where he bought the earrings for her the last time—and he described the eighty-four-bell modest little temple that had intrigued him. Yes, she was younger than him, ten years, perhaps. She had a husband and two daughters.

There was a look of amazement on her face as he'd gone on. When he finished, she was giving him an intense look and he could imagine the questions still playing on her mind. But she looked away.

"It's not like you plan such a thing," he said.

"No."

She became thoughtful, and then abruptly, with a soft smile, she stood up. "I have to go up and talk to my philosopher now. Goodnight, Dad. I love you very much."

His hands lingered over hers as she left. After a while he could hear her voice on the phone. It was a long call. Young love.

The next morning she was up before him, packed and ready to call her Uber. He gave her coffee and fried her an egg first.

"I feel ravenous. I could eat an ox, but an egg is fine."

She had on the mischievous look of a child bursting with a secret. They had not spent much time together, but they had been close. She had not been hurt or scolded him about Mohini, his recklessness. When she was here, her presence was everywhere. She brought life back to the house. She had cooked a dinner for him, and they had had lunch at the heated patio of a bistro on Yonge Street. She wouldn't have beer or wine, and he'd given her a stare.

"I'd like to come and visit you in New York," he said. "I won't interfere in your life . . . just to see you. I can go to a museum, catch a play."

"You can come whenever, Dad. But there's a special occasion I'd like you to come for. I'll let you know when. In the fall."

"Yes? What occasion? Or is it a secret?"

"I'm having a baby."

He paused, not quite surprised, yet still taken aback. Then he stood up and went round to embrace her.

When her car came, she gave him a tight hug on the sidewalk.

"We should talk more about Delhi," she said, and left.

Mohini

ONCE A MONTH ON Tuesdays she went to her parents' house in Gurgaon to help them house-clean and sort things out. There was decades-old stuff to dispose of—what was not claimed by the two daughters was gradually, and sometimes reluctantly, junked.

When Mohini arrived, a girl was there, already on her fours, cleaning the floors, and Mohini made sure she reached the corners and replaced the water in the bucket. These migrant girls, who came from villages in Bihar or UP, had to be taught the ways of the modern city household, and you had to watch them constantly until they learned. Then, inevitably, they left. Six months ago Ma had slipped on a spot of soap residue. Luckily, there was only a minor wrist injury and it received a small cast. This girl was called Sivani, with striking features—small and thin, skin dark and smooth as chocolate, and proudly wearing a chameli in her hair and a stud in her nose. She was going places. When she was done, she scrubbed the pots and pans, and together they cleaned the kitchen counters and the cabinet doors. Mohini gave the girl some food and sent her off. She would be back in the afternoon. Then, while Mohini herself was doing the glass dishes, the other girl came, Damayanti, similarly featured but without the flower in her hair, who cleaned the bathroom and toilet. The girls were fed on their own separate plates, which Ma brought out twice a week when they came. Caste habits die hard.

Sivani had given notice that she was getting married next month, but would send someone else from her village in her stead.

When the house was sparkling clean, Mohini served her father a cup of tea with a brown-bread toast at the table, to which he had brought his copy of the *Express Times*.

"Let's go," Ma said, all dressed up, and Mohini replied, "Let's," and they set off for the Hanuman temple at the nearby corner. It had grown, from a small Sankatmochan temple into a yellow-and-white building with a golden spire, and there were flower vendors and fruit stalls and one chai stall outside, and a Sher-e-Punjab dhaba across the street, a sardarji doling out fresh jalebis, samosas and pakodas, and chana.

Ma was huffing, though they had gone only halfway down the block, and Mohini was concerned. "Ma, are you all right? Did you get your checkup done?"

"I'm all right, it's your bau-ji you should worry about . . ."

"I worry about him, but did you get your checkup done?"

She stopped for an answer, which didn't come.

"Next time I'm going to take you to Dr. Panwakar myself for the checkup."

She wished Aarti, always the favourite, would shoulder some responsibility for their parents. Show some anxiety. But

Aarti was in Bangalore and hardly had time to look up from her conferences and meetings. Always in the fast lane, and poor Mohini bringing up the rear.

The temple visit took a short time. Mohini and Ma joined the queue, walked up to the pandit with flowers and some money, joined their hands and received the blessings. In a few minutes they were out, but already there was a pleasant glow on Ma's face. They crossed the street and had parathas at the dhaba.

These Tuesday visits kept them close. Although Mohini sometimes got weary and complained about the distance and traffic, it was a privilege. It filled her heart, made her feel like a worthy human being. Aarti might be in the fast lane and earn a hundred thousand or more dollars, but she would regret later not having had these moments.

Ma asked her about the children.

"They are all right, Ma, they are good girls. But Asha just does not have her head in her studies. I am worried."

"And Priya?"

"All right too, I think. At least she is in university. But she made sure she was far from us, in Hyderabad."

"You make sure they study. Girls need education. Your father insisted you both got educated, and see how far Aarti has gone. President. You too, though you could have gone further."

"Then I wouldn't have been able to be close to you and Bau-ji, Ma."

Her mother gave the tiniest smile and squeezed her hand. "You were always my good girl."

"But Aarti was the favourite."

"She only demanded more. You were always steady. We could depend on you, our Mohini. We called her Aarti as a prayer ..."

Mohini often wondered about her mother's background. She was from a little town outside Sargodha where, she once said, nothing exciting happened except the daily round to the local water tap and the monthly visit to the cinema in the city, where her in-laws noticed her. She did not finish her education but taught herself to read in English when Mohini and Aarti started school. Now she could read the dailies. It was she who had preserved that photo, air-brushed and painted, two brothers in blazer and shirt against a darkened studio background, smiling. What could go wrong? Everything. And every day she prayed before the gods at home and at temples and shrines for Mohan's return, though he would be almost as old as Bau-ji, so what did she pray for? That an old man would walk in after fifty years and say, Here I am, it is I, Mohan? Mohini had asked her mother slyly once, Were you in love with Mohan? Ma had smiled. "The husband's younger brother is always special." Then she had looked up into the distance, still with that smile, and said, "He wanted to marry me. He was the one who saw me first, at the cinema. But the older brother always comes first. And he has been good." The second "he" was Bau-ji, whose given name, Chand, she had never spoken after her marriage.

When they reached home, Bau-ji was stretched out on the floor, receiving his massage, groaning his satisfaction. The masseur was a strong, stocky girl from somewhere in the east called Bala. When she had finished, Bau-ji sat down at the dining table and had his meal, which Ma had laid out for him. Then Ma herself received a massage, on the couch, and finally Mohini on the floor.

Mohini stretched out on the couch and instantly fell asleep. When she awoke, from a bad dream, it was due to the reassuring clatter of tea things on the table. Sivani had returned for her afternoon one hour, to prepare tea and fry some pakodas. Ma and Bau-ji were already up from their naps.

"Bau-ji, Ma, I have to go," Mohini said, having washed and briefly fixed her face and hair. "Bahadur should be here any minute, we have to beat the traffic."

Even then, it would take at least an hour to get home. There was a text from Asha, meanwhile, saying she was already back and with her tutor. And another one. From Munir. Her face lit up, her heart beat faster. *How are you today?*

Her eye met her mother's, who said, "Come. Come inside for a moment. I want to show you something."

Mohini got up and with her tea cup in her hand followed her mother to the bedroom. Ma went straight to the great almirah which stood against the wall, put a key into the lock and opened it; stooping down, from the back of the drawer at the bottom she withdrew a package wrapped in an old bandhni.

"What is it, Ma?" Mohini asked.

"It's what you gave me to keep. It's not good, what you are doing. What's inside."

"You looked inside, Ma?"

"Yes, I had to find out. Why are you doing this, a good girl like you?"

"You read . . . the letter?"

"No, I didn't. But I saw the earrings. And that newspaper clipping—about Khan. The author you were telling us about."

"Just let it be, Ma." She wrapped the package again and gave it back. "Keep it with you. And don't tell Bau-ji."

"I only pray you'll come to your senses. What has come over you? Are you possessed?"

Yes, she wanted to say. Something has happened to me and I can't help it.

"Your father too was infatuated with a Muslim once."

That came out quietly.

"He was? You never told me! When?"

"Before he met me. A Muslim neighbour's girl. They rejected him, only because he was a Hindu. He came to his senses. We are different, Hindu and Muslim, like day and night . . . But whether Hindu or Muslim, you are a married woman with a home, Mohini!"

"Ma . . ."

She sat down on the bed and cried. Her mother let her, and then said quietly, "Whatever he is, he is your husband. You are tied to him. And he is a good man, Ravi. So come to your senses."

"Can such feelings be controlled, Ma?"

"They had better be."

She dreamed that she had gone to Canada on some assignment. When she emerged from the arrivals gate at the airport, pent up with excitement, looking left and right to see his face again, he stepped forward and shook her hand formally with, "Welcome to Toronto." Shook her hand! And let her roll her own bag to the car. He escorted her to her hotel, waited for her to check in, and left her at the elevator to go up. He was embarrassed to be seen with her—she in her sari and long plait, weary after a nine-teen-hour journey, with her Indian accent. She flew back home the next day, crying, "Ravi, take me back! I am home!" She awoke in a sweat.

Munir

YOUR GRANDSON WILL BE born an American, Aileen.

Proud of her Scottish roots, she had also been a good
Canadian, impatient of any qualification to the goodness. He
used to say that he had to meet fifty HR managers (rounding
off conveniently) before one arranged an interview for him.
"But that's not racism," she would say sharply. He agreed, there
was no proof. It could have been his accent at the time, or his
manner of dressing (overdone, initially) that turned them off.
Wasn't that racism? He had to agree, though, where in the
world did people not discriminate? They had arrived close to
his initial proposition, but that small gap prevented a quarrel.

Now her grandson would be an American. Like most
Canadians of her class, Aileen did not much care for America.
That neighbour was recognized as a cousin and ally, a giant of
a trading partner, but not liked very much. Canada was better
in every way. No arguing. When Munir arrived in the country
as a student, *Canadian* had meant "white." She had not much
cared for that label either. "Didn't I marry you?" "And I you." But

that distinction mattered less and less, and Toronto grew easier; incidents such as the local butcher asking her, "Who is your husband?" when he was standing right next to her not only vanished, but became laughable when recalled. The butcher shop closed, unable to compete with the A&P.

In all their twenty-five years of marriage, they'd visited the U.S. exactly twice. The second time was following 9/11, and she, a solid McKellar, was quizzed at some length by U.S. immigration (this was the weekend following the shoe-bomber incident), while he, a veritable *Khan*, was asked only two questions: Where? and How long? This became a joke to be relayed among friends.

And then Razia, at the end of grade eleven, made the treasonable statement, "I would like to go to university in the U.S."

Aileen objected, threatened: There will be no money from us. Munir cajoled: What's the need to go there, we have perfectly good universities in Canada. But she was admitted to Yale, and what could either parent say then?

Aileen was right in her fear: they lost their girl, in a manner of speaking. If she had stayed in Canada, she would likely have remained closer to them and in Toronto. But that prospect, of losing a child, was exactly what Munir's own parents had been warned against when he dropped his own bombshell, his desire to finish his studies in England: You will lose your son if he goes abroad. And they lost him. That's how it went. Children were to lose. We were a community of immigrants in Kenya, he reflected; we came to a country of immigrants. Rootless; ahistorical; and then he saw that young Indian couple move in a few houses away with their daughter and he thought, I should go to India. Delhi. My grandfather's city. A full circle.

——

Aileen would remind him, fondly, of how she had disliked him the moment she first saw him. It was at his job interview at the corporate finance division of the Bank of Montreal. He was too obviously foreign—his hair too neat, his pinstriped suit and brogues not quite right; and his accent—well. She would smile. He was odd. Hers had been the lone vote against him. He was hired because the bank needed to look diverse, and he was qualified. Gradually she began to look past his strangeness, she said, and appreciated his honesty and openness, his respect for women, when other men were loud and obvious with their innuendoes. He began to act less oddly too. His clothes looked normal (he took a colleague from work to shop with him once) and the abominations in his accent wore away—no longer *cock* for *Coke*.

She was proud and white with a certain restraint, reminding him of some of his British teachers at school. He asked her out the first time because he was scared of her; he dared himself to tame her. And he did. Underneath that waspish veneer he uncovered a person, a woman, as he expected, attractive and often tender. She began to laugh with him, at his jokes about Nairobi, his foibles as an immigrant. The first time they had sex she had to guide him; it was in the back of his car, the way he had wanted to ever since his teens, having seen it done in a movie. His only previous experience had been a visit to a prostitute in Mombasa in the company of friends. After that time in the car they'd gone to his room and done it again. There was no holding him back, and she enjoyed him, decided he was the one for her despite his difference. It had helped, she would admit, that he had a fair skin for an Indian. They had different habits, and in their life together, since he was the immigrant and a male, she often had her way and decided what was proper.

Was it love? A kind of love. There were moments when he adored her, watching her sleeping, looking helpless, her mouth slightly open, the stiffness drained away and the body radiating the night's preserved warmth and she was irresistibly sexy. He was proud of her, her trim looks, her sense of propriety, her animated expressions that were controlled—she was not loud, never embarrassing. There were moments of doubt, initially. Was his a case of the colonized male asserting his manhood? Caliban getting his revenge? That had come out in a quarrel, and she seemed irreparably wounded. It had taken a few days for him to redeem himself, for them to pull away from failure. But they settled down. You have to know someone intimately to become aware of those tender moments, those special attributes, those unstated but very real qualities. You learn the feel of their skin, the smell of their breath, those vulnerable moments of nakedness. They were what made you a couple; in the older expression, man and wife. They are the steady fuel that keeps a marriage going through the years and decades of routine, and over those rocky periods and past impending calamities. They never crashed.

One day his widowed sister Khadija came to visit them. When he had allowed himself enough time to mull over that visit, he admitted to himself that he had been embarrassed by her. She had seemed crude. What a word, for someone who had looked after him when he was young, into whose arms he would run when there was no other recourse. He could hardly recognize her. Her face was jowly and spotted, there were dark shadows under the eyes, and she had grown heavy in the hips, in the manner of Punjabi matrons. Far from the slim and pretty young woman he had left back in Nairobi with a tearful goodbye. Thankfully for her figure, she still wore the salwar-kameez. Her English was barely understandable—or did Aileen exaggerate incomprehension? She did speak loudly and her movements were awkward. She asked them how much their house had cost, how much money they made. She could not hide her suspicion of Aileen, having harboured the belief of many Asians that white people were immoral and dirty. She had only recently come to Canada with a son and lived in the immigrant suburb of Rosecliffe Park. She told him she was sick, and he had sympathized. She begged him to visit her, said she would make him paratha; but he never did, and he did not invite her back. There were always excuses. Aileen wanted nothing to do with her. Once, over the phone, Khadija told him, "I realize it is hard to live two lives; you go ahead and live yours, Brother. Be happy. Jité raho."

Those words ran like a dagger through him. What had happened to him? Had he changed so much? Lost all feeling for the people he had loved? It was a quietly simmering guilt he lived with, spiked with the constant regret that in all the years since he left Nairobi as a boy, he had returned only once, more than thirty years ago, when his mother died. He had a brother in California, an engineer, whom he had not seen since he left home; they had spoken a few times over the phone. There was his younger sister in Nairobi. In Toronto meanwhile he became a writer, recreating that life of a family and community that was now shattered, whose remnants he had rejected. When there was nothing more he could say, he stopped.

Aileen had nothing much to do with her own family either. She had a brother who ran a pub on Toronto's Eastern Avenue, an old working-class neighbourhood. But Munir had discovered after her death that over the years she had sent Christmas presents to her nieces and nephews; and later, money to a niece who had made it to university. So Aileen had cheated on the status quo, their acknowledged aloofness from their pasts.

Perhaps he had taken the easy way out into a marriage—out of loneliness and a need for sex, and to adapt and be accepted into a new life. But they had made a successful life together, they grew into middle age with each other, they brought up a daughter, were members of a club, and travelled. She was proud of his successes and kept a scrapbook of his reviews. More recently, however, she had grown impatient with his inertia, kept exhorting him to snap out of his writer's block. It wasn't a block, he'd protest, just a dead-end.

After Razia had gone away to university, the thought would come fleeting into Munir's mind: Had he and Aileen been married too long? Had he given up—abandoned—too much? And she, too, did she entertain similar thoughts on her part? Surely she must have wished to appeal to her Scottish roots sometimes, be a European, just as he wistfully recalled his father at a qawwali recital in Nairobi, shaking his head and clapping his hands in ecstasy, repeating a phrase with an explosive "*Wah!*", and the radio blaring Hindustani music on weekends.

Their marriage did not crash. But she crashed her car, and he was left to wonder, had he, in some corner of his mind, actually wished her dead?

The police had examined the car following the crash. They returned it two weeks later, and he learned that they had made careful inquiries at his garage. They had asked to see her insurance policy, and got access to her will from their lawyer. They would have loved to pin the classic murder on him—a husband fiddling with the brakes. It was funny, then again, not. Munir knew the brakes worked, he had used the car the previous evening; she had undoubtedly skidded on an ice patch.

One afternoon, some months after the accident, Munir drove downtown and turned onto Eastern Avenue; he ran through a neglected neighbourhood of old brick houses built more than a century ago for immigrant labourers. Seeing a corner bar, the only place of business on the street, he stopped and parked. The bar was dark and dingy inside, a few customers sat on high stools at the counter. On one wall a television mutely showed a soccer match. Munir went and sat at a table on the raised level next to the entrance and ordered a pint of lager from the barman who came over. "Anything to eat?" the man asked, and recommended fish and chips, which Munir ordered. The man, tall and gaunt-faced, the forehead large and broad, first brought the beer and some ten minutes later the food. He hesitated, and then sat down across from Munir.

"You're her brother—Aileen's?" Munir asked. "I saw you at the funeral."

The man twitched his mouth in assent. After a moment he seemed to relax and said, "Her younger brother. She called me Mac."

The funeral service was the only time he had seen Mac, in a black suit, sitting in one of the front rows with a number of young women. In her will, Aileen had left nothing for Mac, but decent bequests for his five children.

"We should have come to see you more often," Munir said.

"Ah well, it's a busy life and to each his own, eh?"

"I suppose so."

There followed an uncomfortable silence, Munir aware of a searching gaze upon him, and then they started to talk. Munir, responding, told Mac what he did, named a few books. No, he agreed, writing was not an easy profession, but he had been lucky and Aileen had been supportive. Mac said he'd lived in this area all his life, it was where he and Aileen had grown up. The neighbourhood was undergoing change, Mac went on, the old industries had mostly gone and the houses were being renovated; there was a theatre nearby and an art gallery. Had Munir seen the Starbucks a block away? A young woman had appeared behind the counter, and Mac called her over, introduced her as Amanda, his second daughter. Emily, the third one, was in university, he said proudly. Studied accounting. Mac refused to accept payment, and Munir stood up to go. They shook hands and promised to stay in touch. Munir said he would bring Razia along when she was next in Toronto. Mac replied, "That would be terrific," adding, "Thank you for dropping by, Munir. It's been good to sit down finally and have a chat with my sister's mysterious Hindoo husband. The world's changed, eh? And better late than never."

Boys in long shirts and caps were playing cricket in the driveway, three teenage girls wearing different-coloured hijabs were heading out towards the entrance of the two-building condominium complex, and a family of three were arriving, pushing a shopping cart, as Munir drove in and parked in the only spot available in the visitors' lot. As soon as he emerged, a boy walked up to him, saying "Munir Mamu?" Apparently he had been holding the spot.

Munir had called Khadija during the week to say he would come to see her on Saturday; this boy, presumably her grandson, was his designated escort. The lobby they entered was crowded but not noisy. The boy, who said his name was Salman, pushed through into the elevator as soon as the door rattled open and motioned him to enter, which Munir to his embarrassment did, bearing the stares of the others.

The apartment was on the seventh floor. Salman had casually pressed the buzzer downstairs, and when Munir entered, Khadija was standing at the door waiting for him. Big sister, little brother. She grabbed him with one arm and pressed him to her, almost strangling him, he thought, and gave a sob. "Bhaiya. It's been a long time. A very long time, my brother."

This was Khadija's eldest son Imran's place, where she was staying; Imran had taken time off from work, as had his wife Shairoz. She stepped forward somewhat shyly, and Munir lightly embraced her, not sure of greeting formalities anymore. Imran had on a bemused, indulgent look the whole time. Imran's sisters Amina and Fatima were the two other adults present, cheerful and chatty and thrilled to meet their writer-uncle. A number of kids were on the living room carpet watching TV. They were quickly shooed off, told to go away downstairs and play, but to remember to return for lunch. The adults sat down. Aileen's funeral had been private, controlled by her instructions, therefore Munir's family had not been present. He had delegated Razia to inform them of her mother's death. Now the small grieving session began, Khadija saying, "She was a good woman, if different," which was the cue, and she put her handkerchief to her eyes and started crying, upon which the other three women joined in, until Munir said, "It's all right, please," and Imran recited the formula, "From Him we come, and to Him we return," and the crying stopped.

"Let's have lunch," Shairoz said and got up.

A feast had been prepared for the prodigal, the like of which he had not had in a very long time, reminding him of Eid days in Nairobi— sweet vermicelli, samosas, and papad to start, followed by lamb biryani, daal, and eggplant bhurta, with naan and pickles, and finally halwa. He was fed by his sister as if he were still a boy. When they were finished, the kids, who had returned back to the television, made a dash for the table and the adults returned to the living room.

It was nostalgia, sweet as the halwa. It felt immensely gratifying to finally reconnect, to heal the sore wound. Aileen would have come around, he was certain, it was only his own weakness that had kept him away from his family. Khadija had five children. Three of them, two sons and a daughter, were in Toronto, a son was in New York, and a daughter, who was the eldest, was in Nairobi. Two of her children had been to university. He took down their particulars, promising to give them to Razia. He was shown the family album and a host of photos on smartphones, and he in turn showed them a photo of Razia with Mark. The wedding had been private and civil, and he could see the disappointment on their faces. Today's kids . . . , they all agreed. Finally he left, with a package of food to take with him.

That night he called Razia; she was not in so he left a message for her, briefly describing his visit to her phupi. He felt so pleased with himself that he also sent a text to Mohini. *I feel so happy, I visited my sister.*

Mohini

MOHINI COULD NOT FORGET her mother's admonition to her to come to her senses. *Have you become possessed?* She couldn't forget her dream, either, his rejection of her when she went to Toronto. She recalled that in the dream, following that handshake greeting, as he drove her to her hotel, his radio was playing some piano music. When she asked him what it was, he said, "Chopin, of course." She commented on how elegant and clean his car was, and then, seeing him negotiate the traffic with ease, at home among streets so different from hers, she said to herself, He's not Indian at all. He's a Westerner. How could I have been so stupid?

Plagued by her insecurity and doubts, she had turned inward. In such moods Ravi dared not provoke her. She did not respond to his exclamations over the paper or the TV discussions, was not keen to go to the Club. Days would pass before she replied to Munir's texts. His were cheerful and full of concern, so *him*, as she had come to know him. One day he wrote that he had finally gone to see his sister, as Mohini had encouraged him to do. *I'm so happy.* She responded instantly, *I'm so happy too.* She recovered. How could she have doubted him?

Before Mohini left her parents' house on that last visit, Ma had put around her neck a Hanuman Chalisa pendant. "But Ma, this is what they sell on TV, those fraudsters!" "I bought it outside the temple. It will help you."

She was wearing it now. Ma had always worn some prayer or charm.

When she was five, they had gone on a holiday to Amritsar. It was the weekend of the Muslim festival of Eid. On the Friday, she had returned from school at lunchtime to find her parents dressed and ready to leave. Ma had packed for all of them. Bau-ji was dressed in a white cotton jacket and dark trousers, like in the old photo with his brother; Ma was in a plain sari.

There was a quiet purposefulness in her parents; not much was spoken as they waited for the auto. Bau-ji had a distant look on his face, an edginess in his demeanour that would remain throughout the trip. He had taken an umbrella and was drumming the ground with it. Ma had a smile on her face, but Mohini sensed apprehension, observed the occasional deep-drawn breath. She wondered if a death had occurred in the family, opened her mouth to ask, then shut it. That's what she was liked for, being the quiet one. The sensible one. Aarti in contrast would have been all over the place, which was why she had been dropped off at relatives'.

"Are you sure you want to take her?" Bau-ji asked at the last moment. "She'll just come in the way."

"She's responsible. I want her to come, and she's already been told," Ma replied. "She has to know."

The railway station was bustling, crowds of people with luggage emerging from it in a daze into the bright sunshine, pursued by taxi touts, or going inside warily, coolies in red jackets running to greet them. "Find out where to go," Ma said to Bau-ji as they stepped out of the auto. As she said this, a red-jacket ran up, and Ma inquired, "Eh, Bhaiya, which platform for Amritsar?" Without a word he snatched the two bags from Bau-ji and ran off, saying, "Don't worry, Platform Four! I'll show where to stand!" Bau-ji shouted after him, "I'll carry my bags myself! Who told you—" And Ma told him, "Go after him, he shouldn't run away with the bags."

It was Mohini who ran after the coolie, into the station, up a flight of stairs, more running, down a flight of stairs, more running. It was exciting! She was laughing, and the coolie, looking back now and then, was laughing with her, knowing perhaps too well her parents' anxiety. They arrived, angry, and haggled with the coolie and paid him.

The red-jacket had a twinkle in his eye as he ran off, saying, "Look after the little girl, don't let her run off. This is Delhi!"

"Bewakoof," Bau-ji muttered, "teaching us . . ." But he turned to Mohini and said, "Stay close to your mother. Don't run off!"

Did she remember all that? She had been little but she could recall much from that trip, and they had reminisced many times, she, Ma, and Bau-ji. What struck her now was that even after fifteen years since the Partition her parents had still kept hope of finding Mohan some day.

Although they had reserved berths, their compartment was packed when they arrived and Bau-ji had to shoo the interlopers away, saying, "Please go, we want to sleep." But Mohini couldn't sleep in her upper bunk, her eyes drawn to the window as they passed slums and villages, the yellow signs proclaiming station names in Hindi, English, and Urdu. Food came, tea came. She didn't know when she finally fell asleep, and when she woke up there was more tea and she didn't want to come out when they reached Amritsar.

"Will we go back by train?"

"Yes, come on."

It was one of her happiest memories; no other journey would be like that, not even in the company of her friends in college, and yet it had a tragic colouring.

They took a tonga, the driver showing them several guest houses before they picked one to stay at, a modest one, where hot water had to be brought in for bathing.

Early the next morning they first visited the Golden Temple. They sat down in the hushed front hall for a while as the kirtans were sung; it was luxuriant and bright, like the inside of a maharaja's palace. After that they got up and went for the bless-ing, and Ma took some time praying before the statue of the guru. Bau-ji did the required, joining hands without lingering, his face as solemn as ever. From here they went to Jallianwallah Bagh, which was not far, and Bau-ji got some animation back, describing the event that was commemorated there. How General Dyer had ordered his troops to shoot at the unarmed protesters who had gathered here in this enclosed space. Mohini put her finger inside every bullet hole, looked deep into the well where women had jumped in to escape the bullets, and had to be held back. "This is how they ruled us, and then they broke up our country and left," Bau-ji said bitterly.

They had lunch near the guest house, then hired another tonga. On the way Ma asked the driver to stop at a temple, into which they entered. Bau-ji again was quick with his worship, but Ma gave Mohini a coin and the two of them took longer with the priest. All the prayers in the world, as Mohini stood beside her mother, her hands joined too, and received the mark on her forehead to say she had been.

Outside the temple, as they came out, Ma purchased a Hanuman pendant.

"For good luck, Ma?"

"Lord Hanuman will help us as he helped Ram-ji."

"Where are we going, then?"

"We are going to a hospital."

"Is someone sick?"

"We are going to see if your Mohan Chachu has been found and brought there. The one who was lost in the Partition."

That familiar reminder of the Partition took away some of the joy of the trip. Everything was still interesting and new and exciting, but now framed by the black of that loss.

The Lady Mary Hospital was a huge building, people going in and out, well, sick, and disabled. A clanging ambulance stopped, people rushed to it, a stretcher came out. For some reason a police car was behind it. Mohini and her parents got off the tonga and entered. It took Bau-ji a lot of pushing and shouting at reception before someone paid attention. A soldier came to escort them down a long corridor, up the stairs, and then down another long corridor. At the end was a hall. The soldier pushed open the door and waited for them to go inside, and when they did so he gave them a salute.

There was a table inside the entrance, where a nurse sat and an attendant stood by. Another soldier stood in a corner. Towards the back of the hall were three cots and three men in pyjamas; one man was lying down, two were sitting on chairs next to their cots. One of the sitting men had a magazine in his hands. He hardly looked sick, and when he heard them he turned a benign look towards them. He had a full beard; the two others merely looked unshaven. All three had close-cropped hair.

Bau-ji gave his name to the nurse and said he was from Delhi; he had received a phone call from the refugee resettlement office directing him to come and verify if one of the men they had cleared in Amritsar was his missing brother Mohan. He told the nurse the story of Mohan's disappearance in the train from what was now Pakistan. It was a long time ago, but like other families, they still had hope.

"There they are," she told him, turning her head towards the men, "all three are Mohans from Pakistan."

They followed the nurse inside, and walked about scrutinizing each man carefully. Body type, face, how much their brother could have changed after more than ten years. "Don't go too close," the nurse warned them softly. "They seem quite harmless, but you never know." Bau-ji would ask each one, "Are you Mohan? Nathu Lal-ji's younger son—from Sargodha?" Only one of them replied, "I am Mohan." But he, one of the two who were sitting, wasn't their Mohan; he was too short, just not right. "He couldn't have shrunk," Ma said. "He just can't be our Mohan." The other two men did not speak. But they were not their Mohan.

Dejected, they shook their heads at the nurse.

"No?"

"No."

"The one who speaks," Ma asked. "Can't he say more? Where he is from? His family?"

"All he says is that he is Mohan. The doctor says he might remember more later."

Bau-ji asked, "If no one is here to claim them, why are they here?"

"Two other families with missing young men are coming later, perhaps tomorrow."

"How did these men end up here?"

"The one who spoke was found near the Wagah border. It was determined somehow that he belonged to our country. The other two, the silent ones, I don't know. Perhaps they had papers, or someone called them Mohan. They are not circumcised."

Ma said, "Anyway, our Mohan was hale and hearty, he would not be in such a state."

"How do you know?" Bau-ji replied.

"Perhaps it's for the better this way," the nurse said. "Assume that your Mohan is with the other Mohan, he is with God."

"Yes, he was a good soul. All he did was go search for a toilet on the train."

As they came out and searched for a tonga, Ma fingered her Hanuman pendant. It had not helped.

Ma would tell her that about a year after their arrival in Delhi, her father-in-law Nathu Lal had written a letter to Hassan, his former employee, whose address he knew, asking him to keep eyes and ears open for any hints about his younger son Mohan. Hassan's reply came some six months after, having been delayed in the post, that he had asked around, even in the villages, and he would continue to look out. He prayed that the family would be united soon. Nathu Lal had not written back. He died soon after, never having recovered from his loss, and his wife followed some years later.

Soon after the trip to Amritsar, Bau-ji was given the teaching job in Shimla. It seemed a good idea to leave the past behind and start anew. The house they had lived in had always seemed haunted by memories of the Partition and reminders of the previous residents, Muslims who had either departed or were slaughtered. Nobody in the neighbourhood wished to visit those memories.

"You can't know what horrors we passed through, during those days," Ma would say. "It was narak. Gandhi-ji was killed just two days after we moved here. It is like a movie that keeps playing and playing in the head . . . Partition turned men into beasts."

And the older they grew the more they missed Mohan.

They were possessed.

Munir

JOSHUA IS BORN.

"Dad, his family's so excited, he's the first male grandchild, and—"

"He's also my first grandchild, Raz—"

"And Ruth will stay with us a few weeks, just to help . . ."

"Who's Ruth?"

"My mother-in-law! I told you about her!"

"I don't think you did. Still, when can I see my grandchild?"

"Give us a few weeks, Dad."

Aileen would never have stood for that. She would be there by now, hovering by her daughter and the baby, jostling Ruth aside. But she and Ruth would have become friends in the end.

Joshua. Sticking to prophets' names, are we. Would she adopt Judaism, Munir wondered. Become a Jew? Was that possible, even? He didn't mind, if she was happy, needed an identity, a base to hold on to, to bring up her child or children in. Something he and Aileen had never given their only child. Was that wrong?

Aileen had once tried to sneak her Scottish heritage in, sending Razia to Glasgow. That had backfired.

Munir would say, We are Canadians, and that's all the identity I need. Facile and defensive, from an immigrant desperate to belong. Meanwhile the stories he wrote had portrayed life in Asian Nairobi. Putting the past to rest, he would say, just giving it a burial.

He looks at the new New Yorker Joshua M. Goldstein on his phone screen. Swaddled in a blue blanket, he looks like all babies. All babies look like Winston Churchill, Munir's father Jehangir Khan used to say. "What's the 'M' stand for?" Munir asked Razia. "We're not saying now, Dad. It's our secret." Well, Josh, you are also a Khan and a McKellar. Remember that. A Pathan and a Scot. Whiskey and halal.

Does it matter, Granddad?

Not really. Perhaps. I don't know, Grandson. Can I call you that? The world is funny. Sometimes it gives you labels you don't need . . . identity is all the rage now.

He has the photo printed and laminated at a local store and drives to Mount Pleasant Cemetery. He reaches Aileen's grave, unfolds his stool, and sits down. Tenderly he holds out the photo.

"Well, here he is, Aileen. Your grandson. Joshua M. Goldstein, Churchill lookalike. 'M' for mystery, by the way. Bless him."

There's a fresh red rose stem leaning elegantly against the headstone. And next to it he sees, to his surprise, wrapped in clear plastic, the volume of Amir Khusrau's poems that had disappeared after he'd placed it there. Well, well. The secret mourner, he's found the book. Does he come frequently; is he more faithful than her husband, Munir Khan? Why does he compete with me with his bigger and better offerings?

Munir turns and looks around for a couple of minutes. The maple trees are in full colour now, glowing yellow in the fall sunlight. It is absolutely quiet and beautiful. How lovely and peaceful Toronto can be. Safdarjung Tomb flashes into his mind for a moment, how different, its monument proclaiming history so casually, pointing to a time when this city and this country were not even a gleam in the eye. In the distance, in the direction of the street, he thinks he sees a figure pacing about, perhaps waiting for him to finish. He looks back at the grave. "Well, Aileen, whoever he is, this boyfriend of yours, he has to wait, while I finish telling you all about your daughter and your grandson."

There was not much more to say, he realized, and soon stood up to go.

It always amazed him, whenever Mohini reminded him, how difficult it was for her to find even a moment of privacy in which to call him. "Can't you just park the car somewhere and call?" "Park where, with all the traffic? And you forget, I have a driver. Bahadur is quiet as a mouse but he listens."

Once, she called him using a friend's phone. But even friends talk. Another time she called him from a grocery shop. The shopkeeper gave her a look. Yet another time, from inside an auto; he could not hear her. And she felt nervous, all the time checking there was no trace left of him on her phone.

He needed to hear that voice, and be reassured, to blow those clouds of doubt and apprehension back beyond the horizon. And when they did connect, even for half a minute, or by hurried text, there was renewed that assurance that they were there for each other, each a part of the other.

"How does it feel to be a nana—a grandpa?"

"I haven't had a chance to play the role yet. But it does feel strange...It's as though I've been extended and there is more of me now, with Joshua ... and you, of course, you're always with me."

"I'm touched, Munir. I so, so wish you were here with me. Now bye."

Just like that, a hurried goodbye.

The apartment is on the seventh floor and modest. It is crowded, and as Munir enters there is a hush and curious looks beam on him, before Ruth—he presumes—comes forward with an extended hand.

"You are Munir, Raz's dad! How are you? And congratulations, you must be thrilled, as are we!"

Those New York vowels, they come at you like the Yankees.

"Thank you, I am thrilled."

"It's so wonderful to meet you, finally! What would you like to drink? Beer?"

He says yes but later, and glances around—Razia is not here, she must be in the bedroom.

He is introduced to Eddie, Mark's dad, and there are Mark's sisters Ellen and Liz, and his brother George, and two girls of about ten. Mark walks in, looking unshaven, unslept, and rumpled, and says, "Hello Mr. Khan—Dad"—he smiles, "come, she's inside," and Munir steps into the bedroom, where his daughter sits on an armchair with the baby in her arms. Josh begins to cry. A thin, baby wail.

He kisses his daughter and stifles a sob. Straightens up. "May I hold him? It's been a while, but the habit doesn't go away, I believe."

Razia gives him a grin. "Have I done a good job, Dad?"

"Yes, you have. I'm proud of you."

"It's small, this apartment. You haven't seen it before, have you? We're looking for a new place, three bedrooms. They are not cheap."

"If you need assistance, Razia, tell me."

"I think we can manage, Dad. Thank you."

"You must be tired."

"No—sit."

He sits on the bed and they talk. Joshua is back in her arms now and Mark comes in to tell her it's time to feed. He pushes a pillow behind her so she can sit up and she begins to feed the child. Munir is embarrassed, looks away. It was not long ago, he thinks, when she was at the breast. Discreetly he gets up and walks out, as Mark sits down opposite his wife.

In the living room the family has laid out a spread for lunch and he eats with them and exchanges niceties. The Goldsteins are a close family, used to all being in the same room, talking at once, interrupting each other. Eddie brings Munir a beer and the two go sit down on the sofa. A girl gets up to give them privacy.

"We've not met before, Munir, but we are so proud to have Raz in our family. She's a wonderful girl. And let me say this in all sincerity, we consider you a part of this family too."

"Thank you, Eddie. I'm afraid I don't have much of a family to offer you in return."

There follows an awkward silence, before Eddie says, putting a hand on Munir's arm, "I'm truly sorry for your loss, Munir. But I would like to reiterate, all of us here in New York are now your family."

"Thank you."

———

Back in Toronto he went and told Aileen about his visit to their daughter in New York. I like the family, Aileen. They are good people. Very warm. And Joshua? I'm afraid he'll be spoilt, Aileen . . . I'm sure you'll love him too, wherever you are. He'll surely come to visit you here. Perhaps Christmas.

As he stepped out onto the pavement of Mount Pleasant Avenue, there was Aileen's other visitor striding towards him, likely on his way to visit her grave.

"Hi, you're Munir Khan . . . may I call you Munir? We met here a few months ago."

"Yes, and you're Ian. Ian Fraser."

"You come to see Aileen McKellar ever so frequently."

"As do you, apparently. May I ask how . . . how you relate to my late wife?"

"We knew each other long ago." Ian paused, then asked, "Say, would you like to sit down for a cup of coffee? And we can get to know each other more."

"Why not?"

They crossed the road and entered a coffee shop. Sized each other up. Knew each other long ago . . . how? Munir wondered.

"You've known about me," Munir said. "But I don't know you—except your name." The question was implicit.

Ian showed the thinnest trace of a smile. He had blue eyes, fading grey hair, and, like Munir, a large forehead. He was slimmer, wore a fall jacket. A plaid logo on the side of his eyeglasses.

"We met by accident once at the Cricket Club—long after we'd parted ways. And then we continued to meet there once in a while. Nothing improper, I assure you." He took a breath.

"There was just a pull . . . from old times. We played tennis a couple of times, then stopped."

So those were the Cricket Club visits. She could have told him about Ian. Her former boyfriend. Introduced him. But she needed her own secret to keep, a cubby hole inside herself. Do we all need that? Perhaps. Mine was my past, which I kept locked away.

"How did you come to know her . . . back then, if I may ask?"

"We went out together while at the U of T. Afterwards . . . well, we parted ways, and I went to work in Calgary and then moved to Vancouver—Scotiabank—then took early retirement and returned to Toronto. I am divorced. Three children— two boys, one girl."

By now they had their coffees; Munir had a muffin, which they shared.

"Well. Thank you for being so candid. I wondered who the other admirer was, who brought a dozen roses for my one stem. And this time a more beautiful one."

Ian laughed, loudly. "That was only the one time—the dozen roses. After that, one stem from me too, and tulips in the spring. That's surely not overdoing it."

"No. And that book of poetry?"

"I put it back, as you noticed."

They resolved to be friends and stay in touch. And they reached an agreement: Munir's day was Friday, Ian's Tuesday.

Well, well, Aileen, you certainly kept secrets. Stayed in touch with your family, and then this man who came from your past.

They must have been intimate. Was Munir Khan, the Indian at the office, the rebound?

Mohini

"I HAD MY EYE ON YOU when you were still a girl in Shimla and I came here for a holiday," Ravi said when they had just got married.

"Liar," she'd replied.

Shimla days, she thought. The town was called Simla then, now they want to call it something else—those were gorgeous days. The happiest days, but they always are, at that age, aren't they. Running in the snow, wearing coats and scarves, sliding, skating. Tobogganing. There were hills and hills to do that. Stopping over at dhabas for paratha and butter and dahi, without a care about waistlines. Sitting by the fireplace listening to stories and munching snacks. Monsoon, and morning mist over the green valleys. And the monkeys! You learned to talk to them so they would leave you alone. I had a favourite, an old mother who always protected me. I called her Janaki. If a youthful monkey came over to harass me on the road to Boileau Ganj she would lope over and smack him. Whenever I told people I grew up in Shimla, they would mention *Love in Simla*. A silly movie, but it struck just the right note. The innocence. The romanticism. Weekends we hiked up to Kamna Devi and in the spring there was always the long hike to Tara Devi. All four of us, Bau-ji, Ma, Aarti and me; Ma and Bau-ji would pause to rest and Aarti and I would head on, betting how long it would take the oldies to catch up. Then Aarti went off—escaped—to Delhi and there were three of us and the spectre of missing Mohan. Aarti always bubbling with energy had kept us in the present; it was hard for me alone. MA studies were a distraction . . . but then *that* happened. The incident.

Did I marry too soon? Because of *that?*

It's a memory I didn't want to see even a shadow of. Why now, when I carry in my heart someone with whom I have experienced my happiest moments? He would understand. But this one beside me, who doesn't know, came around in time and took me away, and unwittingly allowed me to heal.

"You must marry," Ma had said.

And Aarti, who was visiting at the time: "It's a good idea, Didi. You have to do it anyway. You do want to, don't you?"

"And my MA degree?"

"It will work out. Bau-ji will make sure of that."

And all the pressure for me to get married because of Professor Isvara Chinmaya, Ph.D., Bau-ji's friend: "Call me Isvara. You can always come to me for extra help. You've got a good mind, young lady, train it and you'll go far. You're better than Suniti Gopal."

Suniti Gopal, his former student, now a professor at JNU. What is the story there? She never came back to Shimla. And when I saw her once at DRC, I went to greet her, but she claimed she didn't remember me. I know why.

It was the Henry James paper I'd been having trouble with. I had a pass already in my hands, but I was a topper, as they called it, and I had to be exceptional. Only, I was having trouble with context. All the nuances; the European mannerisms, place references; what, even now, do I know about them? The ladies and gentlemen. What was Boston like? New York I knew through American films. I should have picked Kamala Markandaya. Too easy, said Call-Me-Isvara. The department expects more from you. There are British Council scholarships waiting for you, Fulbrights within your reach. You could visit the American Centre in Hyderabad. And then, a year, two years in America!

For some weeks I went to see Call-Me-Isvara, Saturday afternoons. Usually in his office, once at a dhaba. It all seemed like fun and very intellectual, and the other girls were envious. I was flying high, destined for a great future. He knew so much, weaved circles around me, dropping names here and there. Frye, Berlin, Eliot . . . Adler, Reich, and Jung; he had shaken hands with Simone de Beauvoir and Sartre in Paris. These hands—better respect them, girl! The pretty—and liberated— French girls; then the innuendoes came. The West is relaxed about sex, but we still have a lot to learn, despite our *Kama Sutra*. We two hit it off, don't we, Mohini? Peas in a pod, as they say. And Simla is a small pod, ha-ha. Say, how about the two of us travel to Kullu? Like the Bostonians, hey! Only joking. A hike to Tara Devi at dawn?—absolutely inspiring. I refused the whiskey. I refused the wine. And I began to get nervous. This was Isvara, Bau-ji's friend?

Then that Saturday; it had become late. It had rained and now hail was falling, and there was not a soul on the floor. He said, We might have to spend the night here. We were eating pakodas, there was chai from a Thermos, and then reaching out for the Thermos from behind me he pressed against me, hard. Hard. I froze. I squirmed, shouted—why didn't I scream?—he wouldn't release me. His mistake was to put his hand to my mouth and I bit it so hard, blood streamed out. He screamed. Bitch. Whore. Teasing me! And I ran out so fast, leaving him there licking his hand. Don't expect to pass, whore! See where this gets you!

Whom to tell? Who would believe me? I was his fave. I used to glow under his attention. I told Aarti, swore her to secrecy. But she must have told Ma, for the pressure to marry started then.

I failed Henry James, and protested. A bright student, said the comment in the report, but she cannot see through the complexities of her chosen texts. She should have chosen a local author. Bau-ji pulled strings, went to see Call-Me and finally I got a B—below-average—and my MA. But Call-Me's hand was permanently scarred, Aarti told me. Should I be proud? He has a trophy.

The proposals came, and I picked Ravi from Delhi, a junior officer in the IPS, with a bright future. Was it so bad? A trainload of his people came on the Kalka Mail from Delhi and Rajasthan for the wedding. Bau-ji and his relations went to greet them in Kalka and brought them in two buses to Shimla. Many of them were villagers; a trip to exotic Shimla was a treat for them. How fair she is, they said, Shimla girls are truly beautiful. But I am from Delhi, I wanted to shout, and more accurately, I am from Sargodha. Don't be silly, Ma told me. Simla carries prestige; the viceroys lived here, and Gandhi, Nehru, and that fellow Jinnah came to discuss the fate of India right here. Delhi girls are cheap and come by the dozens, and who knows Sargodha?

Which you missed for so long, Ma? But after Bau-ji retired they moved back to Delhi to be close to the grandkids. There is no permanent home for refugees.

We had our honeymoon at the luxurious Cecil, and that is where he told me he had had eyes on me since I was much younger, when he came to visit our town. I never believed him. I felt I had lost something. My bright future. I would have loved to travel, go abroad. Which *he* was able to do, eventually, arranging security for prime ministers.

If I had not bitten that lecher so hard, perhaps squeezed myself out of his grip . . . he wouldn't have raped me, didn't have the guts . . . then would I have been like Suniti Gopal, entertaining Americans and Europeans at DRC, travelling abroad? But I'm a Simla girl, I have principles and dignity.

Munir

THE DELHI RECREATION CLUB had bestowed upon him its coveted membership. When he applied, on the day he departed the previous time, he was advised that he might have to wait a long time for that hallowed status. There was a long list of applicants, some of whom had waited years. It took Munir four months to be approved; perhaps the recommendation of the Indian consul in Toronto helped, and the fact that he would pay a premium for his overseas membership. He could now stay longer, in one of the apartments in a new extension towards the back. His reservation was for six weeks, because he planned to take a few trips outside Delhi this time. And because.

Having checked in early in the morning, he slept a few hours, had his breakfast, and went downstairs to sit on the patio to wait for her. The sun was brilliant, but not excessively hot. The gardens and lawns were being sprinkled, and the pavements were being hosed. A conference was about to kick off in the hall opposite the library, where a crowd had gathered to register. Cars were steadily arriving. It was a pleasant scene.

He saw her approach from the driveway, where Bahadur had dropped her off. Across distance and time she had seemed to recede behind a gauze curtain in his mind, though very much there, and constantly; but seeing her in the flesh, those wide eyes, the little sparkle on the forehead, hurrying towards him, his heart filled up. She was real. Not a pen pal, not a fantasy, not the past but someone intensely special who had come for him.

By this time there was no formality to their greeting, he stood up as she said, "You are here," adding, "let's go to the cafeteria," and shying away when his fingers touched hers, ever so lightly, with "there are people here." As they walked to the cafeteria, now beside each other, she said, "I had to cancel my class. Just for you."

"Well, thank you. But that's a small gesture compared to mine," he quibbled, as they stepped through the outer doors, past the little bake shop and into the lounge. A table against the left wall was empty and they went towards it.

"How, a small gesture?"

"I came all the way from Canada."

She smiled, let out a deep breath and sat down. Watching her across from him, he felt immensely, idiotically happy.

"I'm really happy to be here," he said lamely. "You can't know how much."

"I do, because I'm as happy."

They ordered.

"I've brought a mobile for you with a new SIM card." She pushed the cell forward on the table.

He guessed why.

"It's in a friend's name," she said. "She's called Jayanti."

"How have you been?"

"Very busy. Asha has her exams coming and we are onto the

fourth tutor for her. He's called Amit. I'm convinced that my daughter is a dolt."

"No, she's not. Maybe her interests lie elsewhere, in other subjects."

"Well they're not what she told me they were. She chose science, and that's what she's got. I'm in such despair about her." She suddenly put both her hands to her face for a moment, then looked up. "And you? Tell me about you."

He told her about Razia's visit at Christmas, how she had sprung a surprise on him at the neighbourhood party. And, once again, about his grandson Joshua. He went on, and when he stopped she said, "I'm jealous of you." She said she had accompanied her husband to Gujarat recently, and he wondered if she wanted to make him jealous in turn.

"I had such a terrible dream about you a while ago." She told him how in that dream he had spurned her when she came to Toronto. He gave an uncharacteristically explosive laugh and a few tables looked up.

They got up to go. "I've got to go home and make dinner now for Asha and me."

"And Ravi?"

"He rushed away last night. They captured eight terror suspects in Bhopal."

They became silent. Then he said, "I've brought a present for you. It's in my room . . . apartment . . . shall I go and bring it? . . . would you like to pick it up?"

She gave him an arch look, and they walked out.

"I'll go by the front," she said almost inaudibly, pointing towards the driveway. "You go by the main stairs and I'll see you there. Room number?"

He told her.

After a tight embrace and words of endearment that reac-quainted them physically and reassured them emotionally, they came back down. He'd given her the present he'd brought, a bottle of perfume. He had been forbidden to bring any piece of clothing because she wouldn't have been able to wear it with-out questions. About the perfume, she said, "I'll keep it at my mother's." He looked up, surprised. "It's the bottle—that blue is too conspicuous."

They went to sit on the patio. Soon three young men clad in white appeared and sat down not far from them.

Munir raised an eyebrow. "Them?"

She nodded. "Yes, Jetha Lal's gang. Do you eat beef?" she asked, out of nowhere it seemed to him.

"Very occasionally, and it's not important, just one of the choices. What about it?"

"Last week a Muslim man was lynched by a mob that accused him of keeping beef in his home. He was found hanged. Cow protection groups are springing up everywhere. According to a prominent guru, the next world war will start because of beef. So you watch out. We don't want a war."

"And was there beef in this man's home?"

"I don't know. But you should have seen these Purifiers here. I could have sworn they were celebrating."

They became silent.

"Just be careful, don't walk into crowded areas. Even without a beard you look a Muslim from a mile off!"

What did a Muslim look like to Indians, he mused, as Mohini walked away.

———

On the lawn, under the yellow globe lights, a few people sat on chairs by themselves or in small groups, chatting. It was a balmy evening, as peaceful as one could imagine. After Mohini left, he had napped, and now after a shower and a walk felt wide awake as he sat inside the bar with a snack and a drink, at the same table where they had first met. He had paid a quick visit to the library, where he'd reserved a few books to consult. They were waiting for him at a carrel. He couldn't wait to start.

He felt a strange sense of fulfilment in India, of just-so, of familiarity and ease. Yes, there was the faintest aloofness or dismissal he met sometimes—because he was ultimately a foreigner? A maybe-Muslim, as they saw it? He thought of the recent lynching and other similar violence in the country that he had read about. It was a disturbing feature of this vast and complex country, where hatred and savagery coexisted with sublime thought and heroic nonviolence; where naked igno-rance coexisted with the greatest intellectual achievements. India might have been a different proposition, a different place, if she had not come and sat at his table, this table, that night . . . Wasn't that India too?—its sweetness. He had been uplifted. With Mohini in his life he could laugh again, pick up his pen again. Was she a genie, and he in some fantastic dream? Did he see his Gujarati mother in her? His Punjabi grandmother? They were but distant memories, and she was just she, that husky voice, the matter-of-fact manner that hid a passion and a joy that was infectious and a pain that needed comforting and sharing.

This time she had been wearing white pants and a blue kurta—very different from the usual sari. He forgot to tell her he'd noticed. Of course he'd noticed.

The air inside the bar had turned humid; there came a whiff of expensive perfume. A woman loudly discussed the snack menu with the waiter, a conversation in Hindi that Munir barely understood, but she finally ordered fish tikka.

At a table next to the entrance three men in white kurtas were quietly discussing terrorist bases in Pakistan.

"We should send our CATs in and take out some of these guys. The way the Americans finished off Bin Laden."

"We have the capability."

This was followed by a consensual nod round the table. Who could they be?

"We've always been hesitant—the nice guys of the continent, followers of Gandhi and Buddha. We should have gone after their nuclear arsenal while it was still in its infancy. We had the capability. Then bomb one or two cities to ashes, and that would be it. Peace for a century. Look at Japan."

"Too late now."

"Surgical strikes. They work."

A middle-aged couple in Western casuals sat down, apparently a brother and sister back home from the States.

Munir got up. There was still an hour to go before the library closed.

———

He read.

Perhaps the world had not seen such pomp since Caesar brought Cleopatra as a spoil to Rome, or the Mughal emperor Akbar returned from a conquest. On Tuesday, December 12, 1911, a long procession bearing King-Emperor George V snaked its way from Delhi's Red Fort through the Kashmiri Gate and further north to Coronation Park. As the king sat on his throne, wearing a crown bearing 61,170 sparkling diamonds, as the audience of 100,000 watched and a few more hundred thousand saw from a distance, nawabs, nizams, rajas, and ranas in all their finery came one by one to pay homage, as their predecessors had done to the Mughals and the Turkish sultans.

But the "hydra of terror," as *Hindi Punch* called it, was rearing its head here and there, now and then, and the Empire's guardians sought to club its head down every time. Almost exactly a year later, Lord Hardinge, the Viceroy of India, decided to make a state entry into Delhi. At the front of the procession, heading towards the Red Fort, was a soldier on horseback, followed by an array of eight to ten soldiers. Behind them rode the Viceroy, on the back of an elephant. On the recently paved Chandni Chowk, ticketed seats had been arranged on both sides for people to watch and cheer; black market prices for those seats ranged from fifty to three hundred rupees. As the Viceroy approached Dariba Kalan, a loud explosion was heard. It was, on first impression, as if an earthquake had occurred. People ran in all directions, screaming and shouting, and the mounted soldiers struggled to control their neighing horses. The Viceroy had been thrown off his elephant, hurt and bleeding; the attendant in front of him had been blown to bits. Lady Hardinge lay unconscious on the ground. A cloud of dust had covered the scene.

———

Before he left Toronto, Munir had arranged a meeting with his sister Khadija. "Why don't we go for lunch, Didi. I want to ask you something."

"Only to ask me something you take your sister out for lunch," she said coyly.

She preferred a Chinese restaurant, and so he picked her up and they went to one on Don Mills Road, not very far from her apartment.

"Tell me, Didi," he said, when they were seated at a table and the food had arrived, "Dada used to talk of 'Dariba' sometimes. To me it was just another name for Delhi. Do you know anything about it? What did it mean? What brought them to Nairobi? And the name Hardinge—it was important, wasn't it?"

She reminded him, "They sent you to that English school and you wouldn't speak our bhasha. Punjabi."

"Yes." Her jowly, spotted pink face beaming kindly at him, he reminded himself again of what a beautiful young woman she had been in Nairobi. "Well?" he asked.

"Dada used to work for his uncles in Dariba Kalan. I've been there, you know, Munir? I've seen it. They lived in a gully off this main street. That is where he came from: Dariba Kalan. It is where our roots are."

"And what brought them to Nairobi? What about Hardinge?"

"Laard Hardinge was the governor or something of India. Vice-rai-something. A bomb was thrown at him and he almost died."

"Dada was not involved?"

"No. Bangalis were involved. When the police came chasing

after them, this one Bangali ran into our gully. He would have been caught, for sure, but our dada's chachi-ma, his auntie, was making chapattis in a tava, sitting on a stool behind it. So she told this young man, 'Come over.' He did, and she hid this Bangali in her dupatta and calmly went about her work. Don't ask me how she did it. The police came, looked everywhere, while the women covered their faces. Dada was present during all this, and the police gave him a couple of slaps and took him away. But they had to set him free. He didn't tell them anything. After what they did to Bahadur Shah, he was not going to help them. He could have been rewarded if he had. Or if they had captured this Bangali in that gully, he could have been hanged. And the women put in prison or sent to work in factories. The Bangali stayed with our family for three days, then he left. Nobody knew his name."

Munir stared at his sister. "They told you ... and you remembered all this, Didi?"

"Dadi told me one day. She herself was a niece of Chachi-ma. From Simla."

"From Simla?"

She nodded. "In the mountains. Dadi came from there. Before Dada got any more ideas about freedom-shreedom, he was married to Dadi and they went to stay in Simla. Later they went to Mombasa. Then Nairobi. You know."

They sat in silence for a while.

Khadija added, "Dadi told me that while the police were searching for the Bangali, Chachi-ma managed to flip six chapattis."

They both fell into irrepressible, long-forgotten laughter.

———

Back in his room he tried to read at first, but his mind was distracted. He was flipping through TV channels when a message dinged on his new, Indian phone. *It was so WONDERFUL to see you again!* He replied with a smiley. Soon after, his Canadian phone gave its own distinctive ring, startling him. It sounded like a wrong number, the person at the other end apparently shouting a lot of filth into it in a raspy Hindi. Munir ended the call and was about to turn the phone off when it rang again. It was Dr. Raj Mohan from Gujarat, reminding him that he had agreed to visit Vadodara in two days' time for a lecture. Munir said he remembered. Dr. Mohan had sent him a train ticket by email. Munir thanked him, gave him his Indian number and turned the Canadian phone off. He texted his Indian number to Razia.

He would not be seeing Mohini for a few days, he reminded himself. Four long days of longing. He would be going to Vadodara for a day. They had already discussed this, and she had thought it a good idea for him to see more of the country and meet different Indians. Meanwhile she herself had arranged to take her Ma and Bau-ji to a shrine in Maharashtra. It was Ma's wish, she said, to start her pilgrimages with this one. Aarti and her family would join them, and Ravi would be going too.

Mohini

IT GAVE MOHINI A WARM FEELING inside to have organized her
family's expedition to the shrine. There was something special
to such a family venture, such a gesture of piety. You were overcome by a lightness of spirit and a calm anticipation occluding,
for the time being, your world's worries—even if the purpose
of the visit was partly, for the women at least, to alleviate those
worries. They would be alleviated one way or another, or perhaps not, yet on the way you attained a sense of detachment.
You became aware—once again—of what the great gurus had
always taught, that nothing in this material world really mattered, nothing was permanent. You were part of an eternal,
immovable Existence. Animosities became meaningless, ambi-
tions less urgent. And if you believed, perhaps there was a boon
at the end, which you received humbly.

But there was something different about going to see Sai Baba.
He was not a god, he was human. Whether they worshipped
Ram or Krishna, Shiva-Parvati or Kali-Durga, or Hanuman, and
often it was all of them, many people still kept an image of Sai

Baba on the mantelpiece or a tabletop or their car's dashboard, or even a statue of him in the garden. A simple man in a dhoti and shirt, a casual turban, an unkempt beard and barefoot—he had arrived at Shirdi one day from the hills and put up in a shack; soon he was recognized as someone special, an elevated being, a man-god. Muslims, Hindus, Sikhs, Christians and others came to worship him in the thousands. It was uncertain whether he had been a Muslim or a Hindu. A Hindu authority had recently declared him a Muslim and not to be worshipped by Hindus; send this Baba to Pakistan, he said. Regardless, people came in the thousands, even the educated and the agnostic, admitting that there was more to the world than met your eyes, or that scientists could explain, even if you couldn't tell what it was.

Mohini's parents had been to Varanasi and Haridwar already, the former before she was born, and the latter when she was little, to immerse the ashes of her grandparents in the Ganga; the four of them visited Dwarka during a long holiday in Gujarat when the girls were still in school. Mohini had visited Madurai with Ravi, and had promised her mother a string of pilgrimages beginning with Puri. But, having paid heed to neighbours' chit-chat recently, Ma had said, "Let's go see Sai Baba first. He seems to be listening."

Mohini felt at peace in the taxi van. A warm breeze blew in through the open window, caressing her face, comforting her the way her mother used to when she was little. Asha sat next to Mohini, fast against her, asleep, having read a novel half the night at their hotel room in Nasik. Ma and Bau-ji were in the back seat, Ma acting quite the spoilt child today, wearing a cardigan even in the heat and having demanded the air-conditioning be turned off.

Ravi sat royally in front, upright, an arm across the top of his seat, chatting dryly with the young driver, querying about conditions at Shirdi, the daily crowd numbers, and the seasonal variations, though he probably knew those figures better than the young man. Occasionally he would caution him: "We are not in a hurry, Manu, take your time. We should arrive in one piece." Manu replied once, "You will arrive, sahab, I know these roads well. With Sai Ram's blessings, everyone arrives. I'm just trying to get you there in good time . . ."

They had booked their three-star hotel through an agency in Delhi. Aarti would join them there with her husband and younger daughter—the other was studying in Boston.

In her state, Mohini did not think of Munir. Here she was her Indian, Hindu self. Nevertheless, even dreamily, she was aware of his presence, just outside her conscious mind; a presence, but light as air. Shun all attachments, Mohini, she said to herself, that way lies peace. What did she expect from Sai Baba? A small miracle, regarding this lump of her flesh beside her, Asha; some resolution regarding *him* . . . which *him?* . . . She dozed off.

As soon as they emerged from the car outside the Sat Sai Hotel, two porters came running out to take their luggage away. A young man called Sivadasa approached and introduced himself. He was to be their guide for the rest of the day and the following day.

"You have a rest for a few hours and come sunset I will show you around and take you to the best place to eat. Excellent thali at reasonable price. And tomorrow you go for Baba's darshan."

He went and sat down on the sofa in the reception area and began fidgeting with his phone.

Aarti and family were already in their suite, waiting, and there was a noisy and jubilant family reunion. Kishore and Ravi shook hands heartily, slapped each other on the back, and decided to take a walk out together into town; the two sisters paired off, as did the cousins Asha and Swapna.

Aarti, younger than Mohini, had always remained the more current with the times. Trimmer and fitter than her sister, she was in tight designer jeans and an embroidered yellow shirt open at the neck; her short hair looked recently styled. She was a projects coordinator at Infosys and well travelled, particularly in the United States and Germany. Swapna had just been admitted to Delhi University's prestigious St. Stephen's College in the economics honours program. Mohini, reminded of her own daughter, felt a wave of angst. What could she have done differently with Asha?

Aarti looked into her face with concern. "Don't worry about Asha, Sis," she said. "It's the age. And they can never all be the same. It will all come out right, you'll see."

"I don't know, Aarti. Recently she's begun to question the value of education. She showed me an article from America that said calculus was useless to your happiness. Can you believe that? This comes from putting emphasis on the humanities."

Aarti smiled. She herself used to say literature and history were a waste of time, then she and Mohini would get into heated arguments.

Having exchanged information about their parents, Mohini doing the reporting, the sisters stretched out to rest on the double bed in Aarti's room and fell asleep. The two girls went out for a stroll, clutching their phones.

Sivadasa leading, Mohini and Aarti behind him with Asha and Swapna in tow, and the two husbands chatting politics behind them, they headed out towards Shirdi, pushing gently past throngs of people jamming the sidewalk, which was bounded all the way by a row of vendors selling fruits and vegetables; guavas and oranges were in season. Autos weaved in and out through the hooting traffic, buses arrived constantly to spill out more pilgrims. Touts along their way were selling tickets promising quick entry into the shrine, but Sivadasa said not to pay attention. Every hotel and enterprise they saw was named after Sai Baba. They arrived at a restaurant next to a hotel and parking lot, right across from the shrine complex. When they found their seats, Mohini called up her father, instructing him where to join them. He and Ma would come in an auto.

The fare was sumptuous, making you wonder at the austerity of the man they had come to for blessings. Did there lurk a shade of guilt in all the happy faces gathered here, in expectation perhaps of even greater material gifts? For Mohini, that spiritual high of before had been snapped. But this was family, and you had duties and obligations. She had not become a sadhvi, though she had wished recently that she could lock herself up in some ashram. Bau-ji and Ma were beaming with happiness. They chatted on about the shrines they had visited in the past. Mohini and Aarti recalled the Tara Devi temple in Shimla, right at their doorstep, so to speak—you simply hiked up to there on some Sunday. Bau-ji recalled going with his parents to Vaishno Devi in Jammu. Ma had been ill with typhoid when her own family went; but the goddess had saved her life. Kishore surprised them by revealing that he had been to Ajmer Sharif, the famous Sufi shrine, when a particularly tricky deal for his business was at stake. They all wanted to know what it was like.

Afterwards the men said they would walk back to the hotel, and the rest of them took two autos.

That night in bed she said to Ravi, "You drank beer with Kishore, was it in his room? I could smell it on you. How could you do that when we've come to see Sai Baba?"

"It's not that you yourself don't touch alcohol. What difference does it make when I take it?"

"You know the difference . . ."

But he was already lost in sleep, emitting that low note she'd known since their honeymoon at the Hotel Cecil in Shimla. He never had trouble falling asleep.

At six the next morning they all walked to the shrine complex, Bau-ji and Ma included, despite protests by their daughters. Now Aarti was also in a salwar-kameez, and both Ravi and Kishore were in pure white kurta-pyjamas, which they had purchased the previous afternoon when they went out together. It was a joyous procession, in the company of dozens who had also decided to begin early for a single purpose. If they had gone even earlier, they would have witnessed Baba being bathed. The queues, they had been warned, would be long. And once more a lightness overcame Mohini, and she preferred to walk a little apart, as though seeking that detachment she had experienced before, refraining from all but the necessary conversation. She did not want to think, she wanted the experience; she wanted to float. And then, if only the rest of her life were like that?

Buses were lined up on the road, visitors descending in a daze and making their way to the gate of the shrine. Bhajans were being played in the restaurants. The fruit-sellers were setting up.

The lines were indeed long. Ma and Bau-ji were informed by volunteers that they could go into a seniors' queue, and they headed off, accompanied by Asha and Swapna.

The lines, which began in several spots, moved slowly but steadily, in winding paths, and they were orderly. This was not the place for argument or pushing past and grabbing advantage. Sai Baba's oversized statue became visible ahead and Mohini, in a flutter, asked herself, What to ask? Take whatever comes, she answered, it will all be for the good. When she was in front of the idol—those mesmerizing eyes and the benign gaze, the soft, short white beard—she threw her flowers towards the heap already piled there; Ravi had picked a couple from her basket and he too threw them before Baba. What could he want?—a fleeting thought at the edge of her mind. Mohini then suddenly remembered and quickly held out her plate of boondi offering, and the attendant priest put his hand on the sweet. They moved on. This was it. You should feel different now. Outside, after some effort, they sighted Ma and Bau-ji with Sivadasa. The girls had gone out to the street. Now they moved around the site, walked into the various exhibition rooms displaying photos of other saintly figures, who had been Sai Baba's early followers; there were photos of his first retreat when he came to Shirdi, an ordinary mendicant. On their way out they came upon a nondescript white building, which was the meditation hall. They peeped inside and saw an array of men and women sitting quietly on the floor, reading from small red books resting on wooden desk-stands before them. Mohini told her entourage to keep going, she would meet them later.

Mohini went inside and sat down behind a desk-stand and picked up a red book. She read a few pages of Sai Baba's story, then unwittingly began to reflect upon her own life. She looked up from her desk towards the front of the hall at the benign, holy image of the saint, this saint of the people, his hand raised to give her a benediction, and said, "I am not a bad person, Baba." She would not remember what else she said. She stood up and left.

As she made her way among the throngs of worshippers towards the outside gate, ready to switch on her phone—and the world—and join her family, she saw a mendicant, dressed in a dirty orange dhoti, sitting outside a makeshift shed on the lawn a short distance to her left. Their eyes locked. "Come, daughter," he gestured. "Tell me what troubles you."

She hesitated, then stopped, and said, "I have already prayed to Baba, Guru-ji."

She pointed. But she didn't walk on and he said again, "Come inside."

She stepped onto the grass, followed him into the shed, where he sat down on the ground before a low table on which were flowers and various small objects including a bell. She sat down across from him. Without a prompt, she said, "I want blessings for my daughter. I want her to be successful and happy in life."

"Everyone wants that for their children, my daughter. If Baba grants you this wish, what do you promise him in return?"

"Anything . . . ," she said without a thought, but with a tremor in her voice.

He reached out and she tilted forward to let him place a hand on her head and it felt light. He said, "Be chaste and pure. Give up something dear to you."

"I will try."

"You must. Then he will give. Baba is kind. He is merciful."

"Yes, Guru-ji."

She did a deep pranam and got up. She hesitated, then from her purse she took out a bill and placed it respectfully on the small table. She turned around and went on her way. Instead of joining her family for lunch she proceeded straight to her room. She called her sister to tell her where she was and got into bed and fell asleep.

She was woken by the sound of the door clicking open and shut, as Aarti arrived. She kicked off her shoes, posted two bags on the round table next to the door, and came and sat down on the bed with a sigh.

"Where were you? Why did you abandon us, Didi? We had such a nice lunch."

"I wasn't feeling well . . ."

"You're not going to tell me what ails you, big sister?"

Mohini stared at her. "What d'you mean, what ails me?"

"Ma said you've got yourself into some jam." There was the slightest flash of mischief on Aarti's lips. So she knew. What had Ma told her? "Tell me, Sis."

Mohini paused a long moment, then shook her head. "Sometimes things just happen to you that you can't control."

"I wish they did to me. Now listen, we brought some food for you. Don't tell me you are not hungry after that long day."

"I am," Mohini said gratefully. She got out of bed and went over to the table. She opened the food bag and laid out the vegetarian fare. "What's in this?" she asked, indicating the second bag.

Aarti came over. "I bought some things for you—a Sai Baba photo and pennant, and a little image for the house. And this should please you—Asha and Ravi bought holy threads. Ma bought a lot of stuff to give away to neighbours, and Bau-ji was grumbling."

Mohini gave her sister a hug and suddenly, without letting go, started crying.

"There, there, Sis. Don't cry, please. Everyone has problems. I hope it all works out for you. Coming to Shirdi was the right thing to do. The saint's blessings will heal you."

Munir

HE WAS BEING WATCHED. A young man, almost a boy, dressed in pure white kurta and pyjamas, with an orange scarf round his neck that he was pulling to and fro by its ends, had followed Munir out of the lounge after tea and sat down at the other end of the patio from him, conspicuously within sight. A protegé—or follower—of Jetha Lal, self-styled guardian of purity. Keep your distance from those madmen, Mohini had warned him.

During his last visit, when he had stayed briefly at the guest house on Bahadur Shah Zafar Road, he'd discovered that his laptop had been interfered with. A routine security check, he was told. It had made him angry, then a little wary. And now this shadow in white across the patio? Munir looked, and saw that he had gotten up and gone away. Perhaps it's only my imagination, he thought.

He was sitting in a coach of the Paschim Express, submitting to its rocking and clackety-clack, and memories of train rides in

Kenya as a boy when he would stare out the window in complete absorption. Evening would yield to pitch-dark night, then
beautiful dawn; the landscape went from forest to savannah,
then coast; the weather from cool to humid and hot. Palm trees
and salty air. You would notice zebras and giraffes on the way,
elephants if you were lucky.

He came to, in another world and another time, on another
night train, on his way to Vadodara in Gujarat, having consented
to give a keynote lecture at a conference at the M.S. University
there. "You remember," Dr. Raj Mohan had said, calling him all the
way in Toronto, "when I was in Toronto you promised—if you
visited India you would come to our university and give a lecture?
You kindly invited me to your home and offered me tea and cook-
ies." The resourceful professor, making a routine check of foreign
visitors to Delhi, had discovered Munir's reservation at DRC. "But
that was . . . how many years ago!" Munir had protested. "A long
time ago . . ." Dr. Mohan was unmoved. The subject of the conference was New Trends in Canadian Literature. No amount of
pleading could convince the man that Munir was the wrong
person for the lecture. He did not think in terms of "Literature," he
had no concept of "Canadian Literature," he had written three
books set in Nairobi—which was in Kenya, he reminded Dr.
Mohan—after which he had run out of gas and stopped.

But the professor's resolve was not shaken. "Still, sir, you
must come. Say anything. The students are eagerly awaiting
your arrival."

Now on his way there, he had fully awakened from a restless
sleep, and having gone and washed himself before the morning
traffic got underway, was back at his seat by the window,
making mental notes on what to say in his lecture as dawn

slipped its meagre colours into the grey scenery outside. They were passing a small town, its small, deserted station followed by a settlement with the most elementary dwellings, some of them nothing more than oversized crates balanced upon each other. How long does one live like this, what does one do for a living, does anyone ever manage to escape? The sight of an open countryside with two men crouched in the grass in the semi-darkness, relieving themselves, came as ironic relief.

"You must be from Foreign."

It took Munir a moment to wake up from his reverie, register the full sentence and that it had come from close by and was addressed to him. He shifted his gaze uncertainly. The man, sitting directly opposite him, was smallish, wearing beige pants and a brown sweater in the colour combination that seemed so favoured by Indian men. Was it because the colours didn't fade?

"From Canada," Munir replied.

"You were staring outside, sir. Only foreigners find the poor of our country so interesting."

Munir didn't know what to say and came out with a limp, "It's a pity, this poverty."

"Nothing can be done, there are too many poor people in India."

They took resort in silence. Munir couldn't quite turn away completely from this awkward scrutiny and rewarded the man with a smile. There were two other passengers in the cabin, apparently stirred from their own solitudes by the word "Foreign." One crossed his leg under his open newspaper, and the other leaned forward, a smartphone in his hand. Munir flipped open the dog-eared book on his lap. Down the gangway came the welcome clatter of the breakfast trolley approaching.

"Scholar, sir?" The interlocutor smiled and pointed at the book. "Are you a scholar?"

"I'm a writer." He had always disliked saying that, because somehow it sounded pretentious and it immediately provoked the follow-up, What have you written? and he felt like a child being asked, What grade are you in? He could have said that he was retired. He mumbled the names of two of his books, and was cajoled into admitting that yes, he had been a finalist for one prize, it was called the Governor General's Award. Many years ago. Forgotten.

As soon as he had spoken, the young man with the phone, who was at the other end of his bunk, jumped up, came over in a flurry, and bent down to touch his feet.

How do you respond to that? "Please!" Munir protested, shrinking, "Not necessary . . ." and instinctively put his hand on the man's head, which was a traditional response, a blessing. The man, whose hair was curled and slicked, straightened up and returned to his place. From there he posed the question:

"Your good name, sir? I can Google."

"Munir Khan. Munir Aslam Khan."

The man with the newspaper, sitting diagonally from Munir, made a face and returned to his reading.

Munir's original interrogator's name was Altaf, he was in the merchant navy, and he was visiting Mumbai to see his mother and sister; the young man who had made the exuberant gesture of respect was Rajender, from Odisha. The two plied Munir with questions about Canada, and he did his best to convince them that he was no hotshot. He gave them his phone number and unadvisedly, he would realize later, told them they could visit him when he was back in Delhi, if they wished. He was staying at the Delhi Recreational Club, near Sikandar Gardens.

It so happened that as the train slowed down, screeching to a halt at Vadodara station, there were six people jogging alongside who had come to welcome him. This too was overdone and embarrassing, and only confirmed Altaf's and Rajender's estimations of Munir's greatness. He was indeed a VVIP.

Leading the welcoming pack was Dr. Raj Mohan, whom Munir failed to recognize at first because he looked bigger than when he'd met him the last time, in Toronto. They shook hands, and his small bag was immediately snatched from him and thrust into the eager hands of someone younger, presumably a student. Munir turned and shook hands with Rajender and Altaf, exchanging a brief look with the sneering face of the fourth passenger, who brushed past him and onto the platform, following a porter.

At the conference that afternoon Munir—surprised at his own eloquence on the subject—spoke about how difficult it was to characterize a national literature that was diverse and constantly evolving, from themes of the wilderness and survival to those that were urban and even international in scope, from those that dealt with gender and sexuality to those concerned with memory and history. He could not say if his work was truly Canadian, that was for others to decide; he had written what he had in him. He named a few young writers with immigrant parents who had appeared on the scene recently and discussed what their work signified. He was garlanded and received a bouquet for his effort. Young people came to speak to him, some brought photocopies of his work to sign. He was wined—with whiskey and rum, even though Gujarat was a "dry" state—and dined, and he made a few new friends. He stayed the night, and having declined to speak at other venues, he headed back to Delhi the next morning at eleven.

He had received one text from Mohini the previous night, saying, *Having fun? How did it go?*

Well, he answered, *but all the adulation was embarrassing.*

Indian hospitality, she replied. *Going to bed now.*

He arrived in Delhi the next evening at eight and after depositing his bag and taking a shower, he went down to the dining hall. He waited five minutes while a table was arranged for him, and he ordered the item called "Home-style Food" from the menu, a simple thali with traditional pan-cooked rotis, daal, and two vegetables. He then went downstairs and sat outside on the patio. The air felt cool and bracing. A show ended in the theatre across from the library and a crowd of men and women poured out into the driveway, the latter in colourful saris. A stream of vehicles drove in to pick up their passengers and departed, each time saluted by the watchman.

They were gone. In the stillness now would come a distant insect's chirp, the watchman's plosive cough. Perched on their poles, the globe lamps exuded restrained, misty glows into the thick night air. Except for these silent sentries, there was no one watching him.

Mohini

THEY SAT SIDE BY SIDE on his bed, he playing with her fingers, bending them gently, as he liked to do, putting his own strong fingers through hers. He felt warm to her touch. It was a moment of utmost intimacy. He ran a finger down her bare spine, until she gave a shiver and protested, "Stop, there."

"It doesn't have to be this sordid," she said.

"It's not sordid, it's natural and a manifestation of love."

"But it's sordid because it's in secret and hurried . . ."

She had turned to fix her eyes on him and realized he understood. She gave him much more than he could return. He squeezed her hand.

"Do you mean it?" she asked.

"How can you doubt it?"

"Why can't it remain pure love?"

"Does it make a difference, after everything else, this final act?"

"If it doesn't make a difference, then why is it important?"

"Because it's completion. It's oneness. It's confirmation."

"Go on with your words, you sophist," she said. "It's easy for you to say. You're plain bad. Badmaash."

That word he knew; in Nairobi his elders would use it.

"You really think so? Badmaash?"

She had taken a vow to be chaste and pure. Could she have forgotten so soon, once she was away from that saintly aura? But was it unchaste to desire someone you love, for a few moments to completely abandon yourself to him? He would never betray her, of that she was more than convinced. That dream had just been a dream, a wayward fear. *Give up something dear to you*, the old guru had said. Yes, but not this. He was a gift, her solace. She was not meant to give him up. It was with that resolve that she had come to see him.

"We should be more restrained, that's all," she said, with a sigh.

Then with a smile she told him the story of the great king Pandu, who while he was out hunting in a forest shot and killed a deer that was in the act of coitus. The deer turned out to be a great saint, a rishi, who then, before he died, in his rage cursed the king that he would die in a similar manner, his desire unsatis- fied. Pandu thereupon took a vow of asceticism and celibacy and went off into the mountains, with his two beautiful wives Kunti and Madri. He ate sparingly, suffered bitter cold, wore bark round his waist. Didn't touch his beautiful wives. His five great sons, the Pandavas, were born through the agency of the gods.

"Really? You want me to be like Pandu—and you are what— Kunti? Did Pandu ever die, in this story?"

"Yes, finally."

"How?"

She didn't tell him. One day while Pandu was walking in the

forest with his wives, seeing the beautiful young Madri in front of him in diaphanous clothing, he was tempted. We don't know where Kunti was; Mohini and Aarti had had great fun debating that question as teenagers. Overcome with lust, Pandu approached Madri. Having controlled himself for so many years, now he lost all restraint. He grabbed her from behind, and at that instant he died. The five Pandavas went on to fight the great Mahabharata war, and Madri perished on her husband's funeral pyre, which she entered of her own accord, depriving Kunti the opportunity.

Mohini was ready to go and composed herself before the mirror, while he went to the door and opened it enough to peep out. He motioned to her and she followed him. As they came down the stairs to the reception area, in the waiting annex a few people were sitting on sofas, intently watching a cricket match. A small crowd stood at the counter awaiting attention, among whom was Jetha Lal. His red lips opened into a wide wolfish grin upon seeing them.

"Hello hello, namaskar, Mohini-ji, what brings you here?"

"Hello, Jetha Lal-ji . . . I had to pick up something from Mr. Khan here."

Munir earned what seemed to her a contemptuous look, and she wished she could slap the man right there. But she had to be polite. Form was everything.

"We'll meet at tea, then," Jetha Lal said.

"Let's," Mohini replied.

Outside, she became panic-stricken. "See what you got me into," she said crossly. "You didn't have to walk down with me."

"I should have taken the other way. I'm sorry. I completely forgot."

She walked away from him, and he went and sat down by himself on a chair at his usual place on the patio. She felt sorry for him. She was at fault too, she should have reminded him to take the other exit. It was the guilt racking her, she knew, that brought out these attacks of irritation. The fact that she knew that that wolf knew. He himself would have liked nothing better than to force himself on her.

In the bakeshop outside the lounge she ordered some pastries to take home, but told the attendant to hold the box for her to pick up later. She went inside and ordered a tea and greeted a few people. Was she imagining that she had become the object of speculation? She lost interest in the tea and left.

Munir was still sitting on the patio, looking out, looking thoughtful. He was a lonely man. She came and sat next to him. Jetha Lal passed them just then, on his way from reception to the tea lounge, in the company of a couple of women, and a trail of three young men in white. He gave a quick bow in their direction.

"He gives me the creeps," Mohini said.

"He likes to needle you. Ignore him," Munir said and got up to go. "I think I'll—"

"Where are you going?" she asked.

"I thought I'd go back to my room . . ."

"And leave me here?"

"Didn't you want me to stay away? And our friend there—" He nodded towards the lounge.

"Don't be silly. Do you want me to sit with him? And he's already seen us."

He sat down.

"My husband will meet me for tea at five," she told him. "You are welcome to join us."

"You must be kidding."

Moments of silence later, they heard a loud commotion behind the glass wall of the reception area behind them. There was shouting, two people ran out from the front door, and Jetha Lal came striding out from the lounge followed by his retinue, wielding his phone like a weapon. One of his boys was in tears. When he was closer, Mohini asked,

"What's going on, Jetha Lal-ji? Why is that boy crying?"

The man stopped, stepped sideways towards them.

"Terrorist bombing—" he said, in a voice hoarse with rage.

"Bombing? Where?"

"New Noida Mall." He strode off, muttering angrily. "How many times we have told them . . . bomb them into dust . . . flatten that country . . ."

Munir and Mohini looked at each other. "It must be on the TV inside," Munir said, looking towards reception, where a packed crowd stood watching.

"I wonder if he'll come now," Mohini said, thinking of Ravi.

"There was supposed to be a bombing," she whispered, involuntarily revealing more, "but in a different area . . . He received the wrong information, obviously."

They headed for the lounge and found a place to sit; soon it filled up, buzzing with the news. The bombing had been at a glitzy mall, in a new men's clothing store on the eve of its opening. A number of people had died, it wasn't known how many. The perpetrators were on the run, but it was clear to everybody from where the attack was instigated. Pakistan.

"Doesn't that just make you furious?" she said, feeling bitter.

"It makes me sad," he said.

"Just sad? Not angry? These were Indian lives!" she protested.

"Isn't every life of value?"

That ignited her like a match to petrol, and she responded angrily. "How can you say that? These were *our* people who were killed, this is *our* country that was bombed!" But why was she in tears? "It's easy for you from your civilized and safe Toronto to play the high and mighty, say all deaths are the same. They are not. It's we who are all the time attacked. Mumbai, Hyderabad, Kargil, Pathankot! Anyway, don't say anything like that in public," she muttered.

"I'm sorry. I didn't mean it to come out that way."

Jetha Lal was sitting at his table, gesticulating meaningfully to the people around him. Some had turned their chairs towards him, others had come to stand closer and listen. He was a man of strong opinions, which were evoking shouts of agreement at this emotional moment. "Revenge! We will have revenge!" "You are right, yaar, they can't just walk all over us." "Start with surgical strikes."

She spoke to Ravi on the phone, and he told her to go home. Riots could break out anywhere and in case they did, roads would be blocked. She told Munir she was going home and instructed him not to leave the Club compound and not to express his rash opinions aloud. They got up and walked to the driveway, where he saw her into a taxi. She gave him an eyeful as she got in. He had disappointed her. He had not mustered the appropriate response, outrage, which any true Indian felt at that moment.

Munir

HE WANTED TO EXPLAIN to her that yes, he was from thus-far safe Toronto, up there, out there, and could afford to look with some dispassion at the bombing incident. Such occurrences were in the news every day, many of them more gruesome; hundreds were being killed randomly wherever you turned. How many shows of outrage could you honestly muster? So you lived all the time partly in a state of helplessness and suppressed anger. Still, he realized that he had been insensitive, he should have been more tactful. Should he have faked his fury?

The next day her phone was off all day, which he found odd at first and then worrying, and finally depressing. It was off the following morning. Had he lost her? He attempted stoicism: they had been on borrowed time anyway. He called up the director of the Institute of Advanced Study in Shimla, where he had arranged to spend a few days the following week, and asked him if he could start his visit early. The director asked him when, and Munir replied, Tomorrow. The director said he was welcome, and warned him that it was wet and rainy. Munir thanked him.

It was when he had arrived at Kalka railway station in the Himalayan foothills the following morning, and was waiting for a connecting narrow-gauge train to take him up to Shimla, that she called.

"I rang your room at DRC, and they said you had checked out."

"I'm supposed to be away, not checked out."

"I thought you had abandoned me, having . . ."

She didn't finish; he understood. "And I thought *you* had abandoned me. Your phone was off all day. Maybe you needed time to yourself. To think about who I really was—and so I decided to go to Shimla sooner."

"Munir!"

"Is everything all right?"

"It wasn't a good time to call . . . Sorry."

"I know I disappointed you. I just couldn't fake an outrage, come out with a stock response. I'm not made that way."

"I know, and I like you for that. I was wrong. I am sorry. I thought you didn't show enough emotion, you didn't care about a tragedy that struck our city. But it's easy to show emotion, isn't it. To follow the crowd . . . Patriotism being the last resort of the scoundrel, and so on."

"I thought I'd lost you."

He could hear the tremor in her voice as she said, without any logic, "I don't believe you—you badmaash—or you wouldn't have gone away without telling me. I missed you too, terribly. You will never lose me . . . are you listening? . . . even if we stop seeing each other."

He took a deep breath. "I'll be back next week. You could come to Shimla . . ."

"You know I can't. But let me know when you're coming back. Give my regards to Kamala Singh. She's a friend of mine from university days."

"All right. I'll do that."

They hung up after a moment of silence, articulated only by unspoken longing, a desire to quickly set things right.

The train wound slowly through a landscape of pine-covered hills, making frequent hairpin bends (there were more than a hundred of them, he read in his guidebook), looking down all the while into steep green valleys. The white peaks of the Himalayas rose mysteriously over the horizon. Except for a couple of towns on the way, and the few kids frolicking in the containment of their cabin, he seemed to be in the midst of nature in all its abandonment. This was the route—though traversed by road—that Kipling's hero Kim and the Afghan spy Mahbub Ali had taken. The same one, he surmised, his grandfather Yunus Khan had used when he escaped for a short while to Shimla with his new bride.

He was met at Shimla's small, two-track railway station by Dr. Kamala Singh, a younger colleague called Dr. Girija Sharma, and two graduate students. A welcoming party of four—he was flattered. Upon being introduced, the two students immediately bent down to touch his feet. Dr. Singh was tall and athletic with a jaunt to her pace. Munir remembered to give her Mohini's regards, which raised a curious eyebrow. Dr. Sharma was quiet and respectful. Both taught at the local university, where Mohini's father himself had taught and whom Kamala Singh recalled with affection.

While a porter carried his small hand luggage on his head

(Munir had no say in this) they walked up a narrow road to the institute.

He had come to a different world, as romantic-looking as its reputation; he knew it to be the setting of Bollywood films in which young couples in bright clothes frolicked about in the white snow. It was cool and misty, the air so pure he was inspired to take a few deep breaths. Some of the men and women they passed walked barefoot, their features noticeably hard. The men wore a peculiar embroidered cap, called the Shimla topi. Occasionally, steep concrete steps led down from the ridge along which they walked to houses on the slopes. Behind them upon the hillsides lay a dense sprinkling of white buildings, the town of Shimla. The Viceroy of India's summer residence rose up ahead of them, on one of the highest points in the landscape. His entourage had occupied the many bungalows that were scattered about on the hills and were now in a decrepit state. From here the Raj had been ruled in the summers, while Delhi sweltered. Shimla wore an English veneer.

They arrived at a green wooden gate which, he was informed, was called the Gurkha Gate, and proceeded to make a steep climb up a long, curving driveway. Halfway up he was already out of breath, and his welcome party had to pause for him, much to his embarrassment. At the top of the climb was a gravel plain in front of a great, grey gothic building endowed with a plethora of balconies, verandas, and arches. Showing its age, the former viceregal residence seemed to be crumbling at the edges.

They entered a cavernous hall, muffled in a hushed silence as befitted an institute of advanced studies. Corridors led away on either side. A wide, majestic staircase curved up to the circular corridors of the two higher floors. The predominant motif was wood, deep brown teak brought all the way from Burma. Munir's apartment was on the second floor, a two-room suite once opulent but since run down, with threadbare carpets and collapsed, faded cushions on the sofas and wing chairs. It looked romantic, a memento of another era. When he had placed his luggage inside and washed his face, he came down and joined the women for tea and pakodas at a cafeteria at the side of the building. They were at the edge of a cliff, bound in by a pipe fence, below them a deep green valley covered in mist, in the distance the snowy peaks upon which bobbed and teased the setting sun.

All Munir was required to do during his week-long stay was to give a seminar to the resident scholars, and a reading at the Fire Station Café near the top of the driveway, in the space where the Viceroy's fire brigade had been housed. The rest of his time was his own. Putting in a morning of work at the library, he would go for lunch in the dining room, after which he took the long walk down to the promenade in town called the Mall, a strip of upscale shops and restaurants that during the Raj was restricted to the whites. In the afternoon he sat in on a seminar, or walked around the grounds. His own seminar was on the subject he had covered—so reluctantly!—in Vadodara, and so was the lecture he gave to students at the university. Kamala Singh invited him for dinner one evening at her house, where he met her husband, Inder, a state civil servant. They spoke affectionately of the rather lenient Professor Chand Khanna, Mohini's father. How did Munir happen to meet her? They had shared a table once at the DRC bar, he explained rather inadequately. His red face perhaps further gave him away. He wanted to ask what Mohini was like when they'd known her, but couldn't. Kamala, however, obliged. Mohini had been the brightest and most vivacious of their group.

Daring too. In what way, daring? Well, answering back to gangs
of boys who teased and made lewd remarks to girls passing by;
once she even wrote in the university paper about advances made
by professors. She didn't name any, but the lecherous ones were
well known to the girls. She gave up a bright future and got married suddenly. It was shocking, but that's what happened to many
bright girls. She had a lovely voice, too, and would sing at parties.

Kamala had sensed his stake in her and held him enthralled
with her stories, although he tried not to show it. Inder finally
came to his rescue with, "Mohini married a nice chap, this Ravi,
didn't she? How many children does she have?"

Girija took him on a tour of the Lower Mall, the local market,
which was down a steep flight of stairs from the Mall. Munir's
grandmother's folks had had a store in Shimla, Didi had said,
and it must have been down here in the long, narrow alley,
among the hundreds that sold anything from bracelets and car
parts to jalebi and apricots. Dada had lain low here among his
in-laws, but a police raid on any pretext would have meant
arrest. The wounded Viceroy would have moved into town for
the season, and there were soldiers everywhere on the lookout
for terrorists. Here, a Muslim from Dariba Kalan had arrived
not long following the Outrage. There was a mosque in the
area. He would have gone there on Fridays. And then for some
reason—a good reason—they had left for Bombay and onward
to Kenya. Munir imagined they went by bullock cart and train to
Amritsar, and then the long train ride down half the length of
India to the docks of Bombay. A dhow to Mombasa.

Sitting by himself at the threshold of a chai shop halfway
down to the Lower Mall, Munir wondered at the Providence that
had brought him here to the mountains. Somewhat absently, he

watched the bustle going up and down the steps, the dazzle of colours from the women's clothing. Just outside the entrance, a man sat frying jalebis. Across from him was a small Hanuman shrine. Munir knew no one here, and yet he found himself connected, in a surreal scheme blending fact with fiction, past with present. Dada, a jeweller's apprentice, had escaped Delhi to come to this quaint hill town where Kipling's master spy Lurgan Sahib had run a jewellery shop. Lord Hardinge, perhaps still recovering from the attack on his life in Delhi, would have been two miles away, in that baroque palace that was now the institute where Munir was a guest, staying in a room that Lady Hardinge or her companions might have occupied; the present library was at the location of the ballroom where the English lords and ladies would have danced. The blueprints for India's partition would be drawn there.

And Mohini had lived in Shimla with her refugee parents, down a hillside in an area called Summer Hill. She had been described to him as a vivacious, daring young woman. That same daring was on display as she plunked down at his table at the DRC bar and started chatting with him and challenging him, a total stranger.

The way back to the institute seemed longer, and midway, before he began to ascend, he had to pause on a bench by the roadside. He wondered if, despite what his checkups said, he was really fit after all. He should resume playing tennis. With this thought he felt a tug at his heart as he recalled the little girl he had taken to the courts and taught how to play the game. He pulled out his phone and called Razia. She was lying down, she said. Josh had just fallen asleep. He described to her where exactly he was walking, how beautiful it was, his felt connection to it. His dada and dadi had come to lie low here, before they left for Kenya. He was chatty, drunk on mountain air. Perhaps there'd been something in the masala chai. She had to interrupt him, "But Dad, I would like you to be here, close to Josh and me. Tell *him* your stories." "I am always there for him, don't worry, Razia. I'll be back soon and you can come and visit."

Lighter on his feet, he walked on. He had his walking stick, more like a prophet's staff, presented to him by Kamala Singh, which he swung from time to time to ward off any monkey or stray dog contemplating harassment.

During his few days in the hills, having had tea with a snack late in the afternoon, Munir would opt for fruit and tea in his room instead of a full dinner. He watched a bit of TV, read a lot on his laptop. Late at night, before turning in, he would take a stroll outside, the gravel softly crunching under his feet; a couple of times the sky was pitch-black, the stars clear, bright pinpoints and the haze of the Milky Way plainly visible; it rained two nights, when the earth seemed clothed in a mist as it trundled along its trajectory in the solar system. Over the bounding wall of the institute, thick as a castle rampart, he could look at the lights of the town, spread out in the dark before him like another galaxy. These variations of one stillness transported him deep within himself.

One night he awoke to the sound of muffled thunder in the distance, where the mountain peaks were, and he turned on his back, his heart racing. The gods are angry, he mused. It was pitch-dark and otherwise absolutely still. Then came fierce flashes of lightning, and there appeared on the curtain of the French window the shapely figure of a woman. He stared at her. Common lore at the institute said that some of the viceroys' wives haunted the premises. Don't be silly, he chided himself.

But he turned away from the apparition, not wanting to face her, and started to breathe again. His hair had stood on end. Perhaps, the thought came, it was Lady Hardinge, come to haunt the grandson of the terrorist. Go to sleep. He fell asleep.

It was a night of nightmares. He saw Aileen standing at the bay window of their house in Toronto, telling Razia and Mark, "But he's not here! Don't you see, he's gone away. He's gone away and he's not coming back!" She was in tears, and Razia was on a bed, a baby in a bassinet hollering beside her. Mark was alternately the man at the cemetery and Razia's husband. Razia was in New York and Aileen in Toronto. Razia with a pained look on her face, protesting, "But he's here, Mom, why don't you see him?"

Munir woke up, his heart thumping. There was a loud knocking on the door. Outside the window, dawn was breaking. At the door, the attendant had brought his tea tray, with biscuits. Thank God, he said, taking it, his hands shaking. The man helped put it on the table. Aileen had come to haunt him. Perhaps it was not Lady Hardinge but Aileen all along. But Aileen did not have such an exorbitantly shapely figure. With his tea in his one hand and a biscuit in the other, Munir walked to the French window, which was rattling from the wind. Outside was the wide parapet of the building, with stone railings, a few of them broken. He deduced the obvious—that it was the shadow of a railing, thrown onto his curtain by the lightning, that had frightened him.

There had come nothing from Mohini since he arrived. He had texted several times, called once, anxious to share his excitement. Finally, two days before his departure, a text came. *My father passed away last week. I'm with family.*

He texted, *So sorry. I'll be back on Sunday. Take care of yourself. Thinking of you always.*

Friday night he spent with Kamala and Inder at their home, with four other old-timers, including the vice-chancellor of the university, who had also been a colleague of Mohini's father's. It was a long night of nostalgia that began and ended with Scotch. On Saturday at noon, still barely awake and suffering from a hangover, he took a taxi to Kalka, from where he caught the nightly Kalka Mail to Delhi.

Sitting in his compartment next to the window, as he liked to do, staring at the darkness outside, he reminisced about his visit. He had calmed his nerves after that altercation with Mohini and seen a truly amazing place; he had given greater dimension to his grandfather, the old jeweller of Nairobi, grounding him in a larger India than simply Old Delhi. He had learned more about his dear Mohini. His tea tray came. Before he attended to it, he opened the message that had just buzzed on his phone. Mohini had written, *We would like you to come to dinner at our house. Tuesday. Please come.*

He smiled. He thought he should check his Canadian phone to see what had arrived there. A few missed calls and some messages. He pressed to view the last one, and a chill ran through him. A bright, clear photo flashed on the screen. It was not possible what he saw. Yet it was there, the selfie of himself and Mohini at Safdarjung Tomb. The photo on his phone had come back to him.

He was being warned.

He slept fitfully, and when the train arrived at Old Delhi station in the morning, he was wide awake.

Mohini

WHEN MOHINI ARRIVED on her assigned Tuesday to oversee the cleaning of her parents' house, she found Bau-ji sitting on the sofa in a grumpy mood, complaining about this and that. His breakfast was cold, the plate was not cleaned properly, one of his slippers was gone. Mohini herself noticed that one of his pyjama-coat buttons had come off. The new girl was wiping the floor at his feet, where he had dropped his tea cup and saucer.

"What's wrong, Bau-ji? Something bothering you today?"

"It's not a good day."

After the girl left, Mohini and Ma went for their usual visit to the Hanuman temple. On the way, Ma, breathing unusually hard today, said, "That Khan fellow is back, isn't he?"

"He's not a 'Khan fellow', his name is Munir Khan. Yes, he is here. What's wrong?"

"Have you seen him?"

Mohini said nothing, and Ma continued to puff along beside her.

"Don't walk so fast. I always thought it would be Aarti who would cause me grief, not you."

"What grief, Ma? I have done nothing wrong."

Ma didn't bother with that.

"Your bau-ji has not been feeling well. Last night he stumbled twice."

"And you didn't call the doctor, Ma?"

"He didn't want me to. Where's the pendant I gave you?"

"I forgot to wear it. You know I don't like these cheap magic trinkets. They make me look like some village girl."

It had been a difficult week. First the bombing in the city and her outburst at Munir. She felt a pang when she was told that he'd checked out. Serves me right, she thought. Thankfully he'd gone off only as far as Shimla. She smiled. Life would have become easier if he'd really gone away. But he couldn't, just as she couldn't help feeling pleased that he was still around.

Delhi had fretted nervously, poised for another terrorist attack. There were already loud calls for war from the loony right. And Ravi was in a bad temper, his department bearing responsibility for producing the wrong intelligence. Despite their latest interrogation techniques, they had been fooled. Their information had said Bengali Market would be the target, and it went under tight security, but the bomb was thrown on the Janpath Road by a speeding motorcycle with two men on it. They were shot dead, which was another mistake.

There had been the altercation with Ravi. After two difficult evenings away, he was spending one night at home, and perhaps she should have been more responsive to him. They were in the living room, as was usual when he was around at night, but this time they were not quite together—he watching a heated discussion on television, four screaming guests conducted by a screaming moderator, while she brooding with her own thoughts. The discussion on TV was about security, and Ravi made a few dissenting exclamations to which she paid no attention. Finally he sat back, saying, "Nonsense," and looked towards her. She met his gaze with a blank look. His face clouded, and he turned away; after a moment as he stood up to retire, he asked, pretending to be casual, "That Khan fellow still around?" More accusation than curiosity. She flared up. "Why do you have to call him 'that Khan fellow'? He's a person!" She had fallen into it, and he had his handy response: "What's he to you that you so readily jump to his defence?" "Everything!" she said. He turned slowly, took a step back and hit her across the face. He'd not done that in years. He apologized, over and over, fondled her and kissed her, and then the make-up sex, and her head ringing from the blow. She had only Munir in her mind then, and she knew he could tell. They had reached the end of the road now, but would he let her go? Would the girls or her parents allow her? Would she allow herself?

She and Ma reached home to find Bau-ji sitting on the sofa, looking blankly in front of him. There was no question that he was not all right.

"What happened, Bau-ji?"

"I . . . I . . . I just don't remember how I got here."

"Where were you, Bau-ji? At the dining table? Having lunch?"

"Yes . . . I think so, but I must have got up."

"How long have you been here?"

"Huh? I don't know—can you hear me? I don't know what I'm saying."

Dr. Panwakar arrived in five minutes and immediately called an ambulance. "Stroke," he pronounced. "But it's not advanced."

Ma almost had a stroke herself, barely coherent when the ambulance came, and had to be restrained as her husband was wheeled away on a stretcher. Later that afternoon Mohini and Ma went to see Bau-ji and stayed with him till midnight. He slept, mostly, but occasionally opened his eyes and attempted a smile. The two of them would hold his hands then. Ravi came in the evening at seven, bringing Asha with him. Mohini joined them for a meal and then the two of them left. Aarti would fly in the next morning and Kishore would follow. Aarti was constantly on the phone from Hyderabad. Shall I come, Mamma? No, darling, I'll let you know.

At six the next morning they received a phone call from the hospital. Bau-ji had passed away in his sleep.

Mohini hardly slept the next three days. There were so many arrangements to make, there was no time to dwell upon her grief. Ma needed attention constantly, in her dazed state feeling more loss than grief. There were moments when she thought she was still in Sargodha, or Shimla. She would speak to the absent Mohan— "Your elder brother is dead, Mohaniya, how he worried about you." "Now he is gone, Mohan." Asha would go and stand by her grandmother and hold her hand. Once, breaking into nervous laughter, Mohini said to Asha, "Are you taking her pulse?"

There were friends and relatives to inform, the house to be prepared to receive them, and the priest to call; the body to be bathed; and then the cremation. All of which she accomplished, with some help from Aarti, like an automaton, as her duty to her bau-ji. She would recall each of these tasks seconds later. But if she had paused to reflect at the time, she would have broken down. She and Ravi and Aarti and Kishore took the ashes by car to immerse in the Ganga at Haridwar, where they spent the night in a hotel. Ma stayed back with Asha. On the way back they had lunch at a dhaba outside Haridwar, where they fondly recalled Bau-ji as they had known him at various times, and then it was all over. Bau-ji was no more. It was decided that Ma would stay with Mohini and Ravi for a while. Aarti and Kishore left, flying to Delhi and onward to Bangalore.

There remained a weight upon Mohini's heart, an indescribable oppression, a need to scream it out to the world. She had not been there for her parents, not realized how sick her father was. More so in the recent months, since Munir came into her life. She thought of Gandhi-ji, who had been dallying with his bride at the hour when his father was dying. He never forgave himself. She was not fit even to touch Gandhi-ji's toenails, why compare . . . and Munir was up in Shimla when Bau-ji died, why blame him? After her outburst, she had longed to see him again. Say she was sorry. To be held and told it was all right. All that for herself, and Ma and Bau-ji got neglected. If she had called the doctor right then, when she'd arrived . . . spent time with him then. She had casually walked away with Ma.

Was this her punishment, this gnawing guilt, would God have taken away Bau-ji just to get at her? What about Aarti— who knew what she was up to, with her modern outlook and all her travels abroad? She had taken it all in stride, Bau-ji was an old man, after all. Old people fell sick and died.

"You can't blame yourself for Bau-ji, Moi," Ravi said. "You did more than anyone else. And he did live a long and eventful life. His time had come and he's found his peace."

Throughout, his had been the voice of cold reason. But he did care, she thought. He had been kind to her father.

They were in the living room having tea. Asha was on the floor watching an American sitcom, chuckling away, but she paused to agree with her dad.

"Yes, Mamma . . . old people have to die," she said.

"Didn't you love your nana?" Mohini asked her sharply.

"Of course I did, Mamma. Just saying."

"What's happening to me, I don't know. I'm sorry."

A few minutes later Asha got up. As she passed her, Mohini put an arm out and drew her close in a hug, with a sob. "You must forgive your Mamma—for everything. You know I love you very much."

After that, she and Ravi sat mutely in the room, the silence between them suffocating. Finally an English wicket went down with an uproar.

"Who's playing?" Mohini asked.

"West Indies against England. It's an old match," Ravi said, then asked, "Is . . . Munir . . . still in India? Just wondering."

"Yes, he's gone to Shimla to give some lectures."

"Ah. He's seeing more of India now."

"Yes, he went to Gujarat before that."

"Good for him. There's more to India than Delhi, he should know that. Delhi is an artificial city. Most people who live in Delhi have come from somewhere else. Listen—"

He paused and stared at her. She looked back. "Yes?"

"I received a phone call from a colleague."

"And?"

"You know that time you—he complained about his room being searched at that guest house on Bahadur Shah Zafar Road?"

"Yes."

"It's their job to do these occasional searches. Well, it turns out that this Munir Khan is the grandson of a terrorist. One Yunus Khan of Dariba Kalan. A long time ago, still . . ."

Catch your breath, she said to herself, don't make a fool of yourself again. Count to ten, to a hundred. Why is he telling me this? When she was ready she said, "And that makes Munir Khan a terrorist? That was during British times. Even Netaji Bose was called a terrorist—"

"I just thought you should know."

"Okay. Sorry."

Their eyes met.

"Let's invite him for dinner. I've not had a proper chat with him. When's he back from Shimla?"

"Sunday."

He could have asked her how she knew. Instead he got up and went to the bathroom.

"Would you like the kulfi?" he called out later.

"Yes, thank you."

She picked up her phone and looked at the message which had arrived a short while ago. Upon seeing it she gave an audible gasp.

"What happened?"

"Nothing."

She was staring at the selfie she and Munir had taken at Safdarjung Tomb. At her insistence.

When the kulfi came, she choked on the first bite. With difficulty she forced herself to finish it. Her husband just stared at her.

Munir

ASHA OPENED THE DOOR for him with, "Come in, Uncle," and gave him a shy smile. "Thank you," he said. "It's Asha, isn't it? I've heard so much about you. Nice things only." Her eyes lit up and he walked behind her into a little hallway and then what appeared to be the dining area, with a large table set for four. Mohini had come forward and with a smile guided him to the living room inside, where Ravi Singh was waiting. "Welcome, Munir," he said. He pointed Munir to an armchair and they sat down.

Mohini stood at the doorway. She was in a blue salwar and white kameez. Ravi was in an elegant beige kurta. Munir had put on a newly acquired short blue kurta over his casual pants.

"I'll be back in a minute," Mohini said and left.

There was an awkward moment of silence, before Ravi stood up and walked to a cabinet in a corner. "What will you drink?" he asked. "I'm having whiskey." Munir said he'd have the same, with a little water.

Ravi poured whiskey for Munir and himself, and vodka for Mohini, who had just come in with some water and ice.

She'd remembered he took water with his Scotch.

"So what's happening in Canada, Munir?" Ravi asked, in a dry, drawling voice. "You live in a very stable country. You are lucky. Over here we're constantly at each other's throats."

Munir laughed politely and agreed that Canada was indeed one of the calmer places on the globe currently.

Ravi smiled.

"India is different. India changes day to day, minute to minute—it's hard to keep up. It's a complex country, mind you, but . . ."

And so it went. Mohini got up—"I'll give Asha her dinner first"—and Ravi regaled Munir with GDPs and budgets, poverty statistics, and life expectancies. Very clearly, he cared about his country, and was concerned that China was developing much faster. Munir asked him what kept India behind. At this point Mohini came in to say that dinner was ready.

"My mother is staying with us for a few days, but she's a bit shy to come out. And it's too soon after . . ."

Munir said he understood.

For dinner they had pakodas, palak paneer, bhindi, and karhi, with chapatti and a fragrant pullao. She had asked him if he would like Italian or Chinese and he had said he would prefer traditional Indian. There was an affecting intimacy in eating what she had made with her own hands. Her hands. "Munir was born in Nairobi," Mohini said, to keep the conversation going, and Munir gave his resumé. Ravi himself came from Jaipur; his father was a schoolteacher. He had joined the army and later moved to the home ministry as an information officer.

"There should be a meat dish, dear," Ravi said to Mohini in mild reprimand. "You could have ordered lamb biryani. You know that our guest is non-veg."

"I'm not addicted to meat," Munir said, with perhaps too much emphasis. "I do like vegetarian, especially when it's this good."

There was a pause. A tinkle of cutlery on plates. Ravi said, "That's not right. If you're non-veg, you should remain consistent." Realizing the oddness of the comment coming from a host, he laughed and said, "But of course you are free to eat what you want to eat!"

They all laughed.

"Munir especially likes palak paneer," Mohini said.

She shouldn't have. First the water for his Scotch and now this. He exchanged a sweeping glance with Mohini. The discussion about meat was absurd, for she had told him that Ravi and Asha both ate chicken. And she ate meat occasionally, as he knew, and surely Ravi the information-meister knew that too. They spoke freely and fluently, yet there was an oppressive formality to the proceedings that would not go away, a lurking fear that something wrong might be said.

They returned to the living room. Ravi poured them more whiskey, saying, "Some Indian whiskeys nowadays are better than Scotch." Mohini declined a drink, hovering close to the doorway. Indian women have three jobs, she had said.

"Your family didn't migrate to Pakistan?" asked Ravi, sitting down.

"My grandparents didn't, obviously. I believe my dada's siblings might have gone there—there was a brother and a sister. We didn't keep in touch—at least not my generation. I don't know where they are or what happened to them."

Mohini breezed in, followed by her assistant gingerly carrying a clattering tray of dessert. "Gulab jamun," she said. "I hope you like them. I didn't make them, but there's a very good halwai in the area." She sat down, looking very tense. He wanted to reassure her that everything was fine. Asha came in and sat on the carpet before the TV, which she turned on, keeping the volume low. For a few minutes Munir played the avuncular guest, asking her about herself. She said she liked school. Her favourite subject was business, but not science, and her marks had improved because she had tutoring. She liked dance. She wanted to go to college in Delhi, close to Mum and Dad. Turning a shy, apologetic look on him, she went back to the TV. Her program had started.

The gulab jamun were excellent, Munir said. Yes, he would like some coffee, but afterwards. They were still on the whiskey. It went well with the dessert, he thought. He felt closely observed.

The program on TV was called *The Fresh Prince of Bel-Air*, and they all got a couple of minutes of relieving laughter from it. Munir said his daughter Razia used to watch it. Yes, he had only the one child. And yes, his wife Aileen had died in a car accident not too long ago.

"She was a banker . . . must have left you a good inheritance," Ravi said.

"I have enough money of my own. Most of Aileen's bequest went to our daughter in trust. I own half the house and don't have to pay rent as long as I live. That helps."

He smiled his embarrassment at them.

"We don't speak about money," Mohini admonished her husband.

"Just curious. I know that writing books is not especially lucrative. Unless you write books like *Harry Potter* . . ."

"No, for most writers it's not lucrative," Munir agreed. "I stopped writing a long time ago, but I am quite comfortable.

I inherited from my family, you see. I understand you are in the security services?"

Mohini opened her mouth and almost dropped her dessert.

"Let's say that's another subject we don't speak about," Ravi said with a stiff smile.

"Of course."

But, Ravi said, he was close to retirement and did yoga and meditation. He read the Gita every morning, and sometimes the Upanishads. He had a guru in Rishikesh, whom he visited occasionally. He explained to Munir where Rishikesh was.

Ravi now served Indian brandy. Mohini said goodnight and went to bed. Ravi and Munir sat together and watched the news. They discussed cricket and the great days of the West Indian sides. Munir, of course, had not kept up with recent developments. Finally Ravi walked Munir to the taxi stand and saw him off. The look in his eyes as he closed the car door behind Munir was icy.

There had been no laughter or mirth during that visit except for that distracting minute or two of the sitcom. It had been a sizing-up operation. Munir felt unsettled by the experience, he felt violated; but he would not now have to look at Ravi curiously across a distance. He could wave at him in a pretended friend-ship. But he had also felt like an intruder in that home. A home with a man and wife and a child. But was it that simple? Having alighted from the taxi he had come to sit on the lawn, in a pen-umbral shadow, to wear out the effects of the whiskey and the unnecessary brandy in the cool, fresh air. Occasionally a taxi would arrive and drop someone off on the driveway; otherwise there was no one about save for the watchman and himself.

How would this end? It was too complicated. Perhaps he should simply go away, leave Delhi and never come back. And yet already he longed for her.

Just then five white ghosts emerged from behind him on the right, and while passing, one of them threw a sharp sideways look at him. He was only a boy. At the head was Jetha Lal himself, and there was a determined, purposeful manner in the way they all marched, leaning forward towards something. They reached the driveway and called for a taxi. Soon a few small groups followed, and Munir recalled seeing a poster in the notices cabinet at the entrance about a lecture in the second auditorium, behind the bar. It was titled "Hindu Ritual, Hindu Nationalism."

Mohini

HE LOOKED UP WITH a pleased smile as she arrived. "Where were you? I sent a message . . ."

"I know. You shouldn't have."

It had been a cryptic one, and the caller identity said, Jayanti. But a message saying simply, *I am here* was a dead giveaway.

"I couldn't resist. Today is—"

"Our anniversary! And I've made it, haven't I? Exactly here, at this table, where we first met, and you said—"

He chuckled. "I said you reminded me of the actresses of the old Hindi cinema, and you deliberately misunderstood me—and gave me a chiding."

"I did."

"I arrived early, and stood a round of red wine for the couple that was already seated here. Then I requested them to move. You couldn't come earlier?"

The couple, now two tables away, were smiling benignly at them. If they only knew.

She shook her head. "Duties. Just shopping and traffic took

up half the day." And then there was the meeting in the afternoon with Asha and her tutor. Finally, finally, Asha seemed to
be getting the hang of physics and calculus. A miracle.

It was three days since he had come to dinner. Three anxious
days, and it was a relief to see him, hear his voice, that accent
that was formed in many places, as he once described it to her;
she could see that he was twitching to reach out and touch her.

"You were good at the dinner," she said. "You made a good
impression."

"I'm glad. But that discussion about veg and non-veg was
rather awkward. I felt I was being told that I was different,
would always be different—and should stay different. Why
can't one just *be*?"

She laughed, and a few faces quickly turned to observe them.

"Don't worry. You impressed him."

"I wonder. You were tense yourself."

"A little."

"A lot. And that boo-boo I made—him being in the security
service?"

"Yes. It didn't matter. Just one boo-boo."

All it takes is one. And she was aware of her own gaffes, of
which he didn't remind her.

Just then, a vague acquaintance came by to greet her and
gave Munir a quick appraisal. A waiter stopped at their table
and they ordered paneer tikka and fish cutlets. A bottle of Sula
white. They touched glasses.

"Tell me about that place . . . Shirdi?" he said.

She was startled.

"Why do you ask?"

"Curious. After you went there I kept noticing images of Sai

Baba everywhere. In taxis and autos. In shops. How was the experience? Did it transform you?"

What to say? How to explain? She hadn't yet come to terms with the experience, didn't want to recall it now.

"These places have an aura, a power. They do something to you. Ravi came. And Aarti and her family ..."

"I'm jealous."

"You should be," she said, for no reason, then added, "But you were there with me. I thought about you. I wish you could have come."

A lot had happened since that first time they met. They had felt freer then. She had been chirpy, and he, shy but mischievous. There was the joy and charm of discovery and parrying. Now there was the ecstasy and the pain of passion and love. Fear. Helplessness. Guilt.

A small crowd of people walked in, and the room was filled with excited chatter.

He said, "I quite enjoy the atmosphere in this bar. It's so Indian and yet not completely."

She nodded. "A lot of these people have lived abroad. Or have someone from their family living there. There was a play on tonight," she said. "*Tughlaq*, by Girish Karnad."

"I saw the notice."

"It may be on tomorrow. Go and see it. You might get ideas. I read it in college, it was quite the rage."

He had been casually looking around the room; now he turned and asked softly, "Will you come up? Even a moment?"

"Don't be silly!" she replied, in equal measures softly and sharply. "It's late. I have to go now. But tomorrow afternoon ..." She put a hand on his arm, quick and risky, and he looked startled, then smiled at her. Before he could grab her hand, she pulled it back. But lingered long enough to leave a caress.

"Tomorrow," she said.

She sensed his eyes upon her as she left.

She couldn't help herself. She knew she had to come, despite the late hour. He would be waiting for her. It was their anniversary. It mattered. She couldn't have gone up to his room now, but tomorrow—she had promised. She wanted to be covered by his tight embrace, enveloped completely in his arms, feel the kisses on her face her eyes her mouth. Sometimes she thought she could recall every moment of their lovemaking, every expression on their faces, the tender words.

This is reckless, Mohini. Don't let the world hear you. She entered the car.

You must give up something dear to you . . .

She choked, overcome by a sudden sick feeling; her insides ready to collapse. Goosebumps crawled over her body and she shivered. Why had he reminded her of Shirdi? A moan escaped from her heart and she started to cry.

"Is everything all right, Madam?" the driver asked, his eyes upon her from the rear-view mirror.

"Yes, everything is fine." She sat up and wiped her eyes and blew her nose. "I was just reminded of my bau-ji. Thank you for staying late for me today, Bahadur."

"Welcome, Madam."

She still suspected he was a spy.

Earlier that afternoon, she had walked into the house to see Asha and her tutor Amit sitting at the table, bent over a textbook.

They turned around simultaneously. A beam on Amit's face, a delighted, triumphant look on Asha's.

"What's up, guys?" Mohini asked.

"A miracle, Madam," Amit stood up. "Truly a wonder! She received eighty-six per cent in physics!"

"Really? Asha?"

"Yes, Mamma."

"She's cracked the secret, Madam. And not everyone can do it, I tell you. It's not just knowing the formulas, but how to pose the problem mathematically and solve it. And she's found out. Madam, congratulations!"

"Oh . . ." Mohini gave Amit a hug and he was taken aback. Then she gave Asha a hug.

"You don't think this is a fluke? You didn't cheat, Asha? This is not a one-off?"

"No, Mrs. Singh, no on all counts. I guarantee it."

"Mamma, this is the second quiz."

"Yes, Mrs. Singh, I forgot. We kept the first one a secret, because I wanted to be sure this was no *accident!*"

"And the first one?" Mohini asked.

"Eighty-three per cent."

"And the one before?"

"Sixty-two. But I can see for myself, Mrs. Singh. I set her a problem and she does it seventy-five per cent of the time. We still have to do more practices . . ."

The boy couldn't contain himself. She ordered a pizza for them.

She reached home, gave Bahadur a large tip, and went inside. She went into the living room, saw Ravi, and said, "You are here," by way of greeting. She sat down, absorbed in herself. His eye was upon her, but he let her be. She felt hot and cold, pulled her shawl tight around herself, squeezing her heart which was about to burst. Ravi went to bed, she told him she would sit alone for a while.

Asha's turnaround was the miracle, she was convinced of it. Two test results, but she could see it in her daughter's sparkling eyes, the belief there that she'd not seen in a long time. What will you give in return? the guru had asked. *Something dear to you.* Was it pure accident that Munir himself had reminded her of Shirdi?

Did she even believe in miracles? A few months ago she would have said no. She was modern. She believed in spirituality, but not in cheap miracles, quid pro quo with the gods. That was Ma, and her one big prayer was never answered. She herself went to temples because of their calming atmosphere, and because of her respect for tradition. You placated the priests and you placated the gods, whatever they were. And ultimately we ourselves are God. *Tat tvam asi.* That's spirituality. What's inside you. Your conscience. Your heart.

But she had promised, and you did not fool around with God.

She had not promised to God. Only to a holy man. To be chaste and pure. And she believed sincerely that her love was pure. She wasn't promiscuous. She was modest and generous, she had been attentive to her parents. She had not lied to Ravi... just kept things from him. Between them was the arrangement of marriage; respect and care, duty. Affection too, at times. But nothing like what she felt for Munir, and he for her. She and Munir were meant to be, and they had found each other.

He was what was dear to her.

Ask of me anything else, Baba, and I will give it to you. Not this.

She was woken up by the birds tweeting outside, her cheeks all wet.

Ravi did not ask her why she had not come to bed, and the four of them had their breakfast together. A chirpy Asha then left for school, giving her mother and father each a kiss, and Ma a tight hug. Ravi left with, "*Achha*, see you later." Mohini and Ma finished their tea in silence.

Munir

THE NEXT DAY SHE DIDN'T CALL. Nor the day after. There came no reply to his two messages. The tomorrow she had promised had yet to dawn. He went out for walks, browsed in the bookshops at Khan Market, bought a few apples, had a haircut. He read. He reflected.

On the second evening, after a light supper at the lounge, he walked into the library, which was almost empty. He walked to his carrel, opened his laptop, and stared at a blank page for some time. Then, fatefully, feeling—so he thought—like a child taking its first step, he wrote:

A NARRATIVE OF THE LAST DAYS OF DELHI

One terrible day bled into another following the death of our Sultan Alauddin by poison, and the three princes' gory murders in Gwalior Fort. There was no end in sight to the naib's evil machinations; now a Hindu was installed Sultan of Delhi and the descendants of maharajas strutted about its streets, energized by their polished new idols and charms. The future of Hindustan lay exposed and our own lives hung in the balance from day to day.

Such dark thoughts had returned to play upon my mind as I walked home one evening from a visit to my master Nizamuddin . . .

She called at nine p.m., just before the library closed, and he walked out and answered. She apologized for having been inaccessible. Had Ravi not returned yet? he asked, meaning, was it all right for her to talk?

"He's engrossed in a news program."

He told her what he had been up to, the last two days. The reminder of her broken promise was implicit.

"What are you doing tomorrow?" she asked.

"I'll go to the old city. Do my usual haunts. Look for inspiration. Will you come?"

"Do you want me to?"

"You know I'd like nothing better."

There was a pause. Then softly: "I think he knows. Definitely knows. The dinner was a bad idea . . . but it was his idea . . ." Another pause, then a quick, "Tomorrow. At eleven."

At a quarter to that hour the next morning she phoned that he should wait for her outside the gate, she was on her way. He went down and waited, and soon enough an auto came coughing to a free crawl beside him; she peeped out and he stepped in. Quickly she made way for him, and he could tell immediately that her mood was not right.

"He knows," she said crisply.

"I'm sorry?"

"I'm telling you, he knows."

"We'll just be more careful. No smile today?"

"Yes. And keep your distance, please, the man is watching us."

She meant the driver, who did not even have a rear-view mirror. Her tone surprised him too, as though she were warning off some uncouth male ready to make an advance. Had she come to quarrel with him? Break up? She had promised him a tomorrow that never came. Now this.

They got off at Ajmeri Gate and agreed to take a cycle rickshaw to the eighty-four-bell temple. At the doorway she hit the bell with vigour and almost pushed him back as she entered. There was a priest this time at the shrine. She covered her head, bowed, and quickly did her puja before the gods. She did not wait for him to join her, and feeling hurt he stood behind. They came out back into Sitaram Bazar and walked silently for a while, stopping at a stationers', where she bought a box of greeting cards. They walked on towards the great mosque. On the way they passed Karim's restaurant, which she had introduced to him on their first visit here.

"We can return here for kebabs later," he offered.

"I'm vegetarian now."

Two days ago she had had fish. What had happened in the meantime?

"We'll both eat vegetarian, then."

"No, you must have the kebabs here. I insist. I'll grab a palak or something."

He didn't answer and they walked on. On the way she grumbled at the crowds, the rickshaws, the dirt, and finally the number of steps to go up to the mosque. This had turned out to be an awkward outing. Why had she come? "We don't have to go up," he said finally.

"No, I'm sorry. You must go. We'll go."

They entered the vast courtyard, their shoes in their hands, and stepped onto the red runner. At the fountain, like other visitors, they stood and gazed around at the familiar scene: the four minarets, the immense dome. On the western side, under the dome, the qibla, where a few dozen people were at prayer. To his amazement, she turned to him, tugged sharply at his arm and said, "Don't you want to go and pray?" He was amused. But she was serious. "You are a Muslim, aren't you? You should go and pray. Go!"

He was utterly bewildered. Was this Mohini's double who had come with him today? Irate, offensive, like he hadn't seen her before. Why was she intent on wounding him? What crime had he committed?

"Why do you hesitate? Aren't you a Muslim?"

"All right. I'll go and pray. To make you happy." He paused, then took off his socks, walked over to the fountain where men were washing their hands and feet, and imitated their gestures. He strode up towards the qibla and halfway there went down on his knees, but didn't know what to do then. After a minute or so, he got up and returned to her.

"There, I have prayed. I'm a Muslim. Does that satisfy you? Do I fit into your world now?"

Tears streamed down her cheeks.

"I'm so sorry, I don't know what's got into me," she whispered.

He thought of saying, It's in the air, but desisted.

They took a rickshaw to the Chandni Chowk station, and as

they passed the glittering jewellery market she said, placatingly, "Don't you want to stop here? It's your favourite place."

"Next time," he replied. "When I'm alone."

He had planned to buy a pair of bracelets for Razia, but now he simply wished to call an end to this excursion. He would return another day, before he flew back. He hailed a taxi. Outside the Club gate, he got off and paid the driver, telling him to take the Madam home.

"Goodbye."

"Goodbye, thanks for accompanying me."

Barely conscious of his actions he headed towards the lounge, sat down somewhere at the back and ordered tea. Shock. A ringing in his ears, which had borne their punishment. He could barely hear himself even in his own mind. All around him incomprehensible noise. It took a while for him to breathe easier, in out, several times, then he started silently railing against himself. How stupid and naive he had been. A gullible fool. An idiot. A desperate and lonely widower. A defunct writer. He should have seen that he was a foreigner, and these Indians were aliens. He would never understand them. He had got much out of Delhi, he had attached to it his personal history. He was able to find a home for his grandfather's memories. He was grateful for that. Now he was ready to scram. To run for his life.

Looking up towards the door, he was surprised to see her come in. So she had not gone home. She had many friends here. He saw her glance towards him but paid no notice. Finishing his tea, saying thanks and goodbye to the person who had shared his table, he got up and hurried to his room.

She had wounded him terribly. He had been assaulted, in his intellect, in his emotions. She had found that weak spot in him and pressed it. How could someone who had been intimate with him, who had loved him, turn against him? For the Hinduism she had discovered in herself? Was her spirituality so exclusive and political? For her new-found purity? Or was it his fault, for falling in love with a married woman, taking advantage of her problems? Sitting on his chair, watching through the window the odd person walking or jogging in the park behind the fence, he fell asleep. He dreamt, of her, but later he wouldn't remember what.

There was a light knock on the door. Then another.

He went and opened it. She rushed in, closed the door behind her. Looked at him frantically, took both his hands. "I'm sorry. I'm sorry. I'm sorry . . . please!"

He held her, feeling her hot body against his, her tears drenching his shirt.

He was still hurting and here she was, crying. This was the body, this the soul he had united with. An immense empathy filled him. He gulped to control his emotions, then very tenderly kissed her eyes.

"How will you explain your tears and your state?"

"I won't . . ." Meaningless yet meaningful.

He wiped her tears with his handkerchief. She looked pathetically at him, tried to smile. "I will never let you go, Munir," she said.

They made passionate, reckless love. A fearless consummation oblivious to the fire outside.

———

He called up Razia. It was night there but she was happy to hear from him. And he was relieved to hear her familiar voice, her clear North American accent with the mark of New York upon it.

"Are you all right, Dad?"

"Yes, I'm all right."

"You sound—you know, different . . . How is she?—should I ask?"

"Fine. Don't worry. How is Joshua?"

"A bit cranky. You know something, we were debating whether to expose him to Beethoven at this time . . . or hip-hop! What's your opinion?"

"Both? Afraid he might make the wrong choice?"

"Not me. My mom-in-law sees a new Rubinstein in him. Just from his fingers."

He laughed, and he thought he heard a voice in the background.

"Goodnight, Dad."

"Goodnight, dear."

Mohini

WHAT HAD HAPPENED TO HER? As soon as he stepped off the taxi with a curt "Thanks for accompanying me," her heart sank. She watched him as he hurried away from her and through the gate. And she felt as if she had just broken something, something rare and precious. What had she done? Was there no going back?

She told the driver to stop and return her to the Club. When she arrived there, she sat outside on the patio for some minutes to calm herself before walking into the lounge. He was at the far back and avoided her eyes.

Was that it? All the anxiety and risks, the joy and passion, for nothing? Had she thrown it all away? It couldn't be.

She sat at a table by herself, greeted a few people. Thoughts racing through her mind.

He wasn't like that, unforgiving. She knew him. She had to go and tell him, I'm sorry, a thousand times, a million times, I'm sorry. Let's wipe today clean, it never happened. Let's push it into a black hole . . . out of our memory . . . forever. If only he would look her way.

Who should come by and join her post-haste but the smarmy fanatic Jetha Lal, trailed by two of his followers. He gave off a sweaty odour, despite his pressed, shiny white outfit. Two other young men joined the table. Past the initial greeting, when she affirmed, honestly, "Yes, it's fine, these seats are free," and the man had sidled up next to her on the wide chair, she wasn't even listening to what they were discussing, until he attempted to draw her in.

"Mohini-ji, don't you agree, you have daughters, na?" he said in a low, ingratiating voice.

"Yes," she said, looking at him, "I have two daughters, but what are you talking about?"

"It is our duty to protect our daughters, don't you agree?"

She got a little annoyed. "I agree, but from what? What's the danger?"

"Mohini-ji, Valentine's Day is coming. And boys and girls will, you know . . . but it is not the Hindu way . . . not our tradition . . ."

He gave her a toothy grin.

"They have to be told," said a boy.

"Yes, told," another one put in and nodded.

"We don't live in Saudi Arabia, Jetha Lal-ji! You can't go around checking on couples on the streets! It's their personal business."

If he had cared to read her columns, he would know where she stood on the "anti-Romeo" crusades—zealots and even police stopping couples to demand proof of the legitimacy of their relationships. What happened to freedom?

"Madam," broke in an acolyte earnestly. "But our daughters and sisters need protection—"

"Yes, but from whom? Have you looked at the rape inci-
dences reported daily in our newspapers? Gang rape, child
rape, whatnot? So-called holy men raping girls? You should
address those problems first."

They shut up.

She got up abruptly, paid at the counter, and left the lounge, not
caring if they were watching her as she walked over to the main
building and up to his room. Daughters and sisters . . . there was
no end to madness. There had been the showdown at home last
night. And again this morning.

The mood had been bright around the house the past two
days, especially Asha's. Her entire outlook on her future seemed
to have altered, and they were already discussing colleges for her.
Delhi University was her first choice. Some kind of engineering,
all agreed. Chemical or biological, perhaps. Last night, Mohini
had brought home tandoori chicken, french fries, and a cake.

Ma got up first from the dining table, then Asha lumbered
off. When the two of them were alone at the table, Ravi broke
the longish silence with an unexpected offensive. Her late
arrival two nights ago and the brooding afterwards had not yet
been addressed. For the first time in their married lives she had
not come to bed. Now the consequence.

"This Khan . . . when is he leaving, Moi? He's stayed a long
time, I would say—and he has a family there—"

Mohini lit up. "You've met him, he's come to our home, and
you still call him 'this Khan'? Like he is some object—"

Why couldn't she have taken it easy? Let things be? Munir
would leave in a few days, anyway.

It was too late. There came the eruption, all of Ravi's pent-up anger. "Why does it matter so much to you? Why has he taken such importance in your life? I have noticed, don't take me for an idiot. And I have information—"

"What information?"

"Information. Why don't you go to Canada with him? Become a grandmother in Toronto. What's the baby's name? —Joshua. Become a granny to Joshua. And leave my daughters to me."

"They are as much my daughters as yours! And when did you start caring so much about them, anyway?"

And back and forth, until Asha came out of her room and said, "Mum and Dad, I don't like the two of you fighting. Why spoil everything?" Saying which, she disappeared back into her room.

Later Ravi was in the living room, consulting a bunch of papers from his briefcase, and Mohini began to clear the table.

Ma came in, with purpose.

"Go ahead and break your home. I told you."

"Told me what, Ma? Why are you harassing me?"

"He knows, doesn't he? Your father's ashes still warm and you carry on this sinful affair."

"His ashes we put in the Ganga, Ma."

Trust a mother to know where to hurt you.

"Think of the girl, what will happen to her? Have you thought of that?"

"I've been thinking only of her. And I've done nothing wrong."

"Hm."

She went to join Ravi in the living room. Her phone rang and it was Aarti.

"Is that you, Didi? I want to talk to you alone."

Mohini returned to the dining room, then shifted to the bedroom.

"What is it, Aarti?"

"I should ask you that, Didi. What's going on over there?"

"Nothing. What's Ma been saying?"

"This man . . . Didi . . . it doesn't work."

"You would know."

"Yes, I would. Listen, you have everything to lose. Just swallow the bitter pill and stop it."

Mohini didn't know what to say. Ma had no right to tell tales. But then, she was Ma. And Aarti was her sister.

"Don't you think there can be something genuine to it? Something real? Not all cases are the same. When you know someone is destined for you—is right for you and meant for you but he just got delayed coming to you? And don't you go repeating what I just said!"

"I won't. I understand what you feel, believe me, Sis. Many people reach a dead-end in life. But you have your family, Sis. Please, please, consider this carefully."

"I will."

She came out and saw Ma giving dessert to Asha. Rubbing it in, reminding her she had a daughter.

Then this morning, just having had his tea, Ravi said, "So what are you up to today? Off to DRC again?"

"I'll go where I want," she said sharply. He took half a step to hit her, but Ma was hovering about and walked in. He left.

An hour later, under Ma's condemning gaze, she went out to the auto stand. She picked up Munir outside the Club gate, and then proceeded to hurt him in the place he was most vulnerable.

Going home later that day, after all her sorries and tears, and their reconciliation and dinner, she knew she had resolved nothing. There was no resolution. There was only the now, as he had once told her. They would go on, and on. Distance would bring peace. And longing.

Munir

HE THOUGHT HE SHOULD do a tour before returning to Toronto, see something else of India. A change of scenery, a break to help erase the reminders of recent events. Reception arranged a car to take him to Agra, an obvious choice that he had postponed previously, and then on to Jaipur and Ajmer. Mohini, told briefly about his plans, said it was a touristic schedule, but still a must. While he was waiting for his details to be finalized, he received a phone call, and it would seem later that it had come straight from wonderland.

The caller was Rajender of Odisha, who reminded him that they had met on the Paschim Express not long ago. Munir recalled with a smile the man in his train compartment who had so dramatically jumped up from his seat and touched his feet. He had been acutely embarrassed.

"Professor Munir, sir."

No point in telling him he was not a professor. Even his hosts at the university in Gujarat, who should have known better, had insisted on the honorific, despite his protests.

"Sir, I am in Delhi. I have done research on you . . . I want to come and personally hand you an invitation to come to Odisha."

"Thank you, Rajender. That is kind of you. But I am booked on a tour of Agra and Rajasthan, and after that it will be time for me to return home. You are welcome to come and see me, however."

"Today itself, sir?"

"Later today is fine. Now is fine."

"I will come at five," Rajender said.

At a little before five in the afternoon Munir sat down on the patio to await the man; behind him on the green, more people had dragged out chairs and were sitting around in small, friendly groups; a steady stream of club members were making their way from the driveway to the tea lounge. A man in mufti holding an automatic weapon at the ready stood at the far end of the green, next to the fence, which was suggestive of some political eminence, retired or current, being somewhere on the premises. Munir turned and saw his acquaintance from the train journey walking briskly down the driveway towards him, having got off an auto. As before, he was dressed modestly in a light shirt over trousers; in one hand was a slim black briefcase, in the other a smartphone. Again, with a surprising abruptness he bent down and touched Munir's feet, at which Munir looked helplessly around in case he was seen. He was: curious eyes were already sizing him up.

They went and sat in the outside veranda of the tea lounge, in front of the lotus pond. Over tea, Rajender produced a brochure and a pamphlet and explained that he was an administrator at the Ashoka School for Children in Bhubaneswar, Odisha, founded by a mechanical engineer turned philanthropist called Harish Jain. The facilities in the pictures, Munir observed, looked remarkably modern, with three-storey grey-brick buildings set amidst lush green lawns and flower gardens. The school had some eight hundred student boarders from the villages of the area, brought to receive free education and advance themselves in life. They were taught arts and crafts, English, Hindi, and technological skills, and were given opportunities to play sports.

"I am impressed," Munir said to a smiling Rajender. "This Mr. Jain must be a remarkable man."

Rajender nodded. "Great man," he said, adding that Mr. Jain had received an honour from the president of India.

"We would like you to come and receive an award at the Ashoka School's Annual Day, sir. It is on Friday itself. It has taken me time to arrange it."

Munir was flabbergasted. "What award . . . ? I am interested in the school but . . . an award? For what?"

"You are modest, sir. I've seen your profile on the internet. It took me a long time to find you, sir—I had lost your contact. New phone. But your professor friend in Gujarat finally gave me your number. We would like you to come and speak words of wisdom to the boys and girls at the school. They all come from poor tribal homes. You can tell them how you went from Africa to Canada and became successful. That will be very good." Saying this, he looked at his smartphone, fiddled with it, and held it up for Munir to view a photo of his family. A plain-looking woman in a purple sari, beside Rajender in a brown suit, and a cheerful boy and girl in bright clothes and shiny hair. This seemed like a recommendation as to the worthiness of the man.

Munir said yes. He had wanted a change in scenery, and he had decided on the Taj Mahal, but why not exotic Odisha? He knew little about it beyond what he had once gleaned from a guidebook. He could do the school and the children some good, though the invitation did sound odd, which in itself was nothing unusual in India. Munir knew nothing of Rajender, except what he had been shown by the brochure and the nice family photo on the phone. In the elite ambience of the Delhi Recreational Club, amidst the boisterous political and earnest academic discussions, his visitor—for whom he'd had to sign in the guest book—looked decidedly out of place, a fidgety country mouse.

Through the glass wall on his right, when he took a glimpse inside the lounge, his eyes met Ravi's. He was sitting against the opposite wall looking out, as he usually did, in company with the indefatigable Jetha Lal and a few others. Munir waved briefly but there was no response.

The next day a ticket arrived for him by email. And early morning the following day, a Friday, he flew out east to Odisha.

He stepped down from the plane onto a melting tarmac and walked the short distance to the terminal, a small low-rise building caught in the haze of bursting morning daylight. As he entered the shade, a young man stepped forward and put a garland over his head. He knew it was best not to become too conscious of this, he would remove it at the first opportunity. Immediately afterwards, Rajender came up and touched his feet. The two men accompanied Munir into a small private waiting room which had a table and four chairs around it, where he was asked to sit and offered a glass of water. Rajender was already on his phone instructing a driver to meet them at the front airport entrance. Shortly afterwards they walked outside, where a large white car was waiting. The driver too touched Munir's feet before opening the door for him. Munir was feeling at that moment like a comical fraud or a bumbling idiot and surely the gods were laughing at him. He should not have accepted the invitation, however sincere it had sounded. He couldn't be the right person for what these people had in mind. Now he simply had to go along with whatever awaited him, which thought was accompanied by the mercenary hope that the experience might perhaps be worth storing away for the future.

The hotel was a modern high-rise set away from the road; a long driveway came curving up to the entrance. It was lunchtime, and as Munir walked upon the blue runner to his room on the ground floor he could hear a tremendous clamour coming down from the dining room on the mezzanine floor. He dumped his garland on a chair, washed his face, changed his shirt, and joined his hosts in the lobby, from where they went up to the mezzanine for lunch. After the meal Munir was told he could rest and to be ready at two-thirty, when he would be taken to the campus.

At exactly the designated time he received a call in his room, telling him his ride had arrived. Two young men picked him up in the same white car as before. At the end of a long, moderately busy road they stopped outside an open gate where Rajender stood waiting. He was now in full colour, wearing a crimson vest over an orange kurta. On either side of the gate, standing to military attention were two young women dressed like girl scouts or cadets. As soon as Munir stepped out onto the sidewalk, a third girl appeared from somewhere and put a garland on him. He hurried forward, trying to act casually, and as he reached the gate, much to his astonishment, the two girl scouts suddenly stiffened their postures and saluted him smartly. He had gone from the implausible and mildly quaint to the bizarre.

You have been misinformed! I am only a writer, a mediocre has-been, nobody even knows me anymore in my own country, let alone in India. I am not even flattered by this attention!

Rajender and Munir walked together along a paved driveway, on either side of which were well-tended gardens with gloriously bright flowers. A short distance before them stood a modest-sized new building, into which they entered and went upstairs, where Munir was greeted by various teachers and taken into rooms where the students were ready for him. As soon as he entered they stood up and clapped their hands, faces beaming. In one class, the students were sitting at their computers and learning how to search the web. In another, the boys and girls were painting on easels, and in a third they were at work on the floor, block-printing on coarse pieces of cloth. A sports museum displayed on its walls some framed photos of winning teams and various glass cases displayed sports equipment of special significance. The rugby eleven had attained some fame in international competitions. Finally he was taken to the assembly.

They walked some distance down a path to a large field, at the nearer end of which stood a high platform behind a rope cordon. Munir went up its steps with Rajender and was formally introduced to the redoubtable Mr. Harish Jain, the man who had endowed the school. He was a small-statured man dressed, like Rajender, in kurta and vest, but with a folded beige shawl thrown over one shoulder. A yellow mark on his forehead indicated that he had recently been to a temple or shrine. He welcomed Munir and, to his surprise, asked if he had come from Delhi. Just then, as they stood there talking pleasantries, there came from behind Munir a tremendous applause, and he turned around to face a sea of little people in maroon-and-white uniforms who had all stood up and were cheering. Munir waved briefly at them, following Mr. Jain's cue, after which he sat down among other dignitaries in a row of chairs.

The principal of the school stood up and introduced Mr. Jain, who addressed these children from poor communities in the tenderest manner, telling them of the importance of education, and how once they had succeeded they would be able to help their families. A few other people spoke, after which Munir was introduced by the principal, and there came more thunderous applause as he stood up and walked up to the mike. He spoke in English from notes he had hastily made that morning. He spoke to a myriad of small faces, yet he felt distinctly that he was speaking to himself; they could not possibly understand him, and to Mr. Jain and the others he was merely form, a program item. After he had finished, with much ceremony he was presented with a framed artwork consisting of a fine, intricate etching in an abstract geometric design, and a beige ceremonial shawl with a fine border was put on his shoulder. The principal spoke and dismissed the assembly, and suddenly there were clouds of dust in the bright air. After shaking hands with Mr. Jain, Munir left with Rajender for the gate. It had been too quick. He would have liked to speak more with Mr. Jain and chat with some kids, sit in on a class, see in more detail what they studied. His interest had been genuinely aroused. But Rajender was quiet and preoccupied and handed him over to the driver. There were no escorts this time.

That evening Munir had dinner at the hotel with Rajender and a few locals, including two poets and a man who worked in a tribal area in the hills. It was a jolly evening, though Rajender was again quiet and looked somewhat out of place. He was, after all, a mere administrator. The poets spoke about their work and gave Munir copies of their books. The social worker invited him to visit him in the hills anytime he wished. Looking at the silent Rajender, Munir wondered what his host thought he had got out of him. The following morning a car took Munir on a tour of the city, and he saw many beautiful temples, for which the city was famous. In the late afternoon Rajender dropped him off at the airport, as respectful as ever, and Munir returned to Delhi. Unlocking his room at the DRC, it seemed to him that he had walked out of a dream.

There was just enough time to get dinner, so he hurried to the dining room where a table was found for him. He had a glass of wine. Later he walked around the grounds a few times and then sat down on the patio, recalling his Odisha adventure. He had texted Mohini while walking, and she called. She was getting bolder, he thought, perhaps because he was leaving soon. She gave a bright peal of laughter when he told her of his visit. "At least you saw another place. Now you've seen three different states, and Delhi. You're becoming a real Indian."

Feeling positive after that exchange, musing vaguely about coming days, he closed his eyes. Quite suddenly he sensed a movement and a shadow fell over him, and he opened his eyes to see himself surrounded by six men in white. They pulled up chairs and sat down.

"Good evening, sir," said Jetha Lal in his growly voice, delivered in almost a whisper. "Relaxing?"

"I guess I am. I was having a quiet time."

The man was on his right and moved his chair closer. His acolytes, for some reason, were also leaning forward.

"Mohini-ji didn't come today." A little louder this time.

Munir didn't speak for some moments. Then he said angrily, "What—why are you telling me this? It's her business."

Surrounded by restless white spectres, he now sensed menace.

"Yes. Her business. She's a wonderful woman. Our Mohini-ji. Smart and beautiful, no? A *phataki*."

"I asked you, why are you telling me this?"

"She's a flower of Hinduism. And you are a good Muslim. A pride of the Mohammedans."

"I'm a Canadian. Don't put your labels on me."

"Canadian, sir. But you like Hindu women, I see. Better than Canadian women, no?" He waited. "No doubt. But you are Muslim, sir. *Mlechha*. Different."

"White women not good fuck?" butted in an obnoxious follower.

A round of chuckling.

"You like beef, sir? Meat of mother cow?" spoke up yet another cadre.

"What is it to you?" Munir asked, in a louder voice. "And why have you surrounded me?" He hoped someone passing by would hear him. The spectres became wary and sat back.

"We, sir," Jetha Lal growled, shaking his head side to side, large teeth visible, "are protectors of our sisters and daughters. Hindu. And mother cow."

He stood up, and Munir saw a steely glint in his walking stick, near the top, which then disappeared with a small click.

"You're not scaring me, you know!"

Empty words.

He watched them disappear, then stood up, in a sweat. He went up to his room, had a shower, and ordered coffee. Should he tell her? He couldn't. Surely it was these people who had made that anonymous abusive phone call when he arrived, who sent him that selfie. How did they get hold of it, though? No, he would not frighten her.

Mohini

AARTI FLEW IN WITH Kishore and Swapna on a Friday for three days of a jubilant, noisy family reunion in the house. It seemed like old times for Mohini and Aarti, when they were two sisters under the same roof sharing secrets, sharing everything. Kishore and Aarti took Asha's room, and Asha and Swapna slept on sleeping bags in the living room. They stayed up late into the nights, even Ma, as much as she could, chatting, telling stories, essentially catching up and reaffirming their closeness. The two husbands, starting noon nicely inebriated, were here to indulge their Khanna women. To Ravi's delight, Kishore had brought a bottle of imported single malt and a supply of Sicilian white from his wine club for the two of them to try.

Ma began the first night with the ritual telling of one of her oft-repeated tales from the past, this time about the day the family arrived in Delhi from now-Pakistan. They had been allocated a one-room outdoor shack at the refugee camp, which was outside Ajmeri Gate. They arrived there with their bundles and bags, but before they could go inside, the room had to be swept and cleared of all kinds of rubbish. All around them the bustle of people arriving, people grieving or fighting, exchanging stories of loss. The Khannas had with them Bau-ji's parents and two unmarried sisters. Now, before anything else, Dadi had wanted to go to the toilet, so did Ma, and so did the girls, and off they hustled towards the long queues. Nathu Lal followed them shortly to go to the men's toilets, and Bau-ji was left alone in the midst of the family's possessions. As the ladies departed, a man came up to Bau-ji and said, "There's a sick man lying over there looking for his family. You are from Sargodha itself?" He had cleverly asked the women where they were from. Bau-ji, simple college master, said, "Yes, where is he?" He hoped desperately that Mohan had at last been found. "Follow me," said the man. Bau-ji thoughtlessly hurried behind in great excitement and reached the spot where, apparently, the sick man had been recognized by somebody else and taken away, and Bau-ji returned disappointed, only to find that all their boriya-bistar—the luggage—was gone. Poor Bau-ji was distraught and had to bear all the yelling from his wife and mother.

"I remember Dadi's hoarse voice . . ." Mohini said.

"Yes, she could out-shout a man. But you were not there yet then."

Ma continued her story. A man selling ice cream nearby, who had been watching the scene, told Bau-ji, "Come, I'll take you to your luggage."

"You good for nothing!" Bau-ji shouted at him. "You such-and-such! . . ." Ma hadn't known her husband could speak such language. She tittered.

"Come," said the man, "trust me. I will leave my cold machine here."

Bau-ji followed reluctantly; Ma took command of the ice cream machine and even managed to sell some cones. Bau-ji returned with the samaan, assisted by a nice young man. He said the ice cream vendor had stopped outside a shack and shouted, "Eh, Lalu, bring the man's stuff that you have stolen." The crook emerged, there was a scuffle, and some fellows entered the shack and brought out a lot of bags and bundles. The crook was beaten, he was beaten and beaten until Bau-ji feared he was dead.

That nice young man who helped him carry the luggage back married one of the girls, Suman. They moved to Jaipur, where they had a leather store.

In the camp there were girls who had been raped, she said. Old women. Fit women like her joined the volunteers. They nursed the sick, arranged marriages, looked for lost family members.

"Talk of pleasant things, Ma. We've come a long way from there, thanks to the hard work and resolve of people like you. But it's done."

"What do you know?" Ma said grimly.

Bau-ji would go out to sell ice cream every day, thanks to that good-Samaritan ice cream man. Every time a train came, Bau-ji would be racing towards the coaches. Brought back a few paisa. But then, karma always has a role to play. A man from Sargodha recognized Bau-ji as the teacher, and through some influence got him a flat that a Muslim family had vacated. And a position at a college.

Mohan was always the mischievous one. That time he took the doctor's bike for a joyride . . .

"Mohan again," said Aarti to Mohini as they went to the kitchen to get some snacks. Munchies for their drinks.

"Yes," Mohini sighed. "Mohan again."

"What happened about that doctor's bike, do you remember?" Aarti asked.

"A police-wallah recognized both Mohan Chachu and the bike," Mohini said. "And Mohan got a sound thrashing at home."

They laughed.

"Do you think Ma and Mohan Chachu . . ."

"So you've noticed. Nothing serious, but I think yes. Ma has admitted as such; apparently between younger brother-in-law and bhabhi there's a special bond."

"Convenient."

"Listen—men can have affairs and it's nothing—"

"It's not nothing. It's just accepted and forgotten."

"Why?"

"It's still a man's world, that's why."

"Has Kishore . . . ?"

Aarti turned away.

"Have you . . . ?"

"Don't ask me such questions. We are a happy family. Now you tell me—is that . . . fellow . . . still around?"

"He's not a fellow. His name is Munir Khan."

"You have guts, Didi. And? Where is he?"

"At DRC, though he'll be leaving in a few days."

"And then? Don't think I didn't notice the two text messages you didn't pick up there."

"Don't ask, as you so aptly put it."

Aarti took her sister's chin and turned it towards her and stared into her face. She was about to say something, then changed her mind. Instead she said, "Look, why don't we go for tea at DRC tomorrow?"

A mischievous smile. Mohini returned it. "Let's. Just the two of us."

The four of them, the two couples, ended up going to DRC. Mohini and Aarti went ahead to the tea lounge; the men would follow and meet them in the bar. Later they would all go for dinner together, at the Chinese in the Habitat Centre.

Jetha Lal was present in the lounge, as always, and as soon as they sat down, he came to greet them as though the previous altercation with Mohini had never happened.

"Namaste, Mohini-ji. You brought your sister. How nice to see."

"Yes, this is Aarti," and just to discourage him from sitting down, added, "Our husbands are to meet us here."

"Ah. The wife is the jewel in the husband's crown!"

The two of them giggled as the man left.

Aarti whispered, "Is he here?"

"Yes, outside on the veranda. He likes to stare at the pink lotuses."

Again they laughed.

One of the texts last night had been his: *How are you doing today?* And she'd answered, saying she would be coming with her sister and their husbands that afternoon. As she glanced at him he looked up from his reading and their eyes briefly met.

"Not bad-looking, Sis," Aarti said. "That receding hairline could recede further, though."

"It's not the looks, Aarti."

Aarti leaned forward and said urgently, "It's too late, Mohini. Just let it pass."

"Just like that?"

"Yes. Like in the old film songs, drink your gham, gulp your sorrow."

A text came to Aarti from Kishore; the two guys were already in the bar. As the two women came out, Aarti went to the ladies' room and Mohini quickly took the opportunity to go and say hello to Munir.

"Hi, I'm with my family, as you see."

"Have fun," he said. "Thanks for coming by."

"I escaped."

How lonely he looked.

Munir

HE HAD BEEN WAITING for someone.

The confrontation with the men in white, the Purifiers, as Mohini called them, the protectors of Hindu women and cows as they styled themselves, had shaken him. He had now faced the uglier side of India. Bigoted opinions were one thing; but violence, even threats of violence, were another. They revealed the reality of the menace that lurked, shark-like, beneath the surface of ordinary life in India. When his eyes met Mohini's through the glass wall of the lounge, he had felt gladdened. More so when she came over to greet him. He'd been debating if she would. She did. She was Mohini. What India had come to mean for him.

The previous evening he'd received another unexpected phone call. It was Altaf, the man from the merchant navy, whose interrogation of him during that train journey—"You must be from Foreign"—had been the primary cause of his recent Odisha adventure.

"You asked me to call you in Delhi, sir."

"Yes, yes. How are you?"

Munir had no choice but to invite him to come and see him.

Altaf arrived soon after Mohini left. It being Saturday, the lounge was still fairly full even at this hour. The flies were bothersome in the veranda so they went inside and found a table occupied by a single person. Considerately he soon called for his bill and left. Munir observed that his guest felt uneasy in this environment, shifting around in his chair like a schoolboy, flitting his eyes here and there, and finally saying why didn't they go sit outside on the lawn. Munir declined firmly and told him to place his order, and seeing him confused by the menu, had to do it for him. The man was clearly not used to such a smart place, and the loud talk of Pakistan and terrorism in one corner, and the affected ease and sophistication of America-returnees at the next table, added to his discomfort.

Munir had wondered why Altaf decided to contact him so soon after Rajender had. The answer was simple: the two had exchanged email addresses on the train, and Altaf now received communications from the Ashoka School.

Altaf had come with a request. He wanted Munir to speak to a gathering of Muslim boys and girls in his area. He spoke the word *Muslim* softly.

Munir told him firmly, perhaps sounding pompous because such was the relationship established between them, that he did not subscribe to a religious identity; his wife, who was now dead, had been of Scottish Presbyterian descent, and his only child, a daughter, was married to an American Jew in New York. He would not know what to say to a gathering of Muslim children. Moreover he was a foreigner; how would the kids relate to him? Did Altaf realize that his request was impossible?

He felt irritated at having to explain himself. Why, in this country, did you have to be one thing or the other? Why couldn't the request be for him to speak to *children?*

But Altaf's reply was simple and flat: "Anything you say, sir—it will be valuable."

There was something in the man's dry, unmodulated voice and the blank look in his eyes that took it for granted that Munir had little choice. And indeed, the thought was already nagging: If he could speak to the young aboriginal kids of Odisha, who understood hardly one word he had said, why not here, to some Muslim boys and girls who needed inspiration? Who had to face the likes of Jetha Lal?

They had ended up having dinner in the dining hall. Munir ordered wine with vegetarian, making a point. Altaf ordered lamb, making his point.

The next day Altaf arrived in an auto rickshaw, meeting him at the driveway. He wore a bright white bush shirt over pressed blue denims; his brown shoes had a shine. He paid off his auto and told Munir they would take a taxi, he would pay for it. Nothing doing, Munir said, and asked the uniformed guard to call one.

They rode to Old Delhi, where Altaf asked the driver to drop them off on Chandni Chowk. As they stood on the hectic thoroughfare, a bicycle rickshaw wobbled to a stop near them; they clambered into it and were taken into a narrow and quieter street and dropped off at a broad, somewhat shabby-looking red-brick building. A dissonant clamour of children's voices met their ears. They were outside a primary school, and it was named after Maulana Azad, as the board over the entrance proclaimed in faded letters.

They stepped over a raised threshold into a paved, sunlit courtyard surrounded by some half a dozen clamorous classrooms. The principal, a man with a rich black-and-gold beard, wearing a cap and a long shirt over his fair-sized belly, greeted them effusively with both hands and thanked Munir for honouring his school with his visit. He was called Hamid Sahab. It occurred to Munir that he could have no idea who or what exactly Munir was, but any visitor from the West with a presumed reputation was a great enough honour. Munir had brought one of the few copies of his short story collection that he still possessed and he handed it to him.

The entire place had suddenly become still. And then, in a great flurry, tens of boys and girls of ages between six and twelve emerged, running, girls from one side and boys from the opposite, and in moments had surrounded him. The girls mostly wore hijab over long dresses, a few were in full niqab, and the boys wore white skullcaps and kurtas over long pants. Once more Munir felt utterly like an alien intruder, and he threw an accusing glance at Altaf. What have you done to me? Altaf returned a reassuring nod. The principal instructed the teachers, who had followed the kids out of the classrooms, to bring order to the assembly and sit their charges quietly on the ground. Girls on one side, boys on the other. Lots of nudging and tittering. Meanwhile Munir was given a fragrant chai. His book was passed around to the teachers and admired. Chairs were brought and placed facing the rows of eager boys and girls. Munir sat down with the teachers.

Hamid Sahab stood up and, speaking in Urdu, which Munir only barely understood, greeted and introduced Munir. There was enthusiastic clapping, and the children's smiling faces beamed at him. Hamid Sahab waved his book in the air. More applause. He then gestured to Munir and asked him to speak.

Munir stood up, and having greeted the boys and girls with "Good morning, *adab*," he began by telling them about his life. He was born in Africa, in a country called Kenya; however, his grandfather had come from Delhi, in fact not far from where they now were. He proceeded to tell them about his departure first to England, then to Canada for his education. He exhorted upon them the value of secular education. There was a world out there they must reach out and grab, and become part of.

When he finished, upon prompting by the principal, a forest of hands shot up with questions. They inquired about his family and about Africa, but they were curious mostly about Canada. Munir guessed that they had been coached a little about the country, perhaps had seen a few pictures, and a few even asked him how they could go and live there. At length, Hamid Sahab put an end to the questions, and then the guest had to be garlanded. Pictures were taken. One girl, covered in black niqab, came and stood beside him; her name was Hasina, and after taking a selfie with him, she told him how sorry she was that he had lost his wife. Munir told her hypocritically that it was Allah's will. His wife, Aileen, was now in Allah's presence. She nodded. Through the slit in her veil he thought he detected sympathy in her eyes. He noticed that her dainty feet were just visible under her long dress, inside pink slippers, and she had pink-polished toenails.

"I am willing to marry you," she said.

Munir laughed. It was only later that he realized that she might have been serious.

A long table was brought, around which the chairs were arranged, and he was asked to sit down to eat with Hamid Sahab and the teachers. He removed his garland and put it around the girl who had proposed to him. Sweets and biryani were on offer, and they were delicious.

He was given a plate of the biryani to take with him.

Mohini

MA WAS READY TO MOVE back to her own home; Mohini would have wished her to stay, for Asha's sake and so that she would not be lonely, but Ma insisted and Ravi encouraged her. He valued his privacy; these were no longer the days when three or even four generations of a family tripped over each other under one roof. And so Mohini and Asha took Ma home. Mohini had already had the rooms swept and the furniture dusted the previous day. As soon as they arrived, they hung up a large photo of Bau-ji, garlanded with fresh flowers, on the wall facing the television. It had been taken in Shimla after his retirement party at the university. Mohini put on some tea and sent Ma's daily help, who was back and had wept her tears of condolence, to shop for fresh vegetables. As if on cue, neighbours came to welcome Ma back, reassuring Mohini that they would take care of her mother— wasn't she like their own mother and sister? There were the sympathy tears for her loss but, The end's written for all of us, all agreed. He was a good man and had lived a good, long life.

Bau-ji's clothes were taken away by a neighbour to distribute.

Asha kept for herself a pair of his gold cufflinks, and Mohini saved a gold pen, his retirement gift, for Aarti. She discovered in his drawer four diaries from his younger days and, with a look at Ma, said she would keep them. She also kept Bau-ji's comb, still with a faint smell of his hair cream on it.

Later the three of them walked over to the Hanuman temple, and on the way back stopped at the food shack and sat down for water. It was a hot day, a tense moment, Mohini with more instructions for Ma, and Ma with that admonishing look for her. Back home, the two cooked dinner while Asha did her homework, and when Ravi arrived they all ate together. Bau-ji's absence was palpable, and Mohini worried about Ma as they left her. But her mother had seen much in her life and was perhaps stronger than any of them. Ravi carried a box of Bau-ji's documents and certificates to the car. Mohini followed him, hugging to herself Bau-ji's four hard-backed diaries as though carrying away the last of his bones.

When the ambulance brought Bau-ji home the morning after he died, as the stretcher was rolled out of the back of the van, it was met by loud wailing from the women inside. As the stretcher approached the threshold, Ma had stood up, both arms stretched out to receive him, as Mohini and Aarti stood behind, prepared to steady her. She and a few others had stayed up the night, waiting, while bhajans and verses from the scriptures were recited by individuals or played on tape.

The body was taken straight to the main bedroom, which had been cleared, and placed on a mat on the floor. A new set of kurta-pyjamas had been set aside, with a jug of water and a bowl of dahi. Aarti closed the door to mild protestations from the relations, telling them firmly, "Later." Mohini and Aarti told Ma to hush and be brave, for the sake of his soul, as though they knew anything about it, and she pulled herself together. They removed the sheet that covered him, and his hospital gown. And then, kneeling down, the three of them began to anoint and wash him as ritual required.

They rubbed him lightly with the dahi and sponged him with the water, talking to him and to each other, pretending this was all in a good day's work, ordinary and routine, and he was their baby. How thin he had become. All because he wouldn't eat well recently, would you, Bau-ji? What's that in his hair, let me remove it. I've combed it, there, don't you look smart! Else, how do you cope with touching your father naked? Lying lifeless before you? All those thoughts ready to rush at you through the slightest crack in your wall of composure? His eyes were closed. As if by magic, his body was hardening in their hands in a matter of seconds, so that suddenly he looked stern, as though to reprimand them, This is not funny! You are touching my privates! They wiped him with a small towel and put his pyjamas on him, Aarti and she lifting his legs one by one and Ma pulling up the pant. And then the kurta. Finally he was ready. Looking smart and handsome.

Ma, who had contained herself all this while, even allowing herself an occasional smile, now gave a loud sob. They called in Kishore and Ravi to lift and place the body onto the wood frame, which had been set aside to carry Bau-ji out. They covered him with a clean white sheet and tied his body with twine in three places so it wouldn't roll. Finally they paid heed to the clamour outside and family and friends were allowed in to pay their respects. They walked by, their hands joined, they sat down, some placed offerings of plain shawls—those would end up with the priests—on the body. Marigold garlands and rose petals were strewn across his body. His two sisters, Madhu and Suman, whom he had brought here from Sargodha in now-Pakistan and gotten married, cried uncontrollably.

Mohini and Aarti went with the body in the hearse to the cremation ground. Ravi and Kishore had already gone ahead with two cousins to finalize arrangements. Ma stayed home as was customary, in the comforting care of other women. The road was bumpy and Mohini and Aarti again bantered one-sidedly with Bau-ji all the way. Sorry, Bau-ji, it's a rough road, take care now. Couldn't you have waited a little longer? When Aarti uttered this, they both broke into fits of sobbing, and then suddenly stiffened and recomposed themselves.

Bau-ji had no sons, he was the last of his line. At his crema-tion, his two daughters Mohini and Aarti had undertaken to light the fire that would consume his remains. They stood before the body, their husbands a couple of paces behind them and well-wishers further back, and they acted as instructed by the priest, who was chanting mantras when not speaking to them or attending to the raised pyre. He took away the shawls and the flowers. The twine tying down the body was cut. Then Mohini went around it with a jar of water, sprinkling it on the ground before stopping at their father's head and throwing the jar down with a crash. That symbolized the soul's release. The men helped to lift the bier to the pyre and stepped back, as Mohini and Aarti placed the pieces of firewood atop the body as instructed, leaving a little space below the face.

Finally, Mohini took the flaming torch from the priest, and the two sisters went around the pyre and took turns to light the ghee that had been placed at various spots on the body and, after some moments which seemed to take forever, the heap went up in flames and they watched, and couldn't watch, and the smoke and fire blinded them, thankfully. But this was not over yet. The priest gave her a slight nod. The head. Aarti and Mohini looked at each other. They knew what was required, they had heard of it, seen it from afar, dreaded it. The head had to be struck. After a moment's falter, Mohini took the long bamboo stick from the priest and with a flinch smacked the head and thought she heard it explode. She began to cry, loudly this time.

If anything told you of the ultimate worthlessness of life, this was it.

Then, on the third day at dawn, picking flowers, as they call it, picking up the brittle bones from the ashes at the cremation site, telling the bones from the cinder. A glowing heat welcomed them as they arrived, and the priest poured a cooling mixture of milk and water over it before they began. It still glowed in spots and their fingers burned as they picked. Ashes into a sack, bones into an urn. And then, Mohini clutching the urn, the sack of ashes in the car trunk, they drove with their husbands to Haridwar. When they stopped for a meal on the way, she took Bau-ji with her, hugging him to her chest.

At the riverbank at the Ganga, Ravi and Aarti took care of the arrangements, finding the right ghat, doing the rituals and paying for them, finding the family priest and giving him recent family history, telling him this was the last of the line of the Khannas of Sargodha in now-Pakistan.

Munir

HE WAS EIGHT YEARS OLD and it was the glorious day of Eid. He wore an off-white sherwani and matching pyjamas specially made for him by the family tailor, Parmar. On his head was a white cotton skullcap embroidered in blue and red, an affectation imposed upon him by the adults as he left home with Dada. He looked cute, they would say, and he squirmed. It was Eid, he never remembered which of the two, and he had gone with his grandfather to the downtown mosque for the Eid namaz. Dada wore a lovely brown sherwani embroidered in yellow and blue, and a grey Afghan topee. Inside the mosque, they found themselves in the middle of a row, the hall quickly filling up behind them. He saw his grandfather nod brief greetings at the men to their right and left. All was silence but for the rustle of perfumed new clothes and the occasional murmur. Suddenly the loudspeakers gave a brief piercing squeal and the Arabic prayer started; Dada put a gentle hand on Munir's back and nodded at him. As the rich, throaty recital wound on, Munir followed the ritual actions of those around him. The bending, the turning, the bowing. His knees hurt when he went down on them—why this intense memory of burning knees? He bowed with the others to the One True God and when his forehead didn't quite touch the mat the first time, Dada pushed his head down, and Munir almost toppled forward. The prayer ended with the collective gesture of the men putting their open palms to their faces and murmuring, al-hamdu lillahi, praise be to Allah. Then, as one, they got up on their feet, and as though a volume control had turned, the hall became noisy with Urdu and Punjabi and other languages, and all the men and boys exchanged warm greetings with whomever they could. Then they attached themselves to a snaking queue to file past the elders, who stood in a row in the front to greet you, taking your hands into theirs, Eid Mubarak! Eid Mubarak! When they reached the end of the row they stopped and joined it, and it got longer and longer as more well-wishers arrived, until everyone had greeted everyone else. And then the row broke into pieces and dispersed.

It was a solemn yet joyful occasion. Among the elders had stood the governor of the colony, Sir Evelyn Baring, and the mayor of Nairobi.

Munir's father Jehangir had been present, though he sat separately near the back; after the namaz he came up and gave Munir an affectionate caress on the cheek and twenty shillings, and his own father a tight embrace. Back home, hugs and kisses from Mum and Dadi and his sisters, and shortly afterwards the aunts and uncles arrived, the aunts adding a pinch on the cheek to their gifts of money, which Mum put away for safekeeping. One day he would use these savings to buy a cricket bat with the signature of Don Bradman on it. The laughter and the joy, the feasting. Biryani, sweet seviya, samosas, kachumbar. Games with his cousins.

Eid Mubarak! Why this memory now, arriving after all these years, why Eid and the namaz prayer, when he had put it all behind him, to start his life anew? What's she doing to me, this woman I impossibly love, prompting scenes from my childhood, imposing an identity on me? This is what India does to you.

Munir's father was the younger of two sons, the spoilt one; the older one was upcountry in Eldoret. There were three daughters, Munir's aunts, married with children. For many years Dad and Dada ran the fashionable Kohinoor Jewellers on Government Road. Following the great Asian exodus of 1968, when so many left for England, business waned, and Kohinoor closed. By this time Dada was disabled with Parkinson's. Dada prayed every day, twice, which was enough for progressive, westernized Nairobi. Every evening and morning he had to be helped to go down on his knees, by his favourite servant or by Munir if he was around. At one time Munir could recall in their proper order all the arduous motions of this prayer that so sorely tried his grandfather's joints.

He'd pushed them away, yet over the years these memories would arrive in teasing fragments. Dada's face contorted with pain and his knees cracking as he was helped up from his prayer mat; his crackling voice towards the end. The old man holding him on a knee to tell him stories, about the goodness of that best of men and friend of God, Nabi Muhammad, and about funny, clever men who outwitted sultans and wily animals who outwitted each other. They became distant when Dada was ailing and Munir a bragging teenager—cricket-playing, blazer-wearing, comb-in-back-pocket, hanging out at the new cafés, going to parties and concerts. Discreetly drinking alcohol. The world was racing ahead, with the moon shot and the Beatles, the long hair and the bell-bottoms; his world, and Dada too much of a bygone era and foreign place in which a terrorist or freedom fighter once hid behind the skirt of a woman frying pakodas.

And Dadi? Diminutive Dadi, whom he remembered always cooking or tinkering in the kitchen, at the end had shrunk into herself and her Quran.

There was a photo of Munir in his sherwani taken that day of Eid. Standing by himself, taken at the studio of A.C. Gomes. The hair slicked and parted, with a small puff in front. It had been placed in the family album. He wondered where that album had gone.

In Nairobi he was an Asian; and among the Asians a Punjabi and a Muslim. But at home his mother was an alien, a Gujarati whose Urdu was halting, and a heretical Shia from Tanganyika who had visited Kohinoor Jewellers while on a holiday in Nairobi and ended up, against opposition from both sides, marrying a rambunctious Sunni Punjabi who spent his weekends playing bridge or snooker and drinking whiskey at his club.

Munir would recall her as quiet but determined and always ready with a smile for him. She baked cakes for him, and brought games and books from Woolworths, and was his first stop when he needed something not quite essential. Like her female in-laws and neighbours, she wore salwar-kameez and dupatta and kept a long braid. But on some rare occasions, Zainab Khan came out lithe and beautiful in a sari, and Jehangir her husband would walk out proudly with her to the car. Mummy, wah! You look lovely! Why don't you dress like that always?

There was a period every year when she insisted on going to her Shia mosque daily, and there would be shouting and screaming in the house. Dad would not give her the car keys, but somehow she would have arranged a ride. When she returned from those sessions the makeup would have run down her face as though she had cried, and if Dad was sober enough there would follow another shouting match.

Was there violence? He would not like to think about it. Once she ran out from their room, finger marks on her puffed cheek, tears running down and wailing, straight into Dadi's arms; and Dadi had gone and cussed out her son, telling him, "Find someone your own size!"

One day in exasperation, following an argument about this Shia and Sunni business, Munir had shouted to both of them, "If this is what you call religion, I want nothing of it. I am an atheist. You two have convinced me." He was in high school.

Soon afterwards, the Asian exodus having happened, he was sent to London to complete his high school certificate. He went on to the University of Bath. It was then that Mum died, of cancer, and he went home for the funeral. Soon after he applied to business school in Toronto.

By this time first Dadi, then Dada had died. Dad married a Somali woman he had known for some time, and he lived with her in Eastleigh, not far from their former home. Munir sent him money occasionally.

Munir Khan, Mohini Singh

THIS TIME THEY MET at Khan Market. They did a casual round of the shops first. He bought a notebook, for which she paid, and he picked up the reading glasses he had ordered. Alphonso mangoes were just in season, displayed in fragrant heaps, and she bought a couple for him to eat that evening. He bought gifts for Razia and her family. She bought for Razia and Joshua, and he got a necklace for Asha. Finally, from a jeweller he bought a small pair of earrings for her. "Surely I can do that?" "Yes, you can." "I'll have your ear then." "But not too conspicuous," she said.

They went for a late lunch at a modish restaurant on the market's second floor, where the servers greeted them in English—and looked like teenagers, he observed to her. This was goodbye; he was to leave the next evening. Across their table, he reached out for her hand. The long, slim fingers.

"You know . . ."

She nodded, wiped off a tear and smiled.

"It will be some time before . . ."

"Hm."

"You'll have time to forget."

"Yes."

"You could come tomorrow morning." His flight left late evening.

"I can't."

He told her about his visit to the school in the old city the other day, and she said it was good of him to go there. She would have loved to meet the girls, especially the one who had proposed to him. She took down the name of the school and Altaf's phone number.

"I had a lamb biryani there. It was delicious. They gave me a plate to take with me."

"Now I'm jealous. Do they have biryani on the menu here?" She pored over entrees. "Yes! Let's order it. Lamb. You don't mind? It won't be as good, I bet, as the one you had."

"But you had gone vegetarian, you said."

"That was temporary. Don't judge me."

"How could I?"

Later, over their coffees, she looked at her watch, and he at his. Desperately.

"In six months?" he asked. "A year? We could meet somewhere else."

"Delhi," she said. "Delhi is not far yet," she murmured, misquoting Sheikh Nizamuddin. "But write. Stay in touch. I mean it."

Coming down the stairs in silence, they paused at a landing halfway. There was no one in sight. They fell on each other and embraced tightly.

———

The *Express Times* reported two days later that a man had been murdered in a quiet spot on the track of the Sikandar Gardens. The body had been discovered by joggers in a patch of shade. He had been stabbed multiple times and the corpse had been defiled. The victim was identified as Munir Khan, a Canadian, staying at the Delhi Recreational Club nearby. The murder was attributed to cow vigilantes. A plate of biryani had been found in the refrigerator of the man's room and was undergoing analysis by the authorities for beef content.

Two weeks later the paper reported that its columnist Mohini Singh had met with a tragic accident on the Outer Ring Road near Hauz Khas. The car had caught fire.

A reporter from the paper had spoken to those who knew her at the Delhi Recreational Club.

"She was a fine woman," Pandit Jetha Lal, a friend of the Singh family, said. "She was a beautiful and talented woman. Unfortunately she was pursued by a Muslim man. A terrorist, part of the love jihad against our women. In olden times, our ladies, when their kingdoms were attacked by Mohammedans like Alauddin Khilji, chose to take their own lives, not to fall into the hands of these lechers. The ceremony was called *johar*. Mohini Devi was purified by the fire."

"Do you, sir, believe Mohini Singh committed johar?"

"I did not say that. She died in an accident."

"Who was this Muslim man?"

"He's gone. But the lady did not die, she will return. She's a suttee. As you know, we believe in reincarnation. The body dies but the person returns."

"And the husband of this lady?"

"He has entered an ashram and taken a vow of silence for sixty-one days."

Author's Note

IT'S A PLEASURE TO THANK THE MANY PEOPLE IN DELHI WHO have welcomed me and become friends over the years: Chandra Mohan, whose smiling face was the first one I saw as I came out of the old airport on my first visit so many years ago; Harish Narang, my companion and enthusiastic guide over the years in Old Delhi and many other places, always with many fascinating stories, commentaries, and readings, who also always stood with me outside a certain establishment, waiting for the doors to open; Alka Kumar for generosity beyond the call of friendship in responding to my pestering queries; Neerja Chand for her friendship. And lately, Bharati Bhargava, Jawid Laiq, Lata Krishnamurty, and Ram Jethmalani for their hospitality, and Razi Aquil for his insights. Khushwant Singh was helpful, and understood me, but is no more.

I would like to thank Firoz Manji for finding me a retreat where I could find solitude and write, and Vanda Lima for making it possible.

I must thank my editor Martha Kanya-Forstner for her

extreme diligence and patience; Richa Burman in Delhi for her astute reading of the manuscript and her suggestions; Melanie Little for her thoughtful and rigorous copy-editing; Kristin Cochrane for tea and conversations; and my agent Bruce Westwood for his boundless enthusiasm, as well as Tracy Bohan and Jacqueline Ko for being there during the initial stages of this book. And finally, of course, as always, Nurjehan.

This is a work of fiction. It has been inspired, or called forth, by a certain attitude I have noticed since my first visit to India, and some disturbing trends that have been on the rise recently. It has always bothered me that in India you could not, as a person of Indian origin, just *be*, but were always branded communally— Hindu or Muslim in my experience—no matter your beliefs, background, upbringing, complexities, peculiarities. I don't mean a casual description—we all can be described in various ways—but a labelling of your very essence, who you are. It seems unavoidable. Sometimes even the kindest gestures seem to be directed to your brand. Perhaps that's the nature of India. But that brand or label always comes identified with a politics, a history, a global identity, a status, and an exclusion. Recently and increasingly this division—Hindu and Muslim—has been used politically and at times with hatred and violence. Coming from a time and a place outside of the experience of the Partition of India, and the hatred and suspicion it has left in its wake, I find a communal or religious label antithetical to my very being. During my many travels—my Bharatdarshan, friends called it— across my ancestral homeland, I would sally forth, as myself, known by my (fortunately) neutral last name, an individual:

always annoyed by the presumptions of those who, gleeful classifiers, nevertheless discovered my species and pinned me down; and always nervous lest an accusing finger brought down the weight of a historical and cultural baggage upon me. And so this novel, about a naive returnee to Delhi.

The epigraphs:

The extract from Muhammad Ali Jinnah's speech can be found, with the full reference, at: http://www.columbia.edu/itc/mealac/pritchett/00islamlinks/txt_jinnah_lahore_1940.html.

The song line from *Dhool ka Phool* has been loosely translated.

The *Mahabharata* quote is from the magnificent ten-volume translation by Bibhek Debroy (New Delhi: Penguin).

The MP's remarks can be found easily using the internet.